**I THINK
WE
SHOULD
KILL
OTHER
PEOPLE**

ALSO BY L.M. CHILTON

Don't Swipe Right
Everyone in the Group Chat Dies

I THINK WE SHOULD KILL OTHER PEOPLE

L.M. CHILTON

An Aries Book

First published in the UK in 2026 by Head of Zeus,
part of Bloomsbury Publishing Plc

Copyright © L.M. Chilton, 2026

The moral right of L.M. Chilton to be identified
as the author of this work has been asserted in accordance with
the Copyright, Designs and Patents Act of 1988.

All rights reserved. No part of this publication may be: i) reproduced or transmitted in any form, electronic or mechanical, including photocopying, recording or by means of any information storage or retrieval system without prior permission in writing from the publishers; or ii) used or reproduced in any way for the training, development or operation of artificial intelligence (AI) technologies, including generative AI technologies. The rights holders expressly reserve this publication from the text and data mining exception as per Article 4(3) of the Digital Single Market Directive (EU) 2019/790.

This is a work of fiction. All characters, organizations, and events portrayed
in this novel are either products of the author's imagination or are used fictitiously.

9 7 5 3 1 2 4 6 8

A catalogue record for this book is available from the British Library.

ISBN (PB): 9781035920761
ISBN (ePub): 9781035920778

Cover design: Gemma Gorton | Head of Zeus

Printed and bound in Great Britain by Clays Ltd, Elcograf S.p.A.

Bloomsbury Publishing Plc
50 Bedford Square, London, WC1B 3DP, UK
Bloomsbury Publishing Ireland Limited,
29 Earlsfort Terrace, Dublin 2, D02 AY28, Ireland

HEAD OF ZEUS LTD
5–8 Hardwick Street
London, EC1R 4RG

To find out more about our authors and books
visit www.headofzeus.com
For product safety related questions contact productsafety@bloomsbury.com

**I THINK
WE
SHOULD
KILL
OTHER
PEOPLE**

ARE YOU LOOKING FOR YOUR PRINCE CHARMING?

A NEW TELEVISED SOCIAL EXPERIMENT IS LOOKING FOR YOU

In days of old, a prince would find his bride by searching the land for the fairest maiden in the kingdom. But in 2026, there's no need to saddle the horses. Now, we have the latest artificial intelligence to seek out the perfect princess for our very eligible prince. Could it be you? We're looking for applicants to take part in an exciting new television show:

LOVE SYNCED

If the shoe fits...

YOU COULD BE GOING TO THE BALL

Email applicants@lionsjaw.co.uk with a short video telling us why you're in need of your very own fairy godmother.

ONE

SKARDBALT AIRPORT

What is it about airports that turns people into arseholes?

It's like something in their brain snaps the second they set foot in a terminal, and the simplest things, like the ability to wait in line, empty a water bottle or display the tiniest crumb of human decency, go out the window.

Take the genius currently in front of me. The airport attendant has patiently explained that his suitcase is two pounds over the weight limit, so he'll have to remove something if he wants to check it in. His response? Repack his entire luggage while in the line, leaving me to watch helplessly as he flings open his case and starts wildly pulling out shirts and pants, throwing them in a pile behind him.

'London Heathrow via Oslo, boarding now,' crackles over the PA speaker.

Shit. That's my flight, and I haven't even got through security yet. The airport is pretty much deserted, but somehow

I've managed to get stuck behind a man with more costume changes than Taylor Swift.

'Can I just—' I say, trying to navigate my bags around him to the check-in desk.

He looks up at me, holding a sock in one hand and a toothbrush in the other, his face as red as an overripe tomato.

'Could you *please* give me a second,' he seethes, before muttering under his breath. 'Honestly, you people.'

I clench my teeth and resist the urge to argue – or bite him. Skardbalt Airport is as remote as you can get, with just one flight to the mainland a day, so if I miss mine… well, that is not an option. And yes, I do know I'm meant to get to the airport three hours before flying, but believe me, I've been kind of busy today.

I actually could have made it in plenty of time, except I forgot to factor in one thing: human beings. I don't know who said it, but they were right – hell is other people.

First, the airline guy on the phone refused to change my flight, so I had to max out my credit card on a new ticket. Then, on an island that's less than fifty square miles wide, my taxi driver took the scenic route and ended up stuck behind an uncooperative moose for twenty-five minutes. And now there's this charmer, who's currently putting on a second pair of trousers and stuffing a sock into each pocket.

I'm starting to get the feeling that, actually, it's got nothing to do with airports – people are just arseholes wherever they are.

After he's finished completely repacking, the guy shoves his case back on the scales.

'Sorry, sir,' the check-in assistant says. 'It's still over the weight allowance.'

I dig my fingernails into my palms and try my best not to scream. Above my head, the departures screen showing my flight is now flashing red.

I do not have time for this.

I walk around the guy, lean over the desk and give my best cocktail waitress smile to the attendant.

'Hey, sorry, I don't think he had it on there properly,' I say, slipping my foot under his case to take a bit of the weight off. 'Can you try it again?'

She squints at her screen, then back at me.

'Seems to be fine now,' she says, with zero emotion in her voice.

With that, the guy turns, gives me a grunt of acknowledgement, then slinks off in the direction of the cafeteria. Finally, it's my turn. I push my case onto the scale as I slide my passport towards the clerk. She flips to the back page, then looks up at me. Her eyes narrow as she compares the person in the passport photo with the strange vision in front of her: a woman wearing what is very clearly a wedding dress.

All I can do is stand there, blushing. Roughly eight hours ago, I'd been squeezed into ivory satin, plastered with foundation and blow-dried within an inch of my life. But now, my hair is falling out of its updo, my make-up smeared with tears, and the once pristine dress is covered in scuff marks.

'Um, congratulations?' she offers.

I purse my lips and shake my head.

'Oh,' she says. 'Right.'

My mind flicks back to a few hours earlier. Running out of the chapel, shoving my cases in the trunk of a taxi and begging the driver to please, *please* just run over the damn moose.

She hands me my passport back, and I run-walk to security, dragging my battered carry-on behind me.

Situated on a tiny Norwegian island in the middle of the Arctic Ocean, Skardbalt Airport is one of those small regional airports, pretty much contained in one large building. I've seen bigger IKEAs, to be honest. The combined arrivals and departure lounge has a single check-in desk and a gift shop. Over by the security scanner, there's a small, dingy cafeteria. But once I'd gone past that, to the one and only gate, there was no going back.

Two days ago, when I arrived here, there were a handful of tourists, gambling on a last-chance glimpse of the northern lights, and a few winter-sports enthusiasts, lugging their snowboards through security. But today, it looks like it's just me and Luggage Twat, so with any luck, before the sun comes up, I'll be touching down in cold, grey, rainy, glorious London. I cannot wait to get back home, away from everything and everyone.

See, told you I was a people person.

Once I'm through the security scanner, I pull my wheelie case off the X-ray conveyor belt and head down the short corridor towards the departure gate. But when I push open the door, my heart sinks. Actually, that's an understatement – more accurately, it plunges off a ten-thousand-foot drop, straight to that dark part of the ocean where only prehistoric jellyfish can survive. Because sitting at the gate are five of the worst people I've ever had the misfortune to meet: the Van Batten family.

If hell really is other people, then these guys would probably be the fiends running the place, poking everyone with pointy sticks and whacking up the temperature on the thermostat.

My first impulse is to turn straight around before they can see me (as if they could miss me in this dress). But as I swivel on my heel, I yank my wheelie case round so sharply that the loose wheel flies off, whizzing across the polished floor before coming to a stop at the toe of a well-shined brogue.

I freeze, mouth open, heart pounding, as the owner of said shoe bends down to pick up the rogue wheel.

'Lost something?' he asks, a shy smile spreading across his face, showcasing a perfect set of dimples.

Ladies and gentlemen, my ex-fiancé, Mr Marc Van Batten. *AKA the devil himself.*

TWO

SKARDBALT AIRPORT

Marc holds out the wheel towards me, still on one knee, almost like he's proposing all over again.

He looks tired. His dirty blond hair is unstyled, and there's a smattering of stubble on his face. But, even clearly hungover and exhausted, he still looks annoyingly attractive.

I, however, look like a bride strutting the world's longest walk of shame. I'd managed to swap my ivory satin sandals for trainers and pull on an old hoodie in the back of the cab, but I still have the muddy, snow-sodden train of my dress traipsing behind me.

As I reach out to take the broken wheel, the electronic device around my wrist lights up with a grinning emoji.

'Not now,' I hiss, clasping my hand over it before it can activate. I should have taken the damn thing off and chucked it out of the taxi window, but it's too late now.

Marc's eyes flick to my wrist, and then back at me.

'Hazel,' he says. 'I've been trying to call you, I—'

Before he can say another word, the preppy-looking guy standing behind him marches in between us. He places his palm on Marc's chest, pushing him away from me.

'What the fuck are *you* doing here?' he cries, spitting the word 'you' like he's dragged it from the back of his throat, equally coated in phlegm and derision.

I stare at him blankly.

'Hmm, I don't know, Dante, let me think,' I say, making a show of looking around the gate with a confused expression. 'Oh wait, this is the *airport*? Sorry, I thought it was the annual dipshit convention and you were the keynote speaker.'

He flicks his fringe from his eyes and scowls at me. 'Well, if you're lost, then allow me to help. The exit is right behind you.' He twirls his finger in the air. 'So turn around and piss off back where you came from.'

I take a breath and try to keep my composure. There is absolutely nothing to be gained from getting into a pissing contest with Dante, who's not only Marc's cousin but also his best man. Oh, and a massively self-entitled bellend.

'That is exactly what I am trying to do,' I say. 'I changed my flight to avoid *this exact scenario*. You were all supposed to be flying back to London tomorrow.'

'We rescheduled,' Marc says. 'Forecast says there's a big storm coming. Couldn't risk getting stuck here.'

'Awesome,' I mutter under my breath.

Without warning, Marc's stepmother strides up behind him, immaculately dressed in Dior and six-inch heels, despite the fact she's about to spend the next three hours in a small, uncomfortable chair with zero legroom. She looks me up and down, like I'm an unwelcome guest who's just trodden mud into her shagpile.

'You've got some nerve, showing up here,' she hisses, as if this situation is somehow my fault.

Marc runs a hand across his face. 'Stephanie, just give her a second, I don't think she—'

'I'll give her more than a second,' she snaps back. 'I'll give her a lifetime. After what she did, I never want to set eyes on this woman ever again.'

'You're in luck then,' I say. 'Cos in exactly twenty-two minutes, you'll be tucked up nice and snug behind the first-class curtain, and you can forget I ever existed.'

We both know that the tiny commercial jet taking us to the mainland won't have free peanuts, let alone a first-class section, but you try thinking of witty, off-the-cuff zingers on three hours' sleep and no breakfast.

'I am warning you,' she says, turning away. 'Stay away from my family, otherwise, God help me, I'll…'

'You'll what?' I ask.

Stephanie stops, then slowly swivels back around to face me, her icy gaze aimed between my eyes like a sniper's laser sight. For a moment, she looks like she's going to pull the trigger.

'Well,' she says eventually, smoothing out her blouse as she regains her poise. 'You'll regret it. That's all.'

With a toss of her glossy dark hair, she strides to the other side of the gate, Dante scurrying behind her. Marc shrugs apologetically and follows them, leaving me standing there clutching a plastic wheel and praying the ground will swallow me up.

When that, annoyingly, doesn't happen, I park myself down

as far away from the Van Batten party as possible (which, in a room this size, isn't very far) and pull my hood down, yanking the drawstrings tight.

The truth is, the Van Battens have good reason to hate my guts. Because while Marc Van Batten might arguably be the world's most infuriating man, he's not the one who jilted their fiancé on their wedding day.

That, I'm afraid, would be yours truly.

So maybe it's me, I'm the problem. *I'm* the one with the pointy tail and a penchant for trouble.

I check the time. Just a few minutes until boarding, and after that, I never have to see any of these people again in my life. I can survive that long, right?

But then there's a strange noise from the other side of the gate, like five people groaning in unison. I squint at the small TV hanging in the corner. At first, I struggle to read what it says on the screen, until it flicks from Norwegian to English, then a wave of nausea hits me. Actually, it's more like a full-blown tsunami. The departure time has disappeared, and all that remains is one word, the worst word in the English language:

DELAYED

Bloody *hell*.

THREE

SKARDBALT AIRPORT

'How fucking long?'

Dante's face has turned such a deep shade of red, I'm worried it's about to burst. I say worried, but truthfully, I'd pay good money to see that.

'As I've explained, sir, we are currently looking at a ten-hour delay,' the airline steward says again, his Scandinavian accent only just noticeable. 'I am afraid that no flights can take off until the bad weather clears.'

The steward, tall, fresh-faced and probably still in his twenties, has a light smattering of hair on his top lip that he probably thinks makes him look older. Unfortunately, with his badly fitting bright blue NordAir waistcoat and trousers, he resembles a holiday-camp entertainer more than a serious flight attendant, but I'm guessing he's probably not thrilled about the uniform either.

The group have surrounded the poor guy like a pack of

hyenas. Marc, Dante and Stephanie batter him with pointless questions, none of which are going to change the fact that we are stuck here. Their weird uncle, Gary, dressed head to toe in tweed (imagine Santa Claus, if he was going on a duck hunt in the Cotswolds), stands behind them, hopping from foot to foot.

The only other person at the gate doesn't bother getting up; instead, he lounges in one of the grey plastic seats, hiding behind mirrored sunglasses. I'm keeping my distance too, waiting to see how this plays out. The Van Battens, in my experience, always get what they want, either by throwing money at the situation or, failing that, suing the crap out of everyone within a five-mile radius.

'Ten hours?' Dante is squealing, like a toddler who's dropped his ice cream before taking a single lick. 'Fuck that, let's go back to the hotel.'

Dante isn't the most imposing figure, especially when he's having a tantrum. Only a couple of inches taller than me, with brown hair, combed into a side parting, he's wearing a pristine designer white T-shirt with an expensive-looking gold chain around his neck and an even more expensive chunky metal watch hanging off his wrist.

The steward addresses Dante again, the thin, polite smile never leaving his lips. 'If you wish, you can leave the airport and return tomorrow, sir. Unfortunately, your baggage has already been processed for loading, so you will not be able to retrieve it at this time.'

'So you expect us to wait *here*?' Stephanie says, motioning to her surroundings with a limp hand.

To be fair to her, I don't think anyone would *choose* to spend the night here. It's nothing but a limbo, a sterile, dimly lit holding area between the airport and the plane, where no one is supposed to linger for more than an hour, tops. A TV screen hangs from the ceiling, there's a decrepit vending machine in the corner, and three rows of plastic seats fixed to the polished concrete floor with steel bars. Behind them, huge windows look out onto the snowy tarmac outside, where our plane sits, grounded.

'If you do decide to stay at the gate overnight,' the steward explains patiently, 'I have to inform you all that you do so at your own risk. The airport cannot be held responsible for any damages, loss of income or injury.'

He adjusts his waistcoat and shuffles the papers on his little podium, as if attempting to project an air of authority.

'You're very welcome to apply for reimbursement online,' he offers. 'In the meantime, we can offer a ten-krone voucher for use in the airport café or gift shop.'

'Ten kroner?' Dante cries, getting his phone out. 'You do realise I could buy your poxy little airline? In fact, I might just do that right now. Then I'll be your boss, and the first thing I'll do is fire you.'

'Listen to me,' Stephanie says. 'We have an extremely important meeting with our lawyers tomorrow. It is imperative we get back to London as soon as possible. How much will it cost to resolve this situation?'

'Madam, I can't—'

'Well, if *you* can't,' she says, 'why don't you run along and find me someone worth talking to?'

'Oh, and while you're at it, would you mind terribly rustling up some blankets?' adds Weird Uncle Gary. 'It really is rather chilly in here.'

I can't take any more of this. As much as I would love

to avoid any further interactions with anyone today, I can't sit back and watch someone else get chewed up by the Van Battens.

'Hey.' I stand up and march over to them. 'Newsflash, even you don't have enough money to stop the snow falling from the sky.'

I point out one of the giant windows, where snow is pelting down against the glass at such a pace, the soft thump is like a constant drumbeat. This is more than just your average snowstorm.

'See that? None of us are going anywhere. So how about we all sit down, shut up and stop taking it out on the one guy who's actually trying to help us?'

There's a moment of silence as Stephanie's eyes bore into mine, like she's weighing up whether to slap me or sue me. Eventually Marc places a hand on her shoulder.

'Come on, it's been a long day,' he says, gently leading Stephanie back to her seat. 'For everybody.'

Dante throws his hands up and stomps off, before realising there's nowhere for him to actually stomp to, so he slumps against one of the huge windows, muttering to himself. Only Weird Uncle Gary is left gawking at me.

'But what about my blanket?' he asks.

I stare at him until he shuffles off, then sink into my seat, retreating back into my turtle shell. I feel like I've been having a panic attack from the moment I woke up, but now a tidal wave of exhaustion hits me, and I bury my head in my hands.

I hear footsteps approaching and look up to see the steward.

'Is everything… okay?' he says awkwardly.

'I just want to go home,' I mumble.

He takes the seat next to me and tentatively pats me on the back, like I'm a stray cat that might scratch him at any moment. To be fair, I'm sure comforting distressed brides isn't in his job description.

'Thank you for your, um, assistance back there,' he says.

'I've been Danted a few times myself,' I tell him. 'So I know how it feels.'

His brow furrows, and I cock my head towards Dante, who looks like he's working out how much it would cost to nuke the entire airport. Or at least buy it, bulldoze it and build a shopping centre.

'Oh, *that* gentleman. He forgets that I am also – how do you say? – in the same boat.'

'You have to stay all night too?' I ask.

'This is a tiny airport. Fewer than twenty staff, who will probably be sent home before the roads close. But me? I shall stay,' he says. 'A babysitter, if you will. Somebody has to make sure you do not hurt yourselves.'

'I'm sorry,' I say.

'Dealing with angry, tired passengers is part of the job.' He sighs. 'You know, when I was little, I thought the life of an airline steward would be glamorous, like on the television! But instead, most people treat us like we are their personal waiters. Ring a little bell, and we come running with a snack and a plastic glass of warm wine.'

I smile, for what seems like the first time today.

'Hey, come on, you're more than that. What about that cute little safety dance you do before take-off?' I mimic the routine, as best as I can remember it. 'The exits are here, and here. And don't forget to wear your seatbelt…'

'Ha!' He laughs. 'When is the last time you saw anyone pay attention to that? It is purely for insurance purposes, did you know? If we crash and you die, no one can say that they were not informed!'

My eyes settle on the scuffed NordAir name badge pinned to his waistcoat. 'Emil?' I ask.

'Yes,' he says.

'I'm Hazel,' I tell him. 'And if I'm totally honest with you, I'm not sure I can survive the night in this gate. Is there anywhere else I could wait?'

He shakes his head. 'I am sorry, Hazel. Delayed passengers have to stay in the gate. The rest of the airport will be closed for the night.'

My heart sinks. This is why I hate airports. They're like an independent country, with their own special laws and rules. And like a nuclear bunker or a Las Vegas casino, once you're in them, it's difficult to get out.

'How about a safe room?' I ask. 'Got one of those?'

Emil gives me a dubious look. 'Is there some sort of problem with the gate?'

'Yeah, five of them.'

I jerk my thumb towards the others, currently spread out across two rows of chairs. Dante is now furiously texting on his phone, probably trying to Uber a private helicopter to airlift him out of this mess. Stephanie is berating Marc about his life choices, while Uncle Gary picks at an unsightly scab on the back of his neck. The guy in the sunglasses sits motionless in his seat, trying to ignore them.

'Ah, I see,' Emil says. 'I must say, you do not seem like you are a good fit with these people.'

'That's putting it lightly.' I look over at the Van Battens, with their designer clothes and leather carry-ons, and then down at the chewed sleeves of my hoodie and my three-wheeled case.

'They are not your friends?' he asks.

'Friends? Emil, you might be the only person in the airport who doesn't want to bludgeon me to death with a universal travel adaptor right now,' I tell him.

'Oh,' he says. 'And so why, exactly, are you a thousand miles from home in an airport with these people who want to, um, how did you put it?'

'Bludgeon me to death with a... never mind,' I sigh. 'It's a long story.'

Emil glances at the departures board and then meets my eye. 'I think, perhaps, that we have plenty of time.'

I look over at Marc. He's staring at the floor with the same bemused expression he had earlier today when I struggled to answer the priest's (to be fair, pretty straightforward) question. An expression that I'm guessing didn't change as I ran down the aisle. I couldn't know for sure, because I didn't look back. Even if I had, the tears in my eyes made everything kind of blurry.

'Okay.' I take a deep breath. 'So, you see that guy over there?'

'The one who looks a little like Captain America?'

'Um, okay, yeah, a *tiny* bit. But don't ever tell him that, he's got a big enough head already,' I say. 'That's Marc Van Batten, and he's sort of my ex.'

'Sort of?'

'Well, it's complicated. He's actually the Godzilla of exes. My ex-fiancé, to be accurate. We were supposed to get married today. Hence this ridiculous outfit,' I gesture to my dress, 'and, well, let's just say things didn't exactly work out. And those delightful people with him are his family. Or some of them, anyway. Right now, I am pretty much their least favourite person in the world.'

'And the feeling is mutual, I take it?' Emil asks.

'Well, you met Dante, he's not exactly what you'd call likable. The only reason he's Marc's best man is because they're cousins. They went to boarding school together, I think.'

Emil nods thoughtfully. 'And the lady? She looks very sophisticated.'

Even wedged into what must be the world's most uncomfortable chair, Stephanie does manage a poised elegance. She must be in her early fifties, I reckon, but her face is smooth enough to arouse suspicion.

'Well, sure, in the same way Hannibal Lecter is sophisticated,' I say.

Emil's eyes widen.

'Don't worry,' I reassure him. 'She's not actually eaten anyone. Yet. Not that I know about anyway. Stephanie is the matriarch of the family. And she owes me one, to be honest, since now her illustrious family name won't be sullied by a penniless waitress.'

'And what about him?' Emil points to the slightly portly man with ruddy cheeks and big, bushy white beard, who has now successfully peeled the scab from his neck. 'That gentleman looks relatively harmless.'

'Weird Uncle Gary, harmless? Well, that all depends on how much aquavit he's had to drink. Gary is your classic drunk uncle at a wedding. Little bit handsy. Forced me to watch a card trick and offered me some uppers.'

'Is that why you call him Weird Uncle Gary?'

'Wait for it,' I say, and we watch as Gary pops the scab in his mouth. 'That's why.'

Emil nods again. 'I see. This is all very fascinating. But it does not explain why you are here with the family of a man who is, apparently, no longer your fiancé.'

I take a breath.

'Okay, well, you see the last guy?' I point at the middle-aged man with a haircut that's about twenty years too young for him, an open shirt and extremely white box-fresh trainers. He hasn't taken off his aviator shades since we've been here, even though it's half past seven in the evening and we're inside. 'That's Julian Draper. He's not technically a Van Batten, but he might as well be. You know who Simon Cowell is?'

'Yes, I know of Simon Cowell.'

'Right, well, Julian is the supermarket own-brand version. He created the *Love Synced* TV show. It's his baby; he runs the whole thing.'

'I have not seen it, sorry,' Emil says.

'Don't worry, no one has. Hopefully they never will.'

'So you were all here in Skardbalt to film a reality show?' Emil asks.

'Julian prefers to call it a "social experiment", but yeah, basically,' I say. 'They used artificial intelligence to scour the country for Marc's soulmate, his perfect match, and, lucky me, it turned out to be yours truly.'

I wave my wrist at him. Strapped to it is a black electronic device with a small digital display. It looks like a cheap smartwatch.

'Meet CILLA,' I say. 'Computer Integrated Love Language Algorithm. She's basically an AI assistant who keeps tabs on everything I do and say. Which is actually quite annoying.'

'An AI assistant? Like Alexa?'

'Right, but unlike Alexa, she doesn't just tell you the

weather forecast and turn your central heating down,' I say. 'She can offer relationship advice, settle an argument, even predict likely outcomes, like whether Marc and I were going to be happily married. Although, judging by what happened today, she's obviously had a malfunction.'

Emil peers at my wristband. 'And this CILLA, she is listening to us right now?'

'She's *always* listening. But as the TV show is most definitely over, she's wasting her time. Unless of course she's working out how likely it is I'm going to die, alone and single, at a freezing airport gate.'

I look down at my scuffed Nikes and wonder, if I click them together three times, whether I might magically return home.

'Do not worry,' Emil says. 'I guarantee by this time tomorrow, you will be home safe. All of you.'

When he says that, my wristband beeps, and the display lights up. Before I can stop it, a tinny female voice starts talking.

'Hiya!' CILLA says. 'Hope you're having a great day so far! Sorry to interrupt, I wanted to make a minor correction.'

I lift up my wrist to show Emil. 'See, told you she was annoying. Go on, CILLA, what did I get wrong this time?'

A smiley face flashes up on her screen.

'The actual probability of you getting safely home by tomorrow,' she says, 'is four per cent. Have a great day!'

INTRODUCTION INTERVIEW

LION'S JAW STUDIOS, EAST LONDON

Hazel:
(sits down in a large yellow chair, looks into the camera and waves nervously) Uh, hi? Do I just start talking, or…

Producer (off camera):
You could start by introducing yourself.

Hazel:
Right, that makes sense. My name is Hazel Harper. I'm thirty-two, live in London. I work at Eight Ball… that's a private members' club in Soho, in case you're not a media type or a TikTok celebrity. Rooftop cocktails and lo-fi chillhop, if you're into that sort of thing. My *official* job title is hostess, but I hate that. Makes it sound like I work in a sex dungeon. And I do not work in a sex dungeon. Just to be *super* clear on that.

Producer:
Okay. Why don't you tell us why you're here today?

Hazel:
Because I'm looking for my soulmate… that's the point of this thing, right? And apparently, I am incapable of finding one under my own devices. That's what my friend Tilly thinks anyway. She's the one who talked me into this in the first place. Tilly reckons I'm going to die alone, and they'll only find me, shrivelled up in front of the TV with a microwave meal for one on my lap, when the neighbours complain about the smell. Doesn't actually sound like a bad way to go, to be honest…

(sighs) The truth is, in the past I've found it… difficult to get along with people. I guess I'm sort of… what's that word Tilly used? *Impenetrable*. I don't like to let people get too close. In my experience, if you let someone in, then you've only got yourself to blame if you get hurt. So that's why I want a wristband. Humans are fallible, right? God knows I found that out. But these algorithms, this data, that can't be wrong. The data can't lie, can it? (pauses) Is this the kind of stuff you want?

Producer:
Just keep going, we can edit what we need. You're one of a thousand women who have been given a wristband containing our AI matchmaking software. Tell us why you applied for the show?

Hazel:
Hah, that's a good question. My Aunt Clara loves to remind me that 'the clock is ticking', which pisses me off,

because people never say that to guys, do they? Her theory is I'm actually *allergic* to men. You know how some people, like, can't eat gluten? Well, Aunt Clara says I have a man intolerance. But that's not true. I like men, I just don't have the time or energy to spend weeding out the bad ones. That's what this thing is for, right? (holds up wristband)

Producer:
Why don't you ask her yourself?

Hazel:
Uh, okay. (holds wristband up to her mouth) Um, hello, CILLA, are you there?

CILLA:
Hi, Hazel! It's so nice to meet you! Would you like to chat? You can ask me anything.

Hazel:
(pokes the wristband screen) Are you gonna, like, spy on me then?

CILLA:
Great question, Hazel! As long as you're wearing your wristband, I'll be able to monitor your physical actions, conversations, online activity and physiological data. Once I have collected enough information, I'll use a combination of modelling and statistical analysis to predict which of our applicants is the most likely to have a successful marriage with our bachelor.

Producer:
So how do you rate your chances?

Hazel:
All I have to do is be myself, right? And CILLA here will do the rest. If it's me, great. But if we're not a match, then I haven't lost anything, have I? Probably just had another lucky escape. (laughs)

FOUR

SKARDBALT AIRPORT

Have you ever tried playing I Spy with yourself? It's a lot less fun, but you do win every single time, so actually, I prefer it this way. And having already filed my nails down to the quick, and read every single story on the MailOnline, I am running seriously low on ideas to pass the time.

The fact that I'm famished isn't helping. I keep picturing the untouched wedding buffet and wonder, not for the first time, if I might have made a gigantic mistake.

Luckily, the gate has an ancient vending machine. Unluckily, like everything else in this airport, it seems to have been frozen in time circa 1982 and only accepts coins. As I only have three kroner in my bag, whatever I buy will have to last me for the next ten hours, so I'm appraising every item very carefully. Drumming my fingers on the glass, I gaze gormlessly at the meagre selection of snacks. The least worst option is probably a packet of crisps with a picture of a vegetable on the front so faded and sun-bleached it is almost unrecognisable.

Behind me, the Van Battens sound like they're getting steadily more drunk, and I can't help but feel a little jealous. Next to the vending machine is an old-fashioned water cooler, with a big blue plastic container and a stack of paper cups, and I've drunk about eight of them out of boredom. Alcohol would definitely help this evening go a little faster. Or, better yet, help me forget it completely.

I shove in the coins, one by one, then hold down the button marked F3. The packet jolts, as if it's been suddenly awakened after decades of slumber, but doesn't fall. Instead, it just hangs there, on the brink of tumbling but somehow clinging on for dear life.

'I know how you feel,' I murmur to it, resting my head against the clouded Perspex.

Suddenly I hear a voice behind me.

'I can lend you some cash,' it says. 'There's no need to headbutt it.'

I look up, startled, and see Marc leaning against the machine.

'Uh, no thanks,' I mumble, turning back to the machine and pretending there's something really fascinating happening inside.

But he doesn't move, and I can feel him still looking at me.

'Can I help you with something?' I ask, impatiently.

'No, not really,' he says. 'I was just passing on my way to the bathroom.'

'Well, the men's is over there.' I point to the other side of the gate.

'Out of order,' he informs me, rather too smugly for my liking. 'Apparently we all have to use the women's.' He jerks his thumb towards the toilet door behind him.

I let out a groan. 'So not only am I trapped here for ten hours, I also get to share a bathroom with Weird Uncle Gary? Could this day get any worse?'

Marc shrugs. 'Actually, yeah, I just watched him polish off the three kilos of Norwegian cheese he bought in the gift shop, so I figure it is going to get a *lot* worse.'

I glance back at my trapped packet of crisps, suddenly feeling a lot less hungry.

'So, since we're here, do you wanna, um… talk about it?' Marc asks.

I freeze.

'The crisps?' I ask. 'I mean, what can I say? They're pretty representative of how this day is going so far to be honest—'

'No, not the crisps, Hazel,' he says, not taking his gaze off me. 'What the hell happened today?'

I feel my insides twist. I do not have the answers for that right now. At least, not the ones he wants to hear.

'You really want to do this here?' I ask, keeping my eyes fixed on my reflection in the vending machine. Right now, it's the only person I can trust.

'Why, you have something better to do for the next ten hours?'

'Yes.' I tap on the Perspex. 'Right now, I'm extremely focused on extricating these crisps before I die of starvation.'

Marc shakes his head. 'Right, okay, Hazel.'

He turns to walk back to his family, but then stops.

'You know we did it,' he says, his voice harder now. 'We actually did it. We proved to everyone we really were a genuine match. Soulmates. But then, out of nowhere, you do a runner in front of my whole family and probably a million TV viewers...' He tails off. 'But sure, your snack selection is the pressing issue here.'

'You're seriously blaming this on me?' I snap back. 'After everything that happened, you think this is somehow all *my* fault?'

'You could have told me how you were feeling before our actual wedding day, Hazel. Instead of, you know, when I was standing at the altar with a ring in my hand.'

I'm hit with a wave of guilt. He's not angry; he's hurt. But the truth is, there could not be a worse possible place for this conversation. I know I owe him some sort of explanation, but ideally, when I drop that bombshell, I'll be well out of range of the fallout. I take a deep breath and try to find some words, *any* words that might postpone the inevitable detonation.

'I couldn't... you didn't ever—' I start, before realising I have no idea where to begin. It's too late, too much to explain and I'm too exhausted to think straight.

'Fine,' Marc sighs. 'But if you won't talk to me, maybe you should talk to him.'

He looks over at Julian. He still has his sunglasses on, but even so, I can almost feel the fury emanating from every pore in his body. I grimace. My right hand is still throbbing, a nagging reminder of what's under those shades.

'Do you think he's still going to broadcast the show?' I ask.

Marc rubs his chin. 'After what happened in the chapel, I don't see how he can. But then again, I don't see how he can't either. Lion's Jaw have got millions riding on this thing.'

Lion's Jaw. Julian's production company. Normally they specialise in true-crime documentaries, but *Love Synced* is their first foray into the world of reality TV. Or, at least, it was supposed to be.

'Can't your fancy lawyers do something?'

He shakes his head. 'Did you forget all those release forms we signed? There's nothing we can do.'

'Well, nothing short of bashing his head in, nicking his memory cards and deleting all the footage,' I say.

'Careful,' Marc says, tapping his wrist. 'You-know-who's listening.'

My hand goes to my wrist, instinctively covering the cold metal band clasped tightly around it. I've worn it so long, I almost forgot it was there.

'What happened to yours?' I ask, noticing his wrist is bare.

'Uh, must have left it at the hotel,' he says. 'Piece of crap didn't do a great job, did she?'

'Guess not.' I shrug.

Marc thinks for a moment.

'You know, this flight delay could actually help us out. There's nothing Julian can do with the footage until he gets back to the UK, so maybe, as we're stuck here all night, how do you feel about mending a few fences? If we can convince Julian we don't all want to kill each other, then maybe he'll agree to film a new finale back in London.'

He says 'we', but he means me. And the thought of even talking to that man, let alone begging for his mercy, makes my stomach turn.

'Hazel, if we don't give him something else he can use,' Marc goes on, 'he'll have to broadcast the full wedding. Every cough and spit. And that would not be good for any of us. So how about you come over and play nice, just for a bit?'

'Marc, your stepmother just threatened to kill me. I'm not sure she's up for a game of UNO.'

'Oh, she's just being dramatic. You know what she's like. Besides, I bet you've read every story on the MailOnline twice by now.'

I feel my cheeks burn. 'I do not read the MailOnline.'

'Come on,' he says, leaning over and taking a bunch of paper cups from the water cooler. 'Dante snuck a fourteen-year-old bottle of Scotch through security, and I'd much rather we were drinking it than him.'

'I should really stay here and try and get these out...' I say, pointing to the trapped packet behind the Perspex. 'I didn't have any breakfast and—'

Marc glances at the machine, like he's appraising a second-hand car, and then thumps the side of the machine with his fist. Something falls, clattering on the metal tray at the bottom. He sticks his hand in and retrieves the packet of crisps.

'Problem solved,' he says, waving it at me as he steps backwards towards the others.

'Wait, I thought you were going to the toilet?' I say.

'Oh? Yeah. Hmm, weird, I don't feel the need anymore.' He shrugs. 'So, you coming or not?'

He opens the crisps and pops one in his mouth, then he winks at me, annoyingly.

INTRODUCTION INTERVIEW

LION'S JAW STUDIOS, EAST LONDON

Marc Van Batten:
Hey. (sits down on large yellow chair) This is cool. (pats the chair) We ready to go? (smiles) Alright, let's do this.

Producer (off camera):
Tell us why you agreed to be *Love Synced*'s very own 'Prince Charming'.

Marc Van Batten:
What's that saying about the definition of madness? (laughs) When you do the same thing over and over again, expecting a different result? Well, that pretty much sums up my dating life. Been there, done that. What can I say? God loves a trier, right? I was really flattered to be asked. I mean, 'Prince Charming'? How could I say no? And I've been looking for my soulmate for a long time, you know?

In *all* the wrong places. Quite a lot of wrong places, if I'm honest with you. In hindsight, it was probably unlikely I was going to find her at three a.m. in a Malaysian dive bar. The thing is, I do actually believe in soulmates. I've just been struggling to find mine. So AI matchmaking makes sense. It's just like using Google Maps, right? Don't get me wrong, the long way round was fun, but if the CILLA thing can help me get there faster, that's a no-brainer. If artificial intelligence can tie my shoelaces, then surely it can sort out my love life, right?

Producer:
Um, I don't think it can tie your shoelaces. Yet. But we're working on that. Is it fair to say that you've had serious relationships in the past?

Marc Van Batten:
Serious? Uh, well, that's not the word I would use. I try not to be too serious about anything. I've been accused of being shallow in the past, sure. Not entirely fairly, I might add. I mean, *yes*, the women I've dated previously do all share a certain *look*. But it's just that, because of the circles I mix in, I do tend to end up meeting a lot of... well, a particular sort of person, let's say.

Producer:
Models?

Marc Van Batten:
Hey, they are not *all* models. A few have been professional athletes. Oh, and, actually, I did date a pop star once, but

it wasn't one of the really famous ones. Anyway, the point is, none of those relationships worked out, obviously. Otherwise I wouldn't be sitting here, right? The truth is, every relationship I've ever been in has been a bit of a disaster. So this time around I was hoping to... how can I put it? Prioritise different qualities? Look a bit... deeper, maybe.

Producer:
Some of your previous relationships have made the headlines. Do you have any regrets?

Marc Van Batten:
(runs a hand through his hair, laughs nervously) Okay, I know what you're referring to, and, yeah, fair play, I didn't exactly come out of that, um, situation smelling of roses. I have a past, I know that. And not all of it is good. But this is a new start, and now I've got CILLA to make sure I don't end up with another skeleton in my closet, right?

FIVE

SKARDBALT AIRPORT

Reluctantly, I follow Marc to the other side of the gate, where at least one of the Van Battens seems to be making the most of their situation. Dante is sitting on Stephanie's Louis Vuitton hand luggage, glassy-eyed and swigging from a half-empty bottle of Scotch. By the look of him, I don't think he's stopped drinking since the wedding.

The others are slouched across the chairs in varying degrees of boredom. Stephanie idly flicks through a copy of *Harper's Bazaar*. Weird Uncle Gary is curled up in his seat, eyes half closed, cradling a giant Toblerone bar like it's a newborn baby, while Julian taps his fingers impatiently on his armrest.

As I approach, Stephanie looks over the top of her magazine and tuts.

'Marc, darling, there's a bin over there,' she says. 'You don't need to bring your trash back here.'

Ignoring her, Marc plucks the magazine out of her hands and rolls it up like a megaphone. 'Listen up everyone,' he says through it. 'I'm calling a temporary truce.'

Stephanie exhales theatrically, while Dante leans back, swigging from the whisky with one hand and flipping Marc the finger with the other.

'Seeing as we're all stuck here together for the night,' Marc puts down his makeshift megaphone and continues, obliviously, 'how about we at least try to get along?'

I stand behind him, looking at my shoes and massively regretting every life decision that's brought me to this point. I don't want to 'get along', I want to run away, as fast as I can, in the opposite direction. Unfortunately, right now, that would mean sprinting out into the freezing snow, where I'd end up doing my best Jack-Nicholson-at-the-end-of-*The-Shining* impression.

Sheepishly, I slide into the seat next to Julian and offer him an awkward smile, but he doesn't even look at me. At least, I think he doesn't. Hard to tell with those stupid sunglasses on.

'Hey,' I say, leaning over. 'So, um, about earlier, obviously I lost my temper, and—'

Julian silences me by holding up his palm.

'Too soon, I get it,' I say, slumping back in the chair. I'm beginning to think Dante has the right idea. Hard liquor might be the only way through this.

We all sit in silence for a moment, Julian and me on one row of chairs and the Van Battens across from us. On the other side of the gate, Emil stands behind his podium, desperately trying to ignore us.

'This was a mistake,' I say, standing up. 'I'm going back over there.'

Marc puts the rolled magazine to his lips again. 'Everyone, Hazel would like to say something.'

My mouth goes dry. What the hell am I meant to say? I swear, I had every intention of slipping that ring on my finger today and sodding off on honeymoon. But when the big moment came, I just could not bring myself to say 'I do'. I suppose I could've politely excused myself but, cards on the table, that's never been my style. So instead, I may just have pressed the nuclear button, in front of about three TV cameras and the assembled friends and family of the groom. You know how they say 'go big or go home'? Well, I went big. And now I really want to go home.

'Uh, okay, well...' I sit back down, a row of expectant faces waiting for my big speech. 'So, I know today didn't exactly go as planned. We all said some things we shouldn't have, and—'

'We?' Stephanie snorts. 'You were the only person who made a fool of themselves.'

'Give her a chance to finish,' Marc says.

'I don't really give a shit what she's got to say,' Dante says, putting the whisky to his mouth. 'As of now, I am now officially off the wagon, and all I am interested in is getting very, very drunk.'

'Give me that,' Marc says, snatching the bottle from him before he can take a swig. 'You're not supposed to be drinking, you know that. How did you even get this through security anyway?'

'Slipped the guy fifty dollars,' Dante says.

Marc wipes the top of the bottle with his shirt sleeve, then places the paper cups on Stephanie's luggage and pours a glug of whisky in each.

'If anyone here has a good reason to be upset about today, it's me,' he says. 'So we're all going to have a drink together – not you, Dante, you've had enough – and see if we can't work this whole thing out before we get back to London. Without getting the lawyers involved.'

'If you think I'm about to start downing shots like we're at a frat party…' Stephanie says, surveying the cups.

'Oh come on, Lady Steph,' Marc says, holding out a cup. 'I know it's not exactly a dry martini, but you've never been one to turn down a drink.'

She glares at him but takes a cup anyway. 'Just to be clear, I am not, under any circumstances, performing charades.'

'Fine,' Marc says. 'Uncle Gary?'

Gary nods enthusiastically and picks up a cup.

'Julian, will you join us?' Marc asks, holding a cup towards him.

Julian doesn't respond, so Marc passes the cup to me.

I lift it to my mouth and down the shot. It burns as it hits the back of my throat. I've never been much of a drinker, but if this stuff can take the edge off the next eight hours, then it'll do. Hell, if it can take the edge off the next eight minutes, I'll take the rest of the bottle.

'Alright,' Marc says. 'Has anyone else got anything they'd like to say?'

Stephanie coughs. 'After what she did today, I'm surprised she even has the gall to come over here, dressed like that. She ought to be—'

'Excuse me? What I did?' I cry. 'What about you? You should be ecstatic we didn't get married! You've been against me from the beginning.'

'As a matter of fact, I could not care less about you, Hazel. The only thing I care about is this family, which you have made very clear you do not wish to be a part of. But your ridiculous actions today could destroy everything this family has built. Decades of hard work and sacrifice. Notions that you appear to know very little about.'

'You're lecturing me about hard work and sacrifice?' I scoff. 'The woman who married a millionaire twice her age? You don't know a thing about me, you stuck up cu—'

Marc stands up. 'That's enough! This is getting us nowhere.' He points at the Toblerone in Weird Uncle Gary's hands. 'New rule. From now on, you can only speak if you're holding the Toblerone. That means, Gary, you're up.'

Stephanie rolls her eyes. 'So it appears we are playing charades after all.'

Weird Uncle Gary looks surprised, and actually quite pleased to be involved.

'Oh, well, thank you for the opportunity. I would just like to say, it's been a terribly stressful day, and it would be absolutely wonderful if we could all get along,' he says. 'However, there were a number of hurtful comments made about my character during the ceremony too.'

'Who cares?' Dante grunts. 'We're talking about our family getting cancelled here. I don't think you have to worry about that. The most you're going to get cancelled is your afternoon magic show at a five-year-old's birthday party.'

'Um, excuse me,' Gary says to him. 'You're not holding the Toblerone.'

Dante snatches the chocolate out of Gary's hand.

'My turn now. Thanks to this bitch's meltdown today,' he points at me, 'I am well and truly fucked.'

'It was entirely your choice to get off your face at the stag,' I say. 'I didn't force the cocaine up your nose.'

Dante waves the Toblerone in my face. 'Nuh-uh, you heard Uncle Gary,' he says, then adds in a mocking baby voice, 'No choccy, no talkie.'

Oh, now I really, really want to murder him.

Marc whips the chocolate from Dante, then holds it out towards me, like it's a relay baton. 'Hazel, is there anything you'd like to add?'

I take the Toblerone from him. I could play along. I could apologise. I could beg for forgiveness. But you know what? I'm not sure I really want to. As far as I'm concerned, the Van Battens are responsible for the mess we're in, and they can dig themselves out of it.

Instead, I slide the bar out of its cardboard packet and break off a triangle. Before I can toss it in my mouth, Dante knocks the chocolate out of my hands and sends it skidding across the floor.

'Fuck your fucking Toblerone,' Dante says, picking up the whisky bottle. 'This is bullshit. I'm going to get pissed.'

Slowly, Julian stands up, bends down and picks up the chocolate. 'Does this mean I get to talk now?' he asks, his voice flat, almost bored.

'Looks like the floor is yours,' Marc says.

A thin, unnerving smile creeps across Julian's face. 'Firstly, thank you for this little performance piece; honestly, I've not seen anything quite as embarrassing since, well, since your wedding,' he says. 'Unfortunately, it's been a complete waste of your time. Next week, episode one of *Love Synced* will air, as planned. And once I get back to the UK with the memory cards, the team can edit the footage of the final episode. That's right, the wedding. And believe me, it's *all* going to be in there. So, enjoy yourselves while you can, because trust me, this time next week, none of you are going to be having much fun.'

Everyone stares at him in stunned silence. Marc's face turns ashen. Stephanie looks like she's about to have a heart attack. Dante just growls. Even Weird Uncle Gary seems worried.

'I'm especially grateful to you, Hazel,' Julian goes on. 'For gracing me with a finale to die for. The sins of the Van Batten family exposed, in a chapel, no less! Exquisite. This will make *Love Island* seem like *Countryfile*!'

'We'll sue you for every penny you have,' Stephanie says, coldly.

'You all signed the release forms, so I guess I'll see you in court.' Julian picks up his carry-on bag and pushes past us.

I watch him for a second, then call out after him. 'So you're selling us out? What happened to your so-called "social experiment"?'

He swings round to face me. 'What happened? You know very well what happened, Ms Harper.'

For the first time since we've been here, he reaches up and slowly takes off his sunglasses, revealing a dark, purple bruise around his left eye.

'And if you need reminding, we have *plenty* of footage of the assault,' he says.

A pang of fear spikes through me like I've been jabbed with a cattle prod.

'Fine,' I say, trying to sound tough. 'If you want the whole world to see you getting KOed by a five-foot-four woman in a wedding dress, be my guest, stick it on Netflix for all I care.'

Calling Julian's bluff is risky. If he does broadcast the wedding, I could lose my job, my flat, everything. It's not like

I have a trust fund to fall back on. Or, literally, *anything* to fall back on.

'Oh, don't worry, Hazel,' he says. 'That footage won't be going on television. Oh no, *that* part is going straight to the police. Now if you'll excuse me, it's been a very long day. I've spent the last two weeks watching every moment of your ridiculous lives, and, frankly, I've seen enough.'

He strides to the other side of the gate, where he lies down across a row of chairs and breaks off a big chunk of Toblerone with his teeth.

'Quite honestly,' he says, through a mouthful of chocolate, 'I sincerely hope I never see any of you again.'

The rest of us stand there, dumbfounded. Stephanie looks like she wants to kill him. Dante is gripping the whisky bottle so hard, I'm worried it's going to break. Uncle Gary looks like he's going to burst into tears. And Marc's face is paler than the moon.

Only the howl of the wind outside breaks the shocked silence. The snow is raging hard now, and part of me wants it to cover us so deep we'll never be found.

SIX

SKARDBALT AIRPORT

The second my eyes flicker open, a surge of panic shoots through me. I sit bolt upright, eyes darting around the room.

Where the hell am I? Who are all these people?

In a flash, everything floods back. Oh yeah, that's right, I'm stuck in an airport with my ex-fiancé and his family who hate my guts. Normal Tuesday.

Somehow, I'd managed to doze off in this damn dress, which is a miracle, because it's like a straitjacket, if Vera Wang designed straitjackets.

The gate is dark, it's freezing cold and I really, really need to pee. I scan the room from under the flimsy NordAir blanket that Emil found for each of us, the kind you get on the plane that are so thin you can almost see through them.

The only noise is the wind, and the faint rumble of Uncle Gary snoring. Marc is draped over two chairs, his chest rising and falling slowly. Dante, mouth wide open and dribbling, is spreadeagled, his whisky bottle at his feet. Even Stephanie is fast asleep, her head resting on her hand luggage. The snow is at full gale. With these huge windows, it feels a bit like we're stuck in a reverse snow globe, with the snow on the outside, and us trapped inside.

Julian is the only one I can't see. He must be in the bathroom, I guess, which is annoying, because I'm really desperate now, and after his little outburst, I'm very, very keen to avoid bumping into him in a dark, enclosed space.

I shift my weight, so the plastic chair is not poking into my hip, and check my phone. The battery is down to 11 per cent, and I've only got about fifteen minutes of the airport's free Wi-Fi left. Can I really justify watching thirty-two interior design TikToks in a row, or should I try and eek it out till morning?

I text Tilly, my best friend (and maid of honour), instead.

Hazel:
Tils, you awake? Guess what, I'm stuck at airport. You were totally right to stay at the hotel.

A few seconds later, a reply flashes up.

Tilly:
no way

Hazel:
Way. And guess who's stuck here with me.

Tilly:
shut up

Hazel:
Yep, Marc and the whole Van Batten clan. And Julian. Even their handsy uncle.

Tilly:
Hun I wld die!! We're all holed up at the hotel. Everyone saying it's the worst storm for thirty years! Roads are all closed. Can't get anywhere.

Hazel:
You had a lucky escape, this is a nightmare.

Tilly:
Yeah babes, you're missing out, I got a mini bar n central heating n everything!

Hazel:
Uh, no YOU'RE missing out. I have a Toblerone.

As I type that, I realise Marc ate all my crisps, and I could really go for a chunk of nougaty chocolate. But when I look over where Julian was sleeping, I see the Toblerone has gone. The greedy little wanker must have eaten the whole thing. Unless Gary nabbed it back.

I look over at Gary, and almost fall off my seat. His eyes are wide open, glinting in the darkness and staring straight at me. When he sees my startled expression, he winks. I want to throw up. Was he just pretending to be asleep, but actually watching me this whole time?

Ugh, gross.

I yank my blanket over me, trying to shield myself from

his gaze, but it barely covers my shoulders. There is literally nowhere to hide in this place. How can Julian *still* be in the bathroom? What the hell is he doing in there? On second thought, I don't want to know the answer to that. But I can't hold it much longer. I'll just go in there real quick, keep my head down. Maybe I can get away with a sleepy nod of acknowledgement. Knowing him, he won't miss an opportunity to get a dig in, but I can ignore it, right? Okay, probably not, judging by my track record of absolutely not ignoring people when they come at me, but fuck it. It's either go now or Uncle Gary is going to get a very different show than he bargained for.

Pulling my blanket up over my head, I quickly scurry towards the bathroom. When I push the door, the bright strip lights flicker on, revealing a row of sinks and a mop in a yellow plastic bucket. There's only one cubicle, and the door is closed. I knock on it gently.

'Hey,' I whisper. 'Are you nearly done?'

No answer.

'Jesus,' I say to myself. 'He really did fall asleep sitting on the toilet.'

To be fair, the cubicle is warmer and probably more comfortable than the chairs at the gate, plus there's the advantage of not being ogled by Weird Uncle Gary.

I push gently against the door, but it's locked.

'Hurry up!' I hiss, thumping on the door.

Still nothing.

Sorry Jules, but I really can't wait any longer. I fish around in my hoodie pocket, pull out my emery board and slip it in the gap between the door and the frame. It hits the metal lock and I push it upwards to release the lock. *Voila*, a little trick I learned at Eight Ball when someone had, shall we say, overindulged in the bathroom. The cubicle door swings open, revealing Julian, sat on the toilet, trousers around his ankles, head lolling back. Fast asleep, as I suspected.

I step inside and tap his leg with my foot, resisting the temptation to kick his shin.

'Oi, come on. Wake up, please, I really need to go.'

He doesn't move. I kick him again, harder. This time his head flops forward and I jump back in shock.

His eyes are wide open, and his face is frozen in a terrified rictus. The Toblerone is sticking out of his mouth, like it's been forced in there.

And that's when I start screaming.

- EPISODE ONE -
THE REVEAL

LION'S JAW STUDIOS, EAST LONDON

Producer (off camera):
Today you're going to meet your fiancé. How do you feel about that?

Hazel (sitting in big yellow chair):
How do I feel? I'm freaking out a bit, to be honest. *Fiancé*. How mad is that? Never thought I'd get married, let alone get hitched to a total stranger. It's meant to happen on a rowing boat or something soppy like that, right? Or when you're innocently strolling down the beach gazing at a sunset one evening, and the guy you've been cohabiting with for three long years pretends to trip over. Before you know it, he's waving a rock the size of Gibraltar in your face and asking you to make him the luckiest man in the world. Or at least the luckiest man in East Anglia. But the first

time I'm going to set eyes on my fiancé is in a TV studio in east London, under hot lights and about twenty tonnes of make-up. I'm lucky he's my soulmate, I guess.

Producer:
Do you believe in soulmates?

Hazel:
I mean, apparently we have a lot in common. Racket sports, superhero movies and indie rock music… and we both love a Sunday roast. But none of that guarantees that we'll fall in love, does it? I know we like the same things, but I don't know if he snores, picks his nose or is a terrible dancer. I mean, I am a *great* dancer, as long as I'm drunk, so I guess he must be too? Is that how soulmates work? Everyone's person is out there somewhere, right? So why shouldn't he be mine? I sure as hell don't seem to be anyone else's.

Producer:
What's your usual type?

Hazel:
Warm. Makes me feel super comfortable. Hard to leave in the morning. Wait, sorry, I'm describing my bed again. What was the question?

Producer:
Let me phrase it this way. Would you say you've been unlucky in love?

Hazel:

I'd say I've been very *lucky* to be honest, especially since I developed a zero-tolerance approach – first hint of a red flag, get rid. That helps weed out the dickheads and the incels. Trouble is, after that, you're not left with much. I mean, it's not like I haven't tried. I've been on the apps. But have you seen what we're working with out there? It's like the Wild West, if the Wild West was full of finance bros instead of cowboys. Who's got time for that? The ghosting. The endless exchanging of messages without ever actually meeting up. The hours wasted sat opposite a man in some overpriced restaurant listening to how his ex didn't particularly like asparagus. So if your AI fairy godmother here (waves wristband) can bypass all that... well, that's gotta be worth a try.

Don't get me wrong, I know going on this show – sorry, this *social experiment* – is a bit of a gamble. But it's got to be less risky than hooking up with some rando at a nightclub or matching with a stranger on Connector who turns out to be a serial killer, right? So, when you think about it like that, this makes a lot more sense. (pauses) I mean, I'm assuming you've vetted this mystery guy, right? You've done all the same checks on him that you did on me?

Producer:
(checks notes) Uh... yes, of course.

Chances are, if I'm at a party, you'll find me in the kitchen or, in extreme circumstances, under a pile of coats in one of the bedrooms.

Suffice it to say, I've never craved the spotlight. But here I was, in a brightly lit TV studio in east London, surrounded by TV cameras, about to meet my fiancé for the first time. In a few seconds, the flimsy panel in front of me would open, and reveal the man I was going to – hopefully – marry in two weeks. This was very literally my *Sliding Doors* moment, and I was already starting to regret the three espressos I'd had this morning. Those, combined with a can of Boom and an emergency Snickers in the green room, meant my heart felt like it was about to burst out of my chest.

As per the rules of the show, I hadn't been allowed to know anything about him. I couldn't see his face, hear his voice, even know his name. But, according to CILLA, I was his soulmate, and we were about to get engaged. Back when I'd applied for the show, all we'd been told about the mystery man was he was a very eligible bachelor, under fifty years old, and looking for love. And now, I was about to meet him.

For the initial stage, over a thousand people had been given one of these very expensive CILLA wristbands. The in-built AI assistant had kept track of all our movements, conversations, daily habits, pretty much everything we said and did, working its algorithms until one of us matched with the so-called 'Prince Charming'. And lo and behold, that lucky Cinderella was me.

'We now have the technology to find somebody's soulmate in a matter of weeks,' Julian Draper, the extremely well-coiffured executive producer of *Love Synced* had told me this morning. 'We want to prove that a soulmate isn't a mystical unicorn. It's just a data set that we can crunch.'

It sounded implausible, but on the other hand, in some parts of the world, marriages were arranged from the day you were born. In others, you got married to a man you'd met that night by a guy dressed as Elvis. Besides, I couldn't remember the last time I'd actually made a decision of my own. I let algorithms control every other aspect of my life – what music I listened to, what I watched on TV, what I shopped for online – so why not surrender my love life to the almighty algorithm too?

'Using the last month's worth of your personal data,' Julian had continued, 'CILLA has been able to analyse your entire personality, your values, your interests. She has been tracking not just your daily habits, but your conversations, social media activity, Google searches. We know where you go, who you vote for, what food you order on Deliveroo. When you go to sleep, when you get up, what you have for breakfast, even how often you go to the bathroom—'

At which point I'd made a face, and he changed tack.

'In short, this data is the sum of your life, Hazel Harper.' Julian tapped my wristband. 'Everything you are is in here.'

It felt a bit like he was taking some sort of perverse pleasure in reducing me to a bunch of code. But I kept quiet and let him continue.

'Of course, we did the same for over one thousand others across the country. And after cross referencing the data from each of our "prospective princesses"' – yes, he did the air quotes – 'with our mystery man's own preferences, CILLA has ascertained that you are his most compatible bride.'

He went on to explain that after the reveal, we'd have a fortnight before our wedding day to increase the likelihood of a successful relationship. CILLA would continue to monitor our activities, speech patterns, heart rates, conversations and emotional connection.

Heteronormative bullshit, for sure, but Lion's Jaw, the production company behind the show, had promised to mix it up for future seasons, if this first series was a success. So I guess that made me a guinea pig.

Apparently, Lion's Jaw had spent hundreds of thousands on the matchmaking software, hoping it would give *Love Synced* an edge over all the other dating shows on telly right now. Sorry, *social experiments*. I had to remember, this was a 'social experiment' and definitely, categorically, officially *not* a reality show.

The show was going to be split into seven episodes: the proposal, our first date, meeting each other's friends and families – my episode and his – rehearsing our first dance and the bachelor party, all culminating in the big finale, the wedding. Each one would see me and Marc take a step closer to marriage. CILLA had already decided we were soulmates, but we still needed to prove we were compatible in real life. Her job now was to monitor us throughout each episode and give us a compatibility rating out of 100.

The catch? Total surveillance. Camera crews would shadow us constantly, drones would track our movements, and Lion's Jaw would plant hidden cameras throughout our homes to capture every unguarded moment.

But if we managed to reach 99 per cent before we reached the altar, then we'd get our dream wedding, all expenses paid in a converted castle on the Norwegian archipelago of Skardbalt.

But before that, we actually had to meet each other.

The small studio was divided into two by the sliding door. My half had been decked out to resemble a dressing room, with a small pink armchair and a vase of flowers on a small vanity table. But the intense heat of the studio lights and slightly stale, artificial smell of the set betrayed what it really was: a facade.

'Hazel, are you ready?' Julian called from somewhere behind the cameras.

I snapped out of my daze. I was definitely not ready, but then again, I couldn't recall a time in my life when I had ever been, so I nodded. People like to say 'I was born ready', but I always felt like I was born slightly unsure and a bit surprised to even be here.

There was no mirror to check myself, just the constant buzz of the hair and make-up team poring over every inch of me, polishing out every pore and wrinkle, like I was a second-hand car in a showroom, buffed to oblivion, ready to be paraded on the forecourt.

Julian had picked out a pretty standard black maxi dress for me, with a low neckline and strappy heels that he thought really said 'demure'. But I felt like it was an outfit that said 'she's splurged her pay cheque in Zara after a bad break-up'.

I'd been told to just stand here and wait. There was to be no countdown, and I suspected they wanted to wait till the very last second, just to see me sweat. The idea was the panel would slide up and we'd be revealed to each other for the first time. Then the guy would get down on one knee, ring out, and pop The Big Q. Julian and the researchers loved referring to it as 'The Big Q' but, really, was it even a question? It wasn't like I could say no now. I'd signed all the forms, accepted my fate.

I had asked Julian why I couldn't be the one to get down on one knee, but he got immediately excited and was using words like 'traction' and 'talking point', so I quickly backtracked. There was no way I could kneel in this dress anyway.

All I had to do was stand there, open my mouth in silent awe at the size of the (probably fake) diamond. I'd even practised that bit in the mirror, and I had it down pat. Loosen the jaw, widen the eyes, stick out my ring finger, and giggle as coquettishly as possible.

It came out more like the meow of a hungry cat, and I was sure this would be captured for posterity, snipped up into little chunks and sent onto Lion's Jaw's social media feeds to go viral.

As I stood there, nervously fiddling with a loose strand of my hair (which the nice woman had literally spent three hours setting perfectly), I suddenly felt like running out of the nearest fire exit. There were only three problems with this plan: one, I had no idea where the fire exit was, two, these fucking heels, and three, the door was beginning to slide open.

Could I really go through with this? I'd barely told anyone I was doing this crazy thing, but when all seven episodes dropped, everyone would know. And I mean *everyone*. Old friends, old enemies, random TikTokers picking apart everything I said or did. There would be no hiding it from my family, either. I'd been so sure... but now, actually standing here about to get engaged, something didn't feel right.

'I can't,' I said quietly. 'I can't do this.'

I spun around the studio, desperately searching for one of the researchers, Julian, anyone who could make this stop. There was silence, just the whirr of the cameras, probably focusing in on the rapidly melting make-up on my panicking face.

'I said I can't do it!' I yelled.

The door suddenly stopped moving, juddering to a sharp halt, and Julian appeared. Dressed in a casual sports jacket, chinos and loafers with no socks, he looked as if he'd just stepped off a yacht.

'Talk to me,' he said.

'I'm sorry,' I said. 'I think I've made a big mistake.'

'Take a breath, you're just nervous.'

'No,' I said. 'You don't understand, it's not just nerves. I cannot do this.'

Julian paused for a second, unfazed. 'Okay, let's get Hazel a car,' he said calmly to a fresh-faced runner, who'd appeared like magic beside him.

A wave of relief washed over me.

'We'll be very sorry to lose you, Hazel,' he said. 'You really were the perfect match for our mystery man. Extraordinary, really, given your... background. Now, just to let you know, as you did sign the release form, Lion's Jaw will still be able to broadcast any existing footage that we've filmed so far.'

'Right, whatever,' I said, wiping the sweat from my brow. 'Do what you need to do.'

'And now might be a good time to mention that your father's criminal record came up on our background checks. Involuntary manslaughter, wasn't it? And of course, your own convictions. Petty theft. Affray.'

My jaw dropped. 'That was so long ago... I was a teenager, for God's sake. Those convictions are all spent.'

'I'm sure you understand, we've spent a fair bit of our time and budget filming with you so far, so we'd have to give the viewers an explanation for your sudden departure from the show,' Julian continued.

A bunch of TikTokers slagging off my hair or my Essex accent was one thing, but digging into my past for clicks was something else. If my managers knew, I'd lose my job. The high-class clientele at Eight Ball wouldn't want to be served by a petty criminal with a dad banged up in jail.

Julian put a gentle hand on my shoulder.

'Hazel, this is totally up to you,' he said. 'Here at Lion's Jaw, we don't put pressure on any of our applicants to do anything they feel uncomfortable with. Like I said, if you want to leave, it's one hundred per cent your decision.'

We stood in silence for a second. I looked into his eyes, deep into his soul, and saw what an utter twat he really was.

'Fine,' I said. 'I'll do it.'

'Good girl,' he said, motioning to the production crew to re-set the cameras. 'You know, this really is an incredible opportunity. Trust me, when this goes out, a lot of very jealous people will be wishing they were in your shoes.'

Julian disappeared, leaving me standing in front of the panel. As much as I despised him in that moment, he was right about one thing. This was my decision, and I'd made my mind up a long time ago to go through with it, no matter what. I could do this. I *had* to do this.

I smoothed out my dress, blew a stray curl away from my eye, and positioned myself in front of the sliding panel.

This was it.

The panel began to move again, much faster this time, and a sudden thought flew into my head.

How tall was this guy going to be?

Shit, was I going to be taller than him in these heels? The last thing I wanted was to tower over the poor guy.

Shit, shit shit.

'Wait!' I shouted, kicking off a shoe. But before I could remove the other one, the lights on the cameras turned red, and the panel slid all the way up, leaving me standing there, lopsided, with one bare foot.

I squeezed my eyes shut, half hoping, like a child playing hide-and-seek, that if I couldn't see him, then maybe he couldn't see me either. After a second, I slowly opened one eye to have a peek, and there was my fiancé, standing in front of me. Tall, with blond hair and sparkling blue eyes. When he saw me looking, his face broke out in a big, spontaneous smile, revealing dimples you could swim laps in.

I didn't need CILLA to tell me my heartbeat was racing, but she did anyway.

'Congratulations!' she squeaked. 'Your chances of a successful relationship have risen to ninety-two per cent.'

SEVEN

SKARDBALT AIRPORT

I stumble out of the bathroom like I've downed half a bottle of cheap vodka.

My eyes dart across the room, desperately looking for help. Everyone is still asleep, laid out across the chairs or curled up under blankets. Marc is closest, his six-foot frame squeezed awkwardly across a row of plastic seats, head resting on the makeshift pillow of his leather holdall.

'Marc!' I hiss, shaking his shoulder until his eyes open, slowly, like he's emerging from hibernation.

He blinks, groans and tries to roll over, almost falling off the chairs.

I slap his cheek.

'Wake up!' I say, loudly this time.

'Jesus, Hazel,' he mumbles. 'What is it? It took me bloody ages to get to sleep.'

'It's Julian. Something's wrong... He's in the bathroom, and he's... well, he's not moving.'

'What happened?' Marc sits up, fully awake now.

'I don't know,' I tell him. 'I went to use the bathroom and found him in there. Marc, listen... I think... I think he's...'

Marc swings his legs to the ground and stands up. 'He's what?'

Around us, the rest of the group begin to stir, groggily rubbing their eyes and shooting daggers in our direction. Stephanie is the first to speak.

'Are you two having another argument? For Christ's sake, it's the middle of the night.'

'No,' I stutter. 'It's Julian. I found him in the toilet... He's...' My mouth goes dry as I try to get the words out.

'Spit it out, girl,' Stephanie barks impatiently.

'Dead,' I say loudly. 'He's dead.'

There's a beat, and I see her steely resolve collapsing for just a second. Then, just as quickly, she regains composure.

'Absolute nonsense,' she says and marches off towards the bathroom.

'Stephanie, wait—' Marc calls out, but it's too late. She disappears into the toilets, and seconds later, I hear a scream bouncing off the tiled walls.

Marc runs after her, swiftly followed by Emil, leaving me standing there, shaking.

I pull out my phone and start jabbing the number nine, before I realise I'm not in England, and I have no clue what the emergency number is in Norway.

'What the fuck is going on?' Dante asks me, groggily.

'It's Julian,' I tell him. 'I found him in the cubicle. The Toblerone was shoved down his throat.'

Even as the words come out of my mouth, I can't believe it's real. I have to be dreaming, right? This whole thing is a terrible nightmare, and any second now I'm going to wake up. I try to catch my breath, but I can't, and the gate starts to blur.

Breathe. I need to breathe. Why can't I…

I feel my shoulders begin to shake. This is too much. Everything starts to go black, and I feel my legs turn to putty. Suddenly, I feel an arm around my shoulder and look up to see Uncle Gary's ruddy face.

'You're in shock, dear,' he says, guiding me to one of the seats. 'Come on, sit down.'

He picks up the whisky bottle lying by Dante's feet.

'This will help,' he says, unscrewing the lid and holding the bottle towards me.

'Don't need a drink,' I mumble, pushing it away. 'We need an ambulance.'

'I am afraid an ambulance won't be of any use,' says Emil, emerging from the bathroom looking pale. He's followed by Marc, who has his arm around Stephanie. Her eyes are wide open, staring at the floor like she's in a trance.

'Is he…?' I ask.

Emil nods solemnly.

'But… how? We were all here…' I try to stand up, but my legs immediately give way, and I fall back into the seat again.

'Hey, hey, it's okay,' Marc says, coming over to me. 'That must have been pretty grim, walking in on that. Are you alright?'

'The cubicle door was locked,' I say. 'I don't understand…'

My mind fills with unwanted images. Uniformed police officers swarming the airport, speaking fast in Norwegian, asking questions, demanding answers.

Emil motions to the rows of seats. 'If you would all please sit down for a minute, I will go and alert the authorities that there has been an, uh, accident.'

'And then what?' Dante asks. He's clearly thinking the same thing I am – we are about to be knee-deep in crime-scene tape.

'The emergency services will deal with everything,' Emil continues.

I suddenly remember what Tilly said. The roads are closed.

'How are they going to get here?' I ask. 'No one can get anywhere in this weather.'

'Do not panic. Everyone just wait here, please.' With that, Emil disappears into the airport, leaving the rest of us staring at each other.

I shiver. As the shock of finding Julian subsides, the gate feels chillier than ever. The main strip lights are off, but there's some soft under-lighting running around the room that makes everyone look eerie. I suddenly feel trapped, even more than before. I wish Emil would come back, because there's something about being left alone with these people that makes my skin crawl.

My tiny flat in Southend has never seemed further away. I close my eyes, and I'm there – stretched out on the settee, simultaneously scrolling through Netflix and Deliveroo. Sure, I'd have to navigate past the stack of overdue bills on the doorstep first, then probably deal with the sink full of washing-up that I never quite got round to before I left. But at least the only one who can judge me there is Fergie, my grouchy black cat (and believe me, she can and will judge me, thoroughly). Luckily her affection can easily be bought with Dreamies, unlike the Van Batten family.

'This is an absolute nightmare,' Stephanie says, sitting down and smoothing out her skirt. She takes out a compact mirror and inspects her face, then recoils and snaps it shut.

We sit in stunned silence for a moment before Dante breaks the mood with a whistle.

'What a way to go,' he says. 'I mean, of all the ways you could top yourself… Maybe he just had a really, *really* sweet tooth.'

Stephanie glares at him. 'Please, Dante.'

'What?' he cries. 'What else are we supposed to talk about? The minimalist interior design in here? The exceptional ambience? Would you rather have a philosophical discussion about the nature of reality? Or we could just rank our favourite chocolate bars. That's topical at least.'

Stephanie reaches for her eye mask and slips it over her head. 'Fine, talk among yourselves,' she says, leaning back on her chair. 'I'm not entertaining any of this nonsense. Wake me up when it's time to board.'

I imagine Stephanie is probably used to her enemies conveniently dying. The Van Battens usually deal with any embarrassing problems by sweeping them under what I imagine is an enormous and very expensive rug – then paying someone to roll it up and chuck it off a cliff.

'Oh we won't be seeing dear old Blighty for a long, long while,' Dante says. 'Once the police turn up, we'll be stuck in this freezing cesspit of a country for days, if not weeks, and all because that twat couldn't wait till he got home to off himself.'

'That cannot happen,' I say. 'I have to get home.'

'Why?' Dante sneers. 'To feed your mangy cat? Some of us actually have some important shit to do tomorrow.'

'First of all,' I say. 'Fergie isn't my cat, she's my therapist. And second, I'm sure your golf buddies can tee off without you. I have to turn up to work, otherwise I get fired.'

'Actually,' Dante says, 'we're meeting with our lawyers to start dealing with the fallout from your little outburst at the altar this afternoon.'

I run a hand over my face. Awesome, so by tomorrow I'm going to be stuck in a freezing Oslo police station or stuck in the offices of a stuffy London law firm. Either way, I'm screwed.

Opposite me, Uncle Gary looks equally perturbed as he nervously picks at the back of his neck again. 'What do you mean, off himself? You think Julian did that to himself?' he asks, his voice wavering. 'On purpose? But the steward said *accident*. A terrible accident. That's what he said, wasn't it?'

Accident? The word rolls around my mind, over and over until it loses all meaning. I've seen enough idiots get drunk or high at Eight Ball and end up in an ambulance. But none of them ever had an 'accident' like that. It wasn't suicide either. Julian wasn't depressed last night; he was determined. Determined to fuck up all our lives, but determined nonetheless.

I try to force my tired, cold brain to think back. When I woke up at the gate, Julian was already in the bathroom and everyone else was asleep. Or at least, it *looked* like they were. It's dark, and it's not like I checked.

'Did any of you see Julian go into the toilet?' I ask.

'I was out cold,' Dante says.

'Not surprised, downing half a bottle of Scotch will do that to you,' Marc says. 'I actually did see Julian. I got up to go to the bathroom, and I passed him on my way back. He was going in as I came out. He seemed pretty jittery. Like, scared almost.'

'Did you see anyone else in the toilets?' I ask.

'No,' Marc replies.

'Do we really need to recount the minutiae of the *entire* evening?' Stephanie sighs, not lifting her eye mask. 'This whole experience is intolerable as it is without the play-by-play of my stepson's toilet habits.'

'Sorry, I thought you'd opted out of this conversation?' I say.

'I wish I could, but your incessant chatter is impossible to ignore,' she snipes.

'Okay, so how about you tell us what you saw last night then?' I ask.

'I had this eye mask on all night, so I didn't see anything, if you must know. But I could hear Gary's guttural snoring. It was driving me insane.'

She lifts one side of the mask and aims a withering look at Gary, who takes it on the chin.

'So no one saw *anything*?' I say. 'Everyone was asleep?'

'Everyone except you.' Dante raises his eyebrows at me.

'No,' I say. 'Not just me. Gary was awake too. I saw him.'

'Me?' Gary's eyes widen. 'I was tossing and turning all night. Not exactly the Ritz here, is it?'

Something doesn't add up. Emil said that the door was locked for security reasons, so no one else could have come into the gate. But apparently everyone here was fast asleep and didn't see or hear a thing. So Julian just walked in there and choked himself?

'Why are we still discussing this?' Stephanie says. 'You heard what the steward said. He'll be back soon with someone who actually knows what they're doing. So why don't we wait quietly?'

Before I can protest, Emil walks back into the gate, and we all turn to look at him, expectantly. But something's wrong. He's on his own, and he looks flustered.

'I, uh, have some bad news, I am afraid,' he says. 'There is no one here.'

'What do you mean, there's no one here?' Stephanie asks.

Emil adjusts his waistcoat nervously. 'The airport is... deserted. Everyone must have been sent home before the roads were closed.'

Dante jumps to his feet. 'What the fuck?' he cries. 'And they just left us here?'

'It appears so,' Emil says. 'A small airport like this can lose all power in a bad storm. It seems that no one wanted to risk being stuck here if that were to happen. I have called the emergency services, however with all access to the airport currently closed due to the weather, we will have to wait until morning for any assistance.'

When he says that, there's a sudden eruption of voices, as everyone starts shouting at once.

'Please, there is no need to panic.' Emil tries to make himself heard above the noise, but no one is listening to him anymore. 'I promise you, I have everything under control!'

My heart is racing faster than I can think. Last night, Emil locked the door that led back to the concourse. There is no one else in the airport. That means there's only the six of us here, snowed in. No way in and no way out. Oh, and there's a dead body sitting on the toilet.

One of us killed Julian. One of us is lying. The question is, which one?

EIGHT

SKARDBALT AIRPORT

I need space, somewhere to think, but there is literally nowhere I can go. I back away from the group over to one of the windows, anything to get away from the yelling. I put my hand on the glass and look outside. It's cold to the touch, and all I can see out there is a blanket of white, and the blinking lights of the control tower in the distance. Our little plane is still out there, but there is no chance we are getting on it anytime soon.

The heating system wheezes and rattles overhead, fighting a losing battle against the Norwegian winter seeping through every crack and joint in this flimsy terminal. The fluorescent lights flicker erratically, making everyone look like extras from a zombie film.

I rest my head against the window, squeeze my eyes closed, and pray that when I open them, the snow will have stopped and the sky will be full of air ambulances. But when I peek out to check, I am still very much trapped in a cold, empty airport in the middle of nowhere.

If Julian had got back to London with the wedding footage, it would have been devastating for the Van Battens. I'd spilt all their secrets on camera, exposed their lies and their crimes. But would any of them really have committed murder to stop the show going out?

I look over at them. Dante, pacing the gate, is volatile and impulsive enough to lash out at anyone who wrongs him. Stephanie, despite the situation, looks unflustered, but I notice her hands tremble slightly as she reapplies her lipstick. She would do anything to protect her family's reputation, but choke a man to death? That doesn't seem like her style. Uncle Gary, sat with his head in his hands, muttering, looks harmless, but there's something deeply creepy about him that makes my skin crawl. Then there's Marc, nervously fiddling with his phone. Dumped at the altar, humiliated in front of his friends and family, all his attempts to persuade Julian to shelve the show had failed. Could he have resorted to more desperate measures?

This is pointless. I have no idea what really happened to Julian, and frankly, I'm too exhausted to care. My brain is mush, this dress is cutting into my ribs, and I still haven't been to the bloody toilet. I just need to keep my head down for the next few hours and let the authorities deal with this mess in the morning.

Then a thought hits me like a sledgehammer. What *is* going to happen when the storm clears and the police arrive? As much as I despise the man, Dante has a point. I can see it all now. They'll cordon off the whole terminal, cancel every flight. March us all off to the police station, shove us in individual interrogation rooms for questioning, where we'll all accuse each other. I've seen it on the cop procedurals my aunt watches on an endless loop. I know the drill. I know who they're going to believe.

And it's not going to be the waitress in a filthy wedding dress with the convict father.

I'm the one who conveniently found Julian's body. I'm the one who gave him a black eye. There were cameras filming the whole thing from at least three different angles. And I'm also the one without a fancy big-shot lawyer or readily available bail money. It won't matter what I say. They'll chuck me in jail and throw away the key.

Just like they did to Dad.

I'm done for. Unless… Unless I can figure it out first. But how the hell am I going to do that, when everyone here is about as trustworthy as a sugared-up toddler with a permanent marker? After the last two weeks, I know one thing for sure. I cannot believe a single word uttered by any of the Van Battens.

Then it dawns on me. There is someone I can trust.

Or rather, *something*.

I shield myself away from the group, and whisper into my wristband.

'CILLA,' I say. 'How do you feel about helping me solve a murder?'

NINE

SKARDBALT AIRPORT

There's an eerie pause before CILLA's cheery voice fills the room.

'Hello, Hazel!' she chirps, far too loudly. 'How's your day going so far?'

Suddenly the yelling from the other side of the gate stops, and everyone turns to stare at me. Before I can shut her up, CILLA pipes up again.

'Tell me more about this murder,' she says, 'and we can brainstorm some solutions together!'

'Um, just hang fire a second, will you?' I tell her, as the others circle around me.

'What are you doing?' Emil asks.

'Nothing.' I clasp my hand over the wristband.

Marc tilts his head at me. 'You're asking CILLA for advice? The TV show is over, Hazel. You left me standing at the altar, remember?'

'I am sure I heard it say "murder",' Emil says, folding his arms.

'None of you believe Julian's death was an accident any more than I do,' I say. 'I think CILLA can help us work out what really happened.'

Dante throws his head back and laughs. 'Are you serious? The same piece of junk that thought you and Marc would be a good match?'

'CILLA is the height of artificial intelligence technology,' I say, trying to sound like I mean it.

Dante snorts again. 'Be real. Lion's Jaw built that thing to get people laid, not solve murders.'

Marc shoots him an annoyed look, but turns back to me. 'Dante does have a point, Hazel. All CILLA can do is run probability scenarios until it hits on the most likely outcome. It doesn't know anything that we haven't already told it.'

'But we *have* told it,' I say. 'We told her *everything*. CILLA has been listening to us all over the past two weeks. The dates, the rehearsal, the wedding. It knows all about us. Including Julian. Here, I'll show you.'

I stick my arm in the air so they can all hear.

'CILLA,' I say. 'I found Julian Draper dead in the toilet of Gate One, Skardbalt Airport at about quarter to two a.m. on the fifteenth of April. The cubicle door was locked. As far as we know, no one else came in or out of the gate. What's the probability he was murdered?'

'Hey, Hazel!' she trills. 'What a great question. That certainly is a tricky pickle! Let me get stuck into that right now.'

'Does she have to talk like a twelve-year-old girl?' Stephanie sniffs, and I can't help but think her eyeballs must be in fantastic shape. She seems to roll them approximately a thousand times a day.

'Shhh,' Marc hushes her as CILLA starts speaking again.

'Based on those circumstances,' she says, 'and factoring in Julian's age, there's a ninety-two per cent probability that he did not die of natural causes.'

'Yeah, no shit,' Dante says. 'The prick had a Toblerone rammed down his throat.'

'Wait,' I say. 'CILLA, you heard everything Julian said last night, that did not sound like a man about to kill himself, did it? He couldn't wait to get back to London and ruin all our lives.'

'No, Julian Draper had not been displaying any of the common suicidal tendencies such as low self-esteem, frequent use of drugs or alcohol or extreme mood swings,' CILLA says.

Emil pinches the bridge of his nose. 'This is not at all helpful,' he sighs. 'Please, we need to wait for the proper authorities.'

'They're not coming, Emil,' I snap. 'Listen, I just want to get home, as quickly as possible. That's what we all want, right? But Dante was right about one thing: when the police do eventually get here, they'll keep us on the island for days. Weeks maybe.'

'You don't know that,' Marc says. 'They have forensics and all that stuff. I bet there's fingerprints all over the place. It'll probably all be over in a few hours.'

'CILLA,' I say. 'How long is it likely to take?'

'Great question!' CILLA chirps. 'Based on historical statistics, homicide investigations on Skardbalt last, on average, between four and six weeks.'

I raise my eyebrows and give him an 'I told you so' look. 'Unless we work this out by the time they get here, we're all going to be stuck in this hellhole for a very long time.

Someone here saw something, and the sooner they fess up, the sooner we can all go home.'

'The police aren't going to listen to your silly little wristband.' Dante yawns. 'This is a colossal waste of everyone's time.'

'Fine.' I fold my arms. 'Let's just sit here and wait to be arrested, then.' I motion to our surroundings. Hard plastic chairs, plain beige walls and nothing outside but three feet of snow and a plane without a pilot. Not to mention the dead body in the only bathroom.

'What are you saying, Hazel?' Marc says. 'Because if Julian didn't do this himself, then that means you think it was one of us.'

'That's not what I said...' I start.

He's right though. That is *exactly* what I think.

Marc looks unconvinced. 'You said the cubicle door was locked when you found him?'

'Yeah,' I say. 'It was, but...' I trail off. I don't have an explanation for that.

Dante points a finger at my chest. 'You're the one who conveniently found him in there while we were all asleep. And let's not forget your little tête-à-tête at the wedding. If we're looking for suspects, I'd say that makes *you* numero uno.'

'Me?' I cry. 'You're the one who was off his face on Scotch last night, ranting about how the show was going to ruin your life! And what about Stephanie, she threatened to sue Julian for everything he had.'

Dante walks up to me and gets up in my face. 'Everyone knows the Van Battens,' he points behind him, 'but no one knows anything about you and *your family*. You just turned up two weeks ago. Why should anyone trust you?'

He leans further forward, so close that I can smell the stale whisky on his breath. I lift my arm up, and Dante recoils, like I'm about to punch him.

'CILLA, you heard our alibis earlier, right?' I say into the wristband.

The display lights up. 'I am always listening,' she says.

'Was someone lying?' I ask her.

There's a pause before CILLA speaks again.

'In a stressful situation such as this, the likelihood of deceitfulness becomes significantly higher. In this specific scenario, I estimate that the probability that someone is lying is approximately ninety-four per cent.'

Dante slumps on one of the chairs and waves his bottle of whisky in the air dramatically. 'Whoop-de-do! What a revelation! Let us bow down before our robot overlord!' He takes another swig from the bottle. Marc punches him on the arm.

CILLA continues, 'If someone is not telling the truth, their speech patterns can denote verbal cues such as hesitation and repetition as well as changes in pitch and tone. Other signs of dishonesty include providing too much unnecessary information and avoiding direct answers. Based on these factors, there is an eighty-nine per cent chance that Gary was involved in Julian's death.'

Dante bursts out laughing, and my heart sinks, just a little.
Gary? Weird Uncle Gary?

I run a hand across my face. That can't be right. With his bushy Captain Birdseye beard and rotund figure, you couldn't picture a less threatening looking man. And Gary only arrived two days ago for the stag do; he couldn't have even met Julian before today.

I turn to look at Gary, who's blushing bright red and fiddling with the top button on his shirt.

'Well, that's unusual, isn't it? *Very* unusual. But like I said, we can't really be putting all our faith in a machine, can we?' he says. 'I mean, everyone knows a lot of this modern technology is completely unreliable.'

'He's right. CILLA must be malfunctioning,' Marc says. 'Gary's just your weird uncle.'

'Your uncle, you mean,' I say.

Marc looks at me like I'm speaking French. 'Uh, he's not my uncle. He's *your* uncle Gary, not mine.'

'No,' I say, a shiver running through me. 'I met him at the stag do. He was with *your* wedding party.'

'That chump has nothing to do with us,' Dante says. 'Never seen the guy before he stepped into the chapel.'

'Wait,' Marc says to me. 'You've been calling him Uncle Gary this whole time.'

I look at him like he's gone mad. 'So have you!' I cry.

'Yeah, because I thought he was *your* uncle! That's how he introduced himself, so I assumed he was in your party.'

'I thought he was in *your* party,' I yelp.

My heart is definitely beating faster now.

'So, if he's not your uncle, and he's definitely not my uncle…' Marc says. 'Then who the hell is he, and why was he at our wedding?'

Slowly, we all turn in unison to look at Weird Uncle Gary. All the blood has drained from his face as he takes a step away from us, his eyes flicking nervously around the room.

'I… I can explain,' he stutters.

– EPISODE TWO –
THE FIRST DATE

SUSSEX, UNITED KINGDOM

Producer (off camera):
So, you passed the first hurdle, physical attraction. But physical attraction alone is not a good basis for a happy marriage. On your first date, CILLA will be monitoring your interactions with your new fiancé to see how compatible you really are. We're taking you somewhere away from all distractions, so it's just you and your fiancé, and no safety net.

Hazel:
Okay, so, like, a nice picnic or something like that, right?

Producer:
(...)

Hazel:
... Right?

The mud squelched under my feet as I waded through the field, my brand-new leather ankle boots sinking deeper with each step. I wouldn't have minded but I'd bought them especially for today, and secretly planned to return them to BooHoo afterwards.

After the proposal yesterday, Marc and I had been whisked away to separate parts of the studio to record our pieces to camera. So this was going to be our first proper date, but Lion's Jaw had been tight lipped on exactly what we would be doing.

I'd worn a nice dress and spent ages on my hair, but when the car had dropped me off at the entrance to a large field in the middle of the Sussex countryside, I was a little surprised. Then again, everything about this week had been surprising so far.

It had been a long time since I'd been on a proper date, so even before I saw the muddy field, I was feeling nervous.

'CILLA,' I said to my wristband as I trudged on. 'Any first date advice?'

'Hi, Hazel!' she chirped. 'Got the first date jitters? Don't worry! I'm here to help as always. Try to relax and don't put too much pressure on yourself. Did you know that only fifty-two per cent of first dates end with a kiss?'

'I did not know that,' I replied, squinting into the sun. There was something there, in the distance, but I couldn't quite work out what it was.

'The goal of a first date is to get to know each other. Pay attention to your date's interests and hobbies, and ask open-ended questions to spark meaningful conversations,' CILLA said.

'Okay,' I said. 'Sounds tedious, but fine.'

'And Hazel?' she continued. 'Most importantly, just be yourself.'

I almost face-planted into the mud when she said that.

'Be myself?' I laughed. 'CILLA, babes, that is a terrible idea.'

That's when I realised what was ahead of me – a gigantic orange hot air balloon, bobbing there on the horizon like an angry boil in the middle of the field. I had to resist the urge to turn around and run the other way as fast as I could. And I probably would have, if it was possible to run through mud in these stupid boots.

The sweet-faced, barely-out-of-her-teens Lion's Jaw researcher had assured me that we'd be 'doing something really fun, but we want to capture your genuine reaction when you see it'. Thankfully, there was no camera there to catch my 'genuine reaction' – a raised middle finger paired with a silent scream of frustration.

'It can't be that dangerous, right?' I said out loud to myself. 'I mean, how many hot air balloon accidents are there per year?'

Suddenly the voice from my wristband piped up. 'There are over eighty hot air balloon accidents in the United Kingdom every year,' CILLA said cheerily.

'Thank you, CILLA,' I sighed.

As I got closer, I could see Julian chatting to an elderly man with thick, bottle-top glasses who was standing in the balloon's basket. Their words were barely audible above the roar of the burner filling the balloon with hot air, but I assumed this was the person I was about to entrust with my life. I shivered, despite the warm breeze that drifted across the field.

Julian spotted me and reached out with his usual air kiss, his eyes running over my outfit.

'Hazel! Great! You made it. I see you got the message about dressing down.'

I looked down at my brand-new floral summer dress, which was now splattered with mud.

'Oh, I—' I started.

'So, here's how it's going to work today,' Julian continued. 'We have a drone camera that's been following you since you got out of the car.'

He pointed to the sky, and sure enough, there was a bulky drone hovering above us.

'The drone will continue to fly along beside you during the thirty-five-minute trip. Don't worry, we'll get you mic-ed up so we can capture all the scintillating conversations I just know you're going to have up there.'

I gave him a weak thumbs up.

'Today is all about communication,' Julian went on. 'Up there, two thousand feet in the air, there's nowhere to hide, and nothing else to do but completely open up to each other. Sound good? Lovely. Ah, and here comes your gorgeous fiancé right now.'

We turned to see Marc jogging up the field towards us, dressed in a quilted jacket and – tellingly – wellington boots. Still, he did look handsome, and I couldn't help but feel a little fizz of excitement. Julian ushered us aboard, ignoring Marc's apologies for being late, and gave the old guy the signal to take off. I felt the basket lift off the ground, and beside us, the drone swivelled in my direction, probably getting a nice, big close-up of my uneasy expression.

'Come here often?' Marc said in my ear.

'Yeah, every Tuesday for two-for-one margaritas.' I smiled back.

'Bit much for a first date, isn't it?' he said, looking up into the balloon.

'Yeah,' I said, gripping the edge of the basket as we slowly rose into the air. 'I feel like we got a last-minute Groupon voucher.'

'They used CILLA to pick it, apparently, based on our personality profiles,' he said. 'Guess we both enjoy a high altitude? I skied the Swiss Wall last winter. Sensational views, not that there's much time to look at them when you're hurtling down a black run. At least we get to take in the sights up here, right?'

'Uh, yeah, sure.' I nodded, trying not to look down.

The balloon guy reduced the flame, and the noise of the burner and the wind fell away. We drifted along in satisfied silence for a moment, looking out across the rolling English countryside.

'The crew put a hamper in here somewhere,' Marc said, looking around the basket. He found it and took out a magnum of what looked like it could be champagne, but knowing Lion's Jaw, it was more likely cava. Marc steadied himself as he poured out two glasses, and handed me one.

'You know, it's weird,' he said after a moment. 'But I feel like we've already met.'

'Uh, I don't think so,' I replied. The only place someone like me would have bumped into someone like Marc would've been if I served him at the club, and I definitely would have remembered that.

'—must be because we have all this stuff in common,' he continued. 'Same taste in music, movies, food…'

'And extreme sports,' I added. I looked down for a second, then immediately regretted it. I could see a tiny bright red figure standing in the middle of the field, right by the car that dropped me off. I figured it must be Julian, or the driver, but then again, neither of them had been wearing red. Before I had time to worry about it, my stomach began to swirl, so I focused on a very specific cloud in the middle distance instead.

'Hey, over there.' Marc pointed to a cluster of buildings nestled in the swathes of green fields far below us. 'You can see the house.'

'Your house?' I said. 'You can see that from all the way up here?'

'Yeah, that's the family grounds,' he said.

'Wait, so this is all your land?'

'Uh, well, my dad's, technically.'

'And that would be Malcolm Van Batten?' I said, still staring at my new favourite cloud.

Marc looked at me and raised his eyebrows in surprise. 'You googled me?'

'Of course,' I said. 'First thing I did after the reveal.'

'And?'

'Well, I knew Lion's Jaw had found a "Prince Charming",' I said, 'but I didn't quite expect the heir to one of the biggest soft-drink companies in the world.'

'Europe,' Marc corrected. 'And "heir" makes it sound like I'm actually a prince. I mean, I'm on the board, but I barely show up, to be honest. Dad keeps pushing me to take over, but that sounds exhausting. I'm more interested in my charitable foundation, actually giving something back, you know?'

Most people had heard of Malcolm Van Batten, the charismatic entrepreneur who built a billion-dollar business from scratch in the Nineties, all from a tiny basement in South London. Boom, a gross-tasting but alarmingly effective energy drink, was famous for its red hammer logo and was aggressively marketed with images of base jumpers and free climbers.

'So, I have to ask, why go on a show like this?' I said. 'I mean, you're obviously well off, good-looking... so why are you marrying a woman you've never met, just because a robot says you're a good match?'

He took both of my hands and flashed that smile of his again. 'I want to find my soulmate and fall in love, all of that. You know, dating is actually pretty difficult when people think you're...'

'A billionaire?'

He laughed. 'Let me be clear with you right now, Hazel,' he said. 'I am nowhere near a billionaire. But, yeah, money doesn't make it easier to meet someone, you know. My stepmother is always trying to set me up with the daughter of one of her tedious society friends, or a hot hedge-fund manager from the *Forbes* 30 Under 30 List. And then there's the opportunists, of course.'

'Gold diggers?'

'Right,' he said. 'There's plenty of girls out there who are just after the trust fund. That's what I liked most about *Love Synced*. No preconceived notions. Whoever I matched with wouldn't know who I was, they wouldn't know anything about me, so it would be genuine, you know? I'm a romantic at heart.'

'Yeah, I know,' I said. 'I saw the video.'

His smile disappeared, and he ran a hand through his hair as he looked at his feet. 'Shit.'

'I mean, come on, it's the first thing that comes up on Google. "Socialite Marc Van Batten cheats on long-term girlfriend in an LA nightclub",' I said.

I wasn't kidding. With over ten million views, the TikTok video showing Marc getting rather intimate with a woman in a nightclub had gone viral last year. Worse, it turned out his girlfriend was at home planning his surprise birthday party at the time.

'I wouldn't believe everything you see online,' he said.

'Really?' I asked. 'The video was pretty clear.'

Marc's eyes flicked to the drone camera.

'Look, I can't deny that was me in the video. But I'd broken up with Portia two weeks before. And Portia… well, let's just say she had her own agenda. All that surprise birthday stuff, it wasn't my birthday for months. She just wanted to make me look bad.'

'Uh-huh,' I said. 'The man cheats but somehow it's always the woman's fault, right?'

'I'm not a cheat,' he said, looking me straight in the eye. If he was lying, well, all I can say is he was very good at it. 'I said yes to doing this show because I genuinely want to find The One. I know that sounds corny, but it's true. And Portia definitely wasn't the one.'

'What about the girl in the club?' I asked. 'Was she the one?'

'No,' Marc said. 'But that's the thing, I've been in a thousand clubs, kissed a thousand girls—'

'Okay, wow, I feel really special now…'

'That's not what I meant,' he said. 'Look, I'm trying to say that I was going about this the wrong way. I want to find my soulmate. Someone who shares the same values, the same passions, all that stuff. I know what that video looks like, but that's not me. I'm not a playboy.'

I pulled up a *Cosmopolitan* article on my phone with the headline 'Marc Van Batten: 21st Century Playboy' and showed it to him.

'Second thing that comes up on Google when you search your name,' I said.

He took my phone and shielded his eyes from the sun.

'This is from years ago!' he said, looking at the photo of himself falling out of a nightclub holding a bottle of Patrón. 'I promise, you I got all that out of my system in my twenties. I have different priorities now. I want to get married, have a family of my own. Like, six kids, ideally. Take the Joy Foundation global. Africa, South America, Asia.'

Inwardly, I rolled my eyes. 'The Joy Foundation'. Jesus. *Here it comes, the big speech about saving the world with mental wellness and happy thoughts.* I'd heard it from half the guys who came in the club, in between them popping to the toilet for a line.

'I think we can really make a difference,' he went on.

'Okay,' I said. 'And who's looking after the six kids while you're travelling the world building goat huts?'

'We'll figure it out,' he said.

I folded my arms. 'What you mean is, we'll pay someone else to do it.'

'I get it, you think I'm an idealist too,' he said. 'Just like my stepmother does.'

Oh, he did not just compare me to his stepmother.

'No, I just think you've probably never had to worry about money,' I said, clinging on to the edge of the basket. My voice was getting louder now as I tried to make myself heard above the roar of the jet and the hiss of the wind.

The pilot fired a roar of flame up into the balloon, and we rose higher into the air. A gust of wind blew around us, and the balloon lurched to the right. I stumbled against the edge of the basket. For one horrible second, I thought this was it. This was how I was going to die, falling 10,000 feet onto a random part of Sussex. Or a cow. At least they'd have it all on camera, which would make a fun presentation at my funeral.

Marc put his hand on my arm to steady me, and there was that rush of butterflies again. Why did this man have this effect on me?

'So you think I'm a spoilt little rich boy who's always had it easy?' he said.

The wind was blowing loudly now, and my heart was thumping. Why were we going *up*? Surely we should be going *down* by now.

'Er, we're in a hot air balloon drinking champagne,' I said. 'We're not exactly slumming it.'

'I'm pretty sure this isn't champagne,' he said.

'Well, you would know, I guess.'

'Listen, I can't help who my father is,' he shouted above the noise. 'But I can help people less fortunate than me.'

'That's not what I meant. I just think you're...' I tailed off as the wind blew my hair across my face. 'I think you're a champagne socialist.'

'What? I can't hear you,' he yelled back. 'This is prosecco, I think!'

'Fine! You're a prosecco socialist!'

'What the hell is a prosecco socialist?' he shouted.

'I don't know!' I cried. 'I just made it up! Better than a prosecco fascist!'

The old guy started fiddling with the controls, firing a few bursts of the burner, but the balloon refused to stabilise. I looked at the drone, which was now aimed right in my face, the red light blinking. If it was possible for a drone to look smug, this one was managing it. I looked down to avoid its gaze and felt my stomach churn.

'I think I'm going to be sick,' I said.

Suddenly, the balloon lurched again, throwing me off my feet and straight into Marc. I threw my arms around him and screwed my eyes closed.

'Shit, shit, shit,' I kept repeating. 'I'm going to die here.'

'You're not going to die, we're okay,' he said.

'Okay? We're in a *wicker basket* held up with *cloth* and there's a short-sighted man with a *flamethrower* in charge!'

I was starting to panic; my heart was pounding like crazy.

'Hey, hey, look at me,' Marc said. 'Open your eyes and look at me. Don't look anywhere else.'

I did as he said, and I noticed his eyes were a deep ocean blue.

'Now listen, we're not in a hot air balloon, you're sitting across the table from me in a beautiful restaurant in Florence.'

'This is so stupid,' I hissed.

'Come on, the waiter is here at the table,' he said. 'What shall we order?'

'Um, I dunno, chips!' I yelled.

Marc tilted his head. 'Really? We're in Italy.'

'Yes, specifically French fries dipped in peanut butter.'

'That's so weird,' he said. 'But okay. There's a warm breeze blowing across the piazza, you're eating, um, French fries and peanut butter...'

'Mmm.' I closed my eyes, imagining the salty, nutty taste in my mouth.

Suddenly, I felt a bump. My eyes sprang open, and I rushed to look over the edge of the basket. To my surprise, we were on the ground. We'd landed. For a moment, I really had forgotten where I was.

I breathed a huge sigh of relief and hopped over the basket, just managing to stop myself from kissing the grass. I'd never say a bad word about mud ever again.

I turned to Marc. 'Uh, so… thanks for that, I was sort of freaking out a bit up there. I didn't mean to call you a…'

He grinned back at me. '"Prosecco fascist", wasn't it?'

Before I could explain myself, my wristband display lit up, and CILLA started talking again.

'Hey, guys! That's what I love to see! You didn't kiss on your first date, but you did share a personal moment, and that's even more important. Your chances of a successful relationship just rose to ninety-three per cent.'

As I trudged back through the field, Julian and Marc chatting behind me, I couldn't help but smile. Ninety-three per cent, I thought, not bad. Not bad at all. Maybe this was all going to work out; maybe we'd really vibe with each other, reach 99 per cent and have the perfect wedding.

When I reached the car, I was about to climb in the back seat when I noticed something tucked underneath the windscreen wiper, flapping in the wind like a parking ticket. But there weren't any traffic wardens way out here…

I plucked it out and unfolded it on the bonnet. Then immediately wished I hadn't. My heart had only just calmed down from the balloon ride, but now it felt like it was about to break out of my ribcage again.

I stared at the words, scrawled in jagged black marker across the scrap of paper.

You're in danger. Check the exes.

I spun round, looking for anyone nearby, but the field was empty apart from the balloon, which had now deflated and was lying on the ground like a giant rubber carpet. We were in the middle of the countryside. There was no one here for miles except us.

As Marc and Julian approached the car, I quickly screwed up the note in my fist and put it behind my back.

'You okay?' Marc asked. 'You look like you've seen a ghost.'

'Don't believe in them,' I said, opening the car door and sliding in the back seat before they could ask any more questions.

And not for the first time that day, I wondered what the hell I had got myself into.

TEN

SKARDBALT AIRPORT

'Ow!' Gary squeals as Dante pulls two luggage straps tight around his wrists.

When he's done, Marc pushes Gary down into one of the chairs and pulls the belt out of his trousers. He wraps it around Gary's legs a couple of times before fastening the buckle, leaving him squirming and whining.

Stephanie stands behind them, watching silently. Emil, on the other hand, is pacing around the gate.

'This is a very, very bad idea,' he says, his Norwegian accent becoming more pronounced the more stressed he gets. 'No, no, no, no. We should not be taking the law into our own hands like this.'

To be honest, forced interrogation wasn't top of my list of things to do today either, but once Dante and Marc got the idea into their heads, there was no stopping them.

'This is ridiculous!' Gary cries as he tries to wriggle free.

Marc lands a firm hand on his shoulder, and he stops dead. I kneel down in front of him.

'Tell us who you really are,' I say.

Gary's cheeks burn red as he tries to look anywhere but into my eyes.

'I'm Uncle Gary!' he whimpers.

He's sweating profusely, despite the cold. Looking at him now, it's obvious that under that big bushy beard, he's not a Van Batten. The little hair he has left on top is a mix of grey and rusty auburn, his eyes are brown, not blue, and his stubby, upturned nose would be totally out of place among their classical features. Could this guy really have killed Julian? He looks more like a branch manager at Aldi than a murderer. (Having said that, the manager at my local Aldi does bear a striking resemblance to Ted Bundy.)

'This is hopeless,' I say, standing up. 'He's not going to tell us anything.'

'Is anyone averse to popping him outside in the snow for an hour?' Stephanie suggests. 'That might encourage him to be a little more chatty.'

'Best idea I've heard all day,' Dante says, rubbing his hands.

'No,' Emil says sternly. 'There will be no torturing anyone on my watch.'

He stands at the vending machine, arms folded, eyes trained on Gary, like he's a disapproving head teacher. I'm not super comfy with the whole *Lord of the Flies* vibe either, but I'm running out of ideas. Luckily, I know someone who has loads of them.

I turn away from Gary. 'CILLA, what's the best way to interrogate someone?' I ask my wristband.

The display lights up with a smiley face. 'Great question, Hazel! Interrogation techniques are a fab way to gather accurate information! Why not try using a neutral tone to avoid confrontational or aggressive language and challenging your subject's account by presenting the inconsistencies in their story. Don't forget to appeal to their emotions to encourage cooperation!'

'Okay, got it.'

'Oh, and Hazel,' CILLA says. 'Please remember to prioritise respectful and lawful methods.'

'Fuck that,' Dante says. 'Let's do Stephanie's idea.'

I ignore him and turn back to Gary. 'Gary,' I say as calmly as possible. 'I know you're scared. We all are. We're not going to hurt you, I promise. I just want to get a couple of facts straight, okay? I know you're not my uncle, and you're definitely not related to this lot. So why did you introduce yourself as Uncle Gary at the stag do?'

A single bead of sweat drips down his forehead and slides down the bridge of his nose.

'I am well aware how this looks, but I am begging you to believe me,' he pleads. 'I mean, look at me, I'm just good old Uncle Gary, right? Wouldn't hurt a fly.'

Without warning, Dante grabs him by the throat with one hand.

'You're no one's uncle, you fat piece of shit,' he spits, tightening his grip. 'Now tell us the truth or I'll go get that Toblerone and shove it where the sun doesn't shine.'

'Hey, no aggressive language, remember!' I snap, shoving Dante back. I turn back to Gary. 'Come on, please, you have to give me something. I can't hold off these idiots all night.'

Gary looks at his shoes. 'Very well. I'm a, uh, I'm merely a humble table magician,' he says. 'The production company booked me for the wedding. Check with them if you don't believe me!'

'Check with who?' Dante says. 'The dead body in the cubicle over there?'

Gary shrugs, or at least bobs his shoulders as much as he can with his arms tied behind his back. '"The Great Uncle Gary",' he stutters. 'That's what they call me. Like a stage name, you know?'

Marc kneels down next to me. 'Let's see you do a trick then, mate,' he says.

'Well, that would be rather difficult in my current, um, situation, but if you'd be so kind and loosen my bonds, then I will gladly show you one of my most astounding illusions.'

'Yeah, disappearing into thin air, I bet,' Dante says. 'Sorry chubs, we're not loosening a damn thing until the police get here. Tell us why you did that to Julian, you sicko. You didn't even know the guy.'

'Exactly, you oafs,' Gary pants. 'I had absolutely no reason to kill him. I'm innocent, I tell you. Now let me go.'

'Oh really? Well, let's have a little look at the evidence, shall we?' Dante says, theatrically putting a finger to his mouth. 'Over there, we have one dead body and over here, one twat who's fed us a load of bollocks. So, I'm afraid that equals a big fat no. Sorry, "Uncle Gary", we won't be letting you go, thank you very much. Come on, Marc, I've had enough of this. Let's chuck the sack of shit in the snow.'

Gary looks at me, eyes wide and desperate. The luggage straps are pulled so tight, his hands are beginning to turn white. The more he struggles, the more agitated he becomes.

I put my hand on his knee and make my voice as gentle as I can. 'Listen, I don't think for a second you killed Julian, but you can see the predicament we're in here, can't you? If you don't tell us why you lied to us, Dumb and Dumber over here are going to turn you into a popsicle. So just tell me the truth. Who are you, really?'

'My name really is Gary, I promise you. I've lived on the mainland for years, and I want to get home, just like you guys. I'm only here because the chaps at the castle told me there was some big, posh wedding happening this weekend. I thought I'd pop over to check it out.'

'Seriously? You're a wedding crasher?' I ask.

'Well, actually we don't really like that term—'

Dante raises his palm like he's about to slap Gary, but I stop him with a glare.

'What do you mean you don't like that term?'

Gary looks at me awkwardly.

'You want me to set Dante on you again?' I ask.

'Okay, okay,' Gary stutters. 'Look, it's less crashing *per se*. I'm sort of part of the catering team, you might say. My contact at the castle lets me know when there's a wedding booked, and I pop over with a teeny tiny array of recreational drugs. Really small. Like, minuscule. And nothing too crazy either. Just a smidgeon of weed. Some molly. Maybe a bit of marching powder. Ketamine, if I have it.'

'Uh-huh, sounds *really* small time,' Marc says. 'So you're a drug dealer?'

Gary clicks his teeth. 'That's another label that I don't find particularly useful.'

Dante snarls at him.

'I can't hold him back,' I say. 'So you better start talking.'

Gary gulps. 'Well, it's more like providing a service than dealing, you see. There's a steady stream of rich people coming to Skardbalt for ski trips and weddings. Not much security at the airport here, so it's low risk. I dress up like this, tell people I'm an uncle, a distant cousin or the hired entertainment, no one questions it. My English accent helps. Makes them feel comfortable. Everybody wins. They have a good time, and I get a ready-made customer base, with no police, no prying eyes. I was just as distressed as you, Hazel, when I got to the gate and saw this bloody lot. I'd hoped to avoid everybody by getting an earlier flight back.'

'Yeah, well, that didn't work out too well for either of us, did it?' I say, standing up.

'But you have to believe me, I didn't hurt Julian, I promise you,' he says. 'I'd never met the man until today.'

'Prove it,' Marc says. 'If you're a dealer, where's your stash, huh? Where are all these drugs?'

'I sold everything before I came through security. I'm not a complete ignoramus.'

At Eight Ball, we'd sometimes have to pat down a customer, check the amount of illegal substances they had on them. Normally we'd turn a blind eye to a dab of molly or a discreet line, but we had to make sure no one was dealing inside the club. I run my hands down the inside of Gary's tweed jacket and immediately hit something lumpy in his inside pocket. I stick my hand in and fish out a pack of playing cards.

'No drugs, but look at this,' I say. 'He could have slipped a card in between the cubicle door and pushed up the lock, just like I did with my nail file.'

'Another one of your magic tricks, huh, Great Uncle Gary?' Marc says.

'I'm telling you, I didn't touch the man!' Gary's head slumps to his chest and he starts quietly sobbing.

Dante strokes his chin. 'Okay, listen, he did sell me drugs at the stag do,' he says. 'So that part of the story checks out.'

Stephanie looks furious. 'So it's true? You were high all weekend? You swore to me you were done with all that,' she says. 'You know what the court order said. If that was filmed on camera, you'll be back in front of the judge.'

'It was a special occasion, wasn't it?' Dante says, shiftily. 'How was I to know he was a dealer? I thought he was one of Hazel's weird relatives. Would've been rude not to.'

As they begin shouting at each other, I walk over to the vending machine to join Emil.

'CILLA was right,' I say, keeping my voice low. 'Gary has been lying to us from the beginning.'

'You really believe that this man, um, *inserted* a Toblerone down your producer friend's throat?' Emil asks. 'I think, perhaps, that you may have made a terrible mistake.'

He points at Gary, and I look at the somewhat pathetic overweight man with pattern baldness pointlessly struggling to get his arms under his legs.

'But if it wasn't Gary,' I say, 'then who was it?'

I look at each of the Van Battens in turn. They're arguing between themselves now, chastising Dante for his drug use. If we did tie up the wrong person, then the real killer is standing right in front of me. Each of them had the opportunity and the motive to do it. But then again, someone could say the same about me.

'So what do we do now?' I ask.

'This is a disaster,' Emil says, throwing his head in his hands. 'I have totally lost control of the situation, not to mention my passengers! Do you realise that I was not even supposed to be working this flight?' His accent gets stronger as he loses his poise. 'The airline called me this morning because the girl on duty called in sick. Food poisoning!'

'I'm sorry,' I say. 'That's shitty luck. Now you're in the middle of this mess.'

'My dream was to work for United or British Airways one day. But after this? It is all over. All over!' He goes on, 'I only finished my basic training in July. Since then I've been constantly flying, constantly exhausted. The pay is terrible. The food is even worse. We eat the same as you, you know. This airline is a joke!'

'Yeah, I can tell. They can't even afford uniforms that fit.'

He looks down at his waistcoat, which is so tight it looks like the buttons are about to fly off, and I swear he's going to burst into tears.

'Hey, hey, it's okay,' I tell him, putting my hand on his shoulder. 'We'll figure this out.'

It occurs to me that we aren't so different. I earn my living waiting tables, plastering a smile on my face and pretending it is my dream to fetch fizzy wine for people who don't even look at me when I serve them.

'Look at me, carrying on like this, when I should be comforting you,' Emil says, wiping his eyes. 'I did not say before, but I am sorry about your friend.'

'It's okay. I mean, he wasn't really my friend. If I'm being honest, I hated the guy. Just don't tell the police that, okay?' I force a laugh, but Emil doesn't return it.

'It must have been quite frightening to find him like that,' he says.

'Uh, yeah, I guess.' I think back to the horrific, stretched look of Julian's face, frozen in fear, and shudder.

'You put a – how do you say? – brave face on, but I think you are more scared than you say.'

'I can take care of myself,' I tell him.

'Yes, I am sure of it,' Emil says, a hint of a smile on his face. 'I saw the black eye.'

Before I can reply, there's a loud thud behind us, and I turn to see Gary on the floor. He's managed to wriggle his legs free and squirms around, trying in vain to loosen his wrists, like a gigantic worm. He looks up at us and freezes for a split second, before jumping up and legging it.

Before any of us can move, he's disappeared into the airport, leaving the door swinging behind him.

- EPISODE THREE -
HOMETOWN VISIT

SOUTHEND-ON-SEA, ESSEX

Tilly (sitting in the big yellow chair):
You want to know about Hazel's love life? What love life? (laughs)

Producer (off camera):
She's not had many serious relationships?

Tilly:
Um... she's ghosted every man she's ever dated. I don't think she's ever said 'I love you' to anyone, unless you count her cat. I'm not totally sure she's even capable of that emotion. But I keep telling her, it'll happen, you just have to stay possy. Hashtag PossyLife and all that.

Producer:
Sorry, what does that mean?

Tilly:
Stay positive, of course! It's also the name of my nail salon. Possy Nails. Can I say that on here? It's on Mycroft Road, just down the street from—

Producer:
Um, let's stick to talking about Hazel, shall we?

Tilly:
Oh, okay. Well, Hazel loves my salon! She's in there all the time.

'Here, try this,' I said, leaning over the kitchen counter and shoving a highball glass into Tilly's hand.

She took a sip. 'Gorge. What is it?'

'That's a Ramos Gin Fizz,' I told her. 'One of the trickiest cocktails to make, you have to really shake it.'

I demonstrated with the cocktail shaker and Tilly raised her eyebrows.

'What?' I asked.

'You like this guy, don't you?' she said. 'I've never seen you put this much physical effort into anything.'

I laughed, turned back to the chopping board and started slicing a lemon. We were in my Aunt Clara's tiny council flat in Southend, where I'd lived from the age of sixteen. Back then, I flipped burgers at the greasy spoon down on the seafront (which put me off eating meat for life) and Tilly worked at the nail bar down the road. Our lunch hours were spent eating leftover chips on the beach, and we'd been best friends ever since.

The kitchen area of the flat occupied a corner of the front room, where I was trying to make one of the world's most complicated drinks with extremely limited resources. I'd repeatedly told Julian that I didn't mix drinks at the club, but he insisted we needed 'a visual element to make the episode pop'. Thankfully, I'd watched the bar staff make these enough times to make a decent go of it. At least, I thought I had.

'Tils, he's loaded,' I said. 'Like, *really* loaded. I doubt he's going to be impressed by a homemade cocktail and a bowl of olives.'

'He might be impressed by *this*, though.' Tilly motioned to my dress. Simple, black, and yes, slightly more low-cut than I'd normally wear.

'Do I look okay?' I asked, looking down. 'It's not too much?'

'Too much is never enough, babes,' she said. 'All this for a guy though. That's not like you.'

'It's for a TV show,' I told her. 'It was their idea to have Marc round for cocktails, not mine. Believe me, I do enough of this at work, I have no desire to spend my nights off in a tight dress serving alcohol to guys I barely know.'

'Yeah but *this* guy is different,' she said, taking an olive from the bowl and popping it in her mouth. 'Your AI thingy says you're soulmates! Destined to be together, like Cinderella and her Prince Charming!'

She twirled around the kitchen dramatically, pretending to sing.

'Maybe Cinderella should've stayed with her animal friends instead of settling for a man who had her try on a shoe because he couldn't recognise her without make-up,' I said.

'You are so not a romantic,' she said.

'Yeah, duh,' I told her. 'Why do you think I asked a computer to find me a husband?'

'I still can't believe you actually did that,' she went on. 'Don't get me wrong, I think you're batshit crazy, but I do love this for you. I can't remember the last time you put yourself out there like this.'

'Is it so crazy to want to meet someone without all the hassle of swiping and chatting endlessly online?'

'Those are the fun bits!' Tilly cried. 'That's how you find out if you vibe with each other.'

'Well, call this a shortcut,' I said, pointing to my wristband.

'I can't believe you just lucked out and got a billionaire.' She folded her arms and pouted. 'I've been on Connector for three years and the best I got was a finance bro who tried to pay for dinner with his crypto wallet.'

'He isn't actually a billionaire, you know. Probably not even half that.'

'Oh *right*.' She laughed. 'Just the half bil, then. Poor you. He better not be good-looking too.'

'Uh, well…' I blushed. 'He's probably not *your* type, but yeah, he's attractive. And he was actually pretty sweet in the balloon, especially when I thought I was going to die.'

'Oh Hazel, maybe he really is your person!'

Now, whenever anyone used the phrase 'your person', I had to try extremely hard not to vomit. But I had to remember what I'd signed up for, and maybe Tilly was right. I had to put myself out there, take a risk, leave myself vulnerable. Otherwise, I really was going to die alone in my aunt's flat surrounded by 1970s kitsch.

'Am I his though?' I said. 'I mean look at this place. Look at me. I'm not exactly country-club material.'

'Hey, I have an idea,' Tilly said. She grabbed my wrist and shouted into my wristband. 'CILLA! What's the best way to impress a date?'

After a second, CILLA started talking. 'Hello!' the voice squeaked. 'Did you know only thirty-seven per cent of second dates lead to a third? In order to impress, pay attention to details like lighting or music to set the mood. Think about what your date likes to eat and drink.'

'He definitely likes olives, right?' Tilly asked.

'Uh, I didn't ask. Everyone likes olives, though, don't they?'

Fergie snaked around my legs and looked up at me, eyes wide and hopeful, like the cat from *Puss in Boots*.

'I'm certain *you* don't like olives,' I told her.

Just then the buzzer rang, and Tilly grabbed me by the arms and opened her mouth in a silent scream.

'He's here!' she squealed.

I suddenly felt nervous. I loved my aunt's flat, but with its decades-old settee and scruffy carpet, it couldn't possibly compare to that gigantic mansion where Marc grew up.

I put my hands on Tilly's shoulders. 'Remember, just be yourself,' I told her. 'On second thoughts, be a much chiller version of yourself.'

I pressed the button to let Marc in, and seconds later, he appeared at the door, followed by a scruffy Lion's Jaw producer balancing a camera on his shoulder.

Marc handed me an expensive-looking bottle of wine, then kissed me gently on the cheek. He smelled amazing, a mix of the fresh sea air and a citrusy aftershave, and was dressed in casual, unbranded jeans and a sweater – the kind that look plain but are probably so designer that I wasn't even meant to know who made them.

'Nice pad.' He nodded appreciatively. 'The wallpaper is cool, very retro. And you must be Tilly.' He stuck out a hand towards her, but she stood frozen on the spot, staring at him.

'I know you!' she stuttered. 'You're the energy drink guy, aren't you? Wait, didn't I see you in that…'

'… that online video?' Marc said.

Tilly blushed the colour of her nails.

'Uh, why don't you have a seat, and I'll get some drinks,' I said. 'Tilly, why don't you give me a hand?'

I motioned to the sofa, and Marc sat down, jabbing a cocktail stick into an olive. Fergie immediately jumped on his lap.

'Oh, hello,' he said. She gave him a friendly headbutt, pushing her cheek against his. Marc laughed as she repeated the action.

I left them to bond and went over to the kitchen area, followed by Tilly.

'You didn't tell me he's a Van Batten!' she hissed. 'That's like one step down from the Beckhams!'

'Remember what I said about chilling out?' I poured the cocktail out into three glasses. 'Just be cool, okay?'

'Wait, what if she's the one who sent the note?' Tilly asked.

'What are you talking about?'

'The ex-girlfriend! You know, the one your new boyfriend cheated on in the video? I read somewhere she was so distraught after it happened, she got sent to a psychiatric hospital.'

'Tilly!' I gave her a pointed look and tilted my head towards the cameraman. 'Not now!'

Of course, I'd done what the note told me to do: *check the exes*. Portia was the only one of Marc's exes I knew about, and there wasn't much to check. A few old articles online about her make-up range, a MailOnline piece on her viral 'cheating' video and a winter-sports photo shoot with her posing in a cherry-red ski suit on top of a mountain. But nothing after 2024. I'd checked her social feeds, and noticed she'd done a couple of promo campaigns for Boom, but her last video was ten months ago, face plastered with green goop at an expensive spa. After that, there was nothing. No reposts, no likes or comments. It was like she'd disappeared off the face of the world. Was that what the note meant? Was I supposed to find out what happened to Portia? Was that what was going to happen to me? I hadn't told anyone about the note apart from Tilly. I didn't know what to do about it yet, and I wasn't sure I wanted Marc to know. But it was too late now – he was looking over.

'What note?' he called from the sofa.

'Oh, it's nothing,' I said. 'I found a stupid note pinned on the car after the balloon trip. Probably just someone's idea of a joke.'

'Whad dib id say?' Marc asked.

Tilly and I turned to look at him, confused. Why was he talking like that?

Then we looked at each other in alarm. Tilly audibly squeaked. Marc's lips had roughly doubled in size, and they now resembled two chubby sausages.

'What are you two looking at?' he asked, although it came out more like 'whub are you doo loobing ad?'

I put the drinks down and rushed to the sofa.

'Uh, Marc,' I said, sitting next to him. 'I, um, think there's something, um, a bit wrong with your face.'

'What?' Marc mumbled. His whole face was now puffing up like a balloon.

'Okay, don't panic, but I think we *might* need to get you some help,' I said.

I looked at the camera guy, who was just standing there, gormlessly, pointing his camera right at Marc.

'Don't you have a first aid kit or something?' I asked.

He shrugged, but didn't move the camera away from Marc's increasingly gigantic head.

'It must be a reaction to something,' Tilly said. 'The drink? The olive?'

I whacked the olive out of Marc's hand, and it went spinning across the floor, where Fergie immediately started sniffing it. We both looked down at Fergie, who blinked up at us, a picture of innocence.

'Duh cat!' Marc gasped.

'Fergie!' I picked her up and looked her in the eye. 'Was this you? Did you do this?'

She wriggled out of my hands and scarpered off towards the bedroom.

'Are you okay, can you breathe?' I asked Marc.

He nodded with some uncertainty, rubbing a hand on his throat.

'He needs some air,' I cried, jumping up. I swung open the front door and ushered Marc down the stairs onto the street.

'Go with him!' Tilly said. 'Don't worry about me!'

I did as she said, and found Marc outside, leaning against the redbrick wall of the building, taking deep breaths. It was still light, and there were a few teenagers hanging around the estate, who luckily weren't paying too much attention to us.

'I'm so sorry,' I told him. 'There's a pharmacy down the street.'

'Whad aboud him?' he wheezed.

He tilted his head, and I looked behind me to see that the cameraman had followed us outside and was still recording. I marched over and jabbed my finger at the camera.

'Do you really need to film this?'

The guy shrugged again, seemingly his favoured method of communicating, but didn't put the camera down.

I glared at him, then turned to Marc. 'You good to run?' I asked.

'What?' he said.

'I'll take that as a yes,' I told him.

With that, I swung round, grabbed the camera and popped out the memory card. Then I chucked it into the bushes, before shoving the camera back in the guy's hands. He stood there, mouth open, but before he could react, I took hold of Marc's hand.

'Run!' I cried.

I sprinted down the street, pulling Marc behind me. I looked back to see the camera guy frantically looking through the shrubbery. Eventually, when we were far enough away, we stopped, bent over, panting.

'Julian... gonna... kill us.' He laughed in between breaths.

'Ah, well, Julian can go to hell,' I said. 'We'll make it up to him on the next date. That is, if there is one?'

'Yeah, but only if you promise not to try and kill me again.'

After stopping at the twenty-four-hour pharmacy for

antihistamines, we walked along the seafront. The evening sun was beginning to fade, and I slipped my arm through Marc's. His features had returned to their normal, admittedly handsome, state. When we passed the pier, there was a chain hanging across the entrance.

'Down here,' I said, pulling him towards it.

'It's closed!' Marc said, hesitating.

I ducked under the chain and held it up so he could follow me. 'Come on, I used to do this all the time as a kid.'

We ran down the pier like a couple of teenagers skiving off school. Halfway down, we sat on the warm wooden slats, kicked off our shoes and dangled our legs above the water. Marc put his hand on my knee, and I couldn't help but feel… what was it? Butterflies? Nerves? I'd never really felt this with a guy before.

'So this is where you grew up?' he asked.

I felt a flush of embarrassment and wondered how much to say.

'Actually, no. But when I was little, my dad would bring me up here every summer to visit my aunt. He said it wasn't like the beaches his parents took him to back home. But I loved it… I—' I stopped, the words catching in my throat.

'What is it?' Marc asked.

The sky was beginning to turn a deep shade of pink. Behind us, the town was a distant blur of lights.

'He left,' I said. 'I was just a kid. I didn't understand why he had to go. My mum told me he was a bad man, which just confused me even more, because to me, he was the greatest.'

'Another woman?' Marc asked.

I paused.

'Prison,' I said quietly but firmly, and looked him straight in the eye to see if he would flinch.

'I'm sorry,' he said, not turning away. 'That must have been... hard.'

I could remember the day the police came to the house like it was yesterday. It was his birthday. We were sitting at the kitchen table about to slice into a wonky homemade coffee cake, and Dad was just blowing out the candles when there was a knock at the door. Mum told me to go to my bedroom and shut the door, straight away. I did as I was told, but I sat there with my ear pressed up against the door. I heard everything. The police reading him his rights, the snap of handcuffs around his wrists after he told them to go to hell. And worst of all, my mum's tears, her relentless and tormented tears that I thought would never stop.

When I came downstairs, way past my dinner time, she was still there, crying at the kitchen table. She told me what he'd done. At first, I wouldn't believe it; later, when I had to accept he wasn't coming back, that denial turned to anger, and I punched a hole in my bedroom door. Finally, I begged her to let me see him and hear it from his own mouth.

But Marc didn't need to hear all that, especially not on our second date.

'A couple of years after he went inside, my mum met this guy, Steeeve.' I elongated the vowels. 'That's what I used to call him. Steeeve. He was alright, I suppose. Safe, stable, the total opposite of my dad. And me, to be honest. But he was totally smitten with Mum, and she clung on to him for dear life. I don't blame her. Not many guys would've bothered with a single mum with an ex-husband in jail. And then they had a baby. My sister, Sandra.'

'Sandra? That's kind of an old-fashioned name,' Marc said.

'Tell me about it. They were big Sandra Bullock fans,' I said. 'Anyway, after that it felt like they had their own little family unit, you know? One that I wasn't a part of. I didn't talk like them, didn't act like them, hell, I didn't even look like them. I felt like I was a remnant of a past life that my mum wanted to forget. So, I came here to live with my Aunt Clara instead.'

I didn't tell him that after Dad went away, I started acting up, getting in trouble with the police and ended up dropping out of school. Aunt Clara gave me a chance to start afresh, while Mum found her own way to survive, I guess. It can't have been easy for her. As much as I couldn't stand the guy, Steve offered her an escape ladder of her own. A nice three-bedroom semi in Kettering, deep in the suburbs. Car boot sales, community theatre, a bake sale every time a monarch died, got married or had a baby. Not really my scene.

'My mum's not that interested in what I do these days. So I haven't told her about *Love Synced*. She'd only tell me it's a stupid idea and try to talk me out of it.'

I didn't tell him that, actually, her head would probably explode, and I didn't think her nice neighbours would appreciate that. Even Aunt Clara didn't approve, which explained her tactical retreat to her book club today.

'Julian's going to be furious when I tell him none of my family are coming to the wedding,' I said.

'Well, Julian can go to hell, right?' Marc smiled.

I put my hand over his, grateful for the support. I never really talked about my family to anyone, because once people heard your dad had been in prison, they tended to act differently around you. And by differently, I mean turn into judgmental arseholes.

'Sorry,' I said. 'It's kind of hard for me to talk about.'

'That's okay. I know what it's like growing up without a parent,' Marc said.

'Your mum?' I asked. In everything I'd read about the Van Battens, she was never mentioned. Like she'd been erased from their history.

It was his turn to pause.

'Yeah,' he said eventually. 'She died when I was twelve. Huntington's disease. It was sudden. People live perfectly healthy lives into their thirties and forties before they realise anything is wrong. That's how it was with Mum. She wasn't much older than I am now when she was diagnosed. After that, she went downhill pretty quick.'

'What was her name?' I asked.

'Joy,' he said, still looking at the horizon.

And that's when it dawned on me. Of course. *The Joy Foundation*.

'You set the foundation up for your mum,' I said.

'That's right.' He nodded, a sad smile spreading over his face. 'Hey, look at us, bonding over our shared grief, huh?'

A warm breeze blew across the pier, and I looked down at my toes. I wriggled them, just to check I was really here, watching the sun go down with Marc Van Batten, and this wasn't some kind of joint hallucination.

'I've been thinking about what you said in the balloon,' he said. 'You were right. I can't be a majority shareholder of a multinational at the same time as running a charitable foundation. The business is Dad's passion, not mine.'

'And what does your dad think about that?' I raised my eyebrows.

'Hah, I'll let you know once I've got the courage up to tell him.' He smiled. 'He's got enough going on right now. And, well, so have we, right? Wedding in less than two weeks.'

'You think this can work?' I said.

'I think it's worth a try.'

'You know, I almost did a runner before I even saw you.'

'Are you glad you stuck around?' he asked.

'Yeah,' I said. 'Yeah, I am.'

'You don't sound convinced!' He laughed.

'Tell you what, let's ask the expert,' I said. 'Hey, CILLA, how did we do today?'

His wristband lit up, and CILLA's voice rang out. 'Hi, Hazel! You and Marc communicated really well today! Couples who listen actively and express themselves clearly tend to have better relationships, so good news, you are now ninety-five per cent compatible!' she said.

'I feel like we should high-five or something,' Marc said. 'Even though you almost suffocated me.'

'Uh, yeah, sorry about the whole face thing,' I said.

'How does it look now?'

I tilted my head and put a finger to my mouth. 'Mmm,' I said. 'You know, maybe I preferred it the way it was twenty minutes ago. It had a certain puffy charm.'

'It does still feel a bit swollen,' he said.

'Where?'

'Here.' He pointed to his forehead.

I leant in and kissed him very lightly on the forehead.

'And here,' he said, pointing to his cheek.

I kissed where his finger was.

'Oh, and definitely here,' he said, pointing to his lips.

'Oh yeah?' I smiled, looking closer. 'They look fine to me.'

'Are you sure? I reckon they need closer inspection.'

I shuffled a bit closer to him until our faces were almost touching. It would be so easy, I thought, to move a few centimetres more, and we'd be kissing, effortlessly. But something inside stopped me. Not now. Not yet.

Suddenly, above us, a seagull screeched loudly. I flinched, and the moment shattered.

'Come on, it's getting cold,' I said, standing up. The wind was no longer just a breeze; it was a constant, solid push. 'We should head back and rescue the cameraman. He's probably had his phone nicked by the kids down the parade by now.'

'You don't want to watch the sunset?' Marc asked.

'I've seen a million of them. I live here, remember?'

'But have you ever seen one with me?' He smiled.

'We have our whole lives for that,' I told him as I headed back towards the promenade. Truth was, I always preferred sunrises to sunsets. Sunrises were the universe saying hello, but sunsets were a goodbye, an ending.

Marc followed me down the pier. I slipped my fingers through his, and he squeezed my hand. As we walked, I snuck a glance back, just in time to see the sun dip below the horizon.

ELEVEN

SKARDBALT AIRPORT

Gary is gone, and we're just standing there staring, slack-jawed, at the swinging gate door.

'Shouldn't we go after him?' Marc asks. 'I mean, he killed Julian, right? We can't just let him get away.'

Dante lies back on the row of seats, stretching his legs out. '"Uncle" Gary is an overweight middle-aged man with his hands tied behind his back. How dangerous can he be?' he says. 'Let the fat fuck tire himself out running around an empty airport.'

'What if he comes back? He might hurt someone else,' Marc says.

'I will not let that happen,' Emil says. 'It is my responsibility to keep every passenger safe.'

'And you're doing a fabulous job so far,' Stephanie says drily. 'Only one of us is dead. Do keep up the good work.'

She taps Dante's legs and he obediently swings them to the

floor. Then she sits down next to him and takes her eye mask out of her handbag.

'I agree with Dante. We should lock the gate door and wait here until the authorities arrive,' she says.

'Okay, that makes sense,' Marc says. 'Safety in numbers, right? We stay here, keep warm, wait it out.'

As he says that, the strip lights above us flicker ominously.

'And what if the power goes?' I ask. 'We'll freeze to death in here.'

'Do not worry,' Emil says. 'Every airport has a backup generator. If the worst happens and the blizzard severs the power lines, it should kick in.'

Prior to today, if you'd asked about my worst nightmare, I might have said a thousand tiny spiders each with the face of Elon Musk. Or maybe being chased by my secondary school geography teacher, Mr. Davies, naked (him, not me). But never in a million years could I have imagined a night with the Van Battens, *IN THE DARK* with no toilet *and* a dead body ten feet away. How did this happen? Did I step on too many cracks when I was a child?

Another horrible thought keeps nagging at me. What if Gary is telling us the truth? What if he didn't murder Julian? Because if he didn't, then one of the others did. And that means I am about to be locked in this room with a murderer.

I shake my wristband. 'CILLA,' I say. 'When someone is missing, what's the best strategy to find them?'

The display lights up, showing a thinking emoji face. 'Hey, Hazel!' she says. 'Great question! The most effective option to cover the most ground when searching for a missing person is to split up.'

'Split up?' I scoff. 'I wish you'd given me that advice two weeks ago.'

I try to figure out where Gary would go. It's a tiny airport; he can't hope to hide in here for long. The corridor from the gate leads to the security X-rays, and beyond that is the arrivals/departures lounge, where the café and the gift shop are. If he tries to leave the building, he won't get far in this weather, and even if he could hot-wire a car with his hands tied, the roads are closed. I'm almost freezing to death inside, let alone out in the snow.

I shiver and stick my hands in my hoodie pockets. My fingers curl around something cold and plastic in there. I pull it out. It's the wheel from my carry-on. I look over at my little three-wheeled case, and it dawns on me.

'Where's Julian's bag?' I say.

'What?' Emil asks.

'His carry-on,' I say, running over to where Julian had been sitting last night. I bend down, and sure enough, under the seat is his leather holdall. The zip is already open, so I turn it over and empty it out on the polished floor of the gate.

'What are you doing?' Emil asks.

'Last night, Julian said he would ruin us all, remember?' I say, not looking up. 'I think he meant Uncle Gary too.'

Rummaging through Julian's belongings, I pick up items at random and quickly discard them.

Passport, iPhone charger, a hardcover biography of Alfred Hitchcock, a washbag.

But no memory cards.

Lion's Jaw had been filming everywhere at the wedding venue. If Gary was dealing drugs, he probably got caught on camera doing it, which means Julian had footage on those memory cards that would incriminate him.

Maybe, when he couldn't find them in Julian's bag, he followed him to the bathroom to try and persuade him to edit him out. Julian refused, and things got... a little heated.

If Gary wants to destroy the evidence, he'll have to be looking for those memory cards. And if Julian didn't have them on him, there's only one other place in this airport they can be.

That's where I'll find Gary.

Without saying another word, I push past Emil and head through the gate door.

I run down the short corridor, through the scanner to the security checkpoint. There's a big glass box there. I'd seen it on my way in. An amnesty box, where staff put any confiscated items before you go through security. I peer inside. It's full of bottles of water and aerosols but also corkscrews and scissors. I can even see what looks like a flare gun in there. But it's securely locked, annoyingly.

After security is the cafeteria, and then it's a short walk to the main concourse where I checked in hours ago. It had been brightly lit and filled with noise then, but now the large, empty room is eerily quiet. This airport is really nothing more than a functional box of concrete and steel, hunkering down against the relentless wind and snow. There are no windows, and the only light is coming from the flickering screen on the wall that says 'All flights suspended'. There's an old-fashioned payphone on the wall. If only I hadn't wasted my last coins on a packet of crisps, I could call... I don't finish the thought. Who would I even call?

I look up at the signs above my head. They're written in

Norwegian, but each word is accompanied by a little symbol, like a cup of coffee, an aeroplane, and the little man and woman that signifies a restroom.

Oh man, my bladder aches when I see that. I rush in, checking the men's first for any signs of Gary, then go to the women's. Afterwards, I splash cold water on my face and shake out my curly brown hair. From what I can make out in the mirror, I look like shit, which is no surprise. The adrenaline rush of the last few hours is beginning to fade, and the lack of sleep is catching up with me.

I go back into the main concourse and spot the symbol I'm looking for: a little silhouette of a suitcase. Baggage reclaim. Following the sign towards another short, dark corridor, I keep going until I reach a smaller room with an empty carousel. This must be where passengers pick up their bags after a flight.

'Gary?' I shout, pointlessly. There's no one here.

The air is stale, musty almost, and there's a couple of luggage trolleys lined up haphazardly against the wall. The monitor above the carousel is blank, which makes sense, as there haven't been any arrivals.

The conveyor belt makes a perfect loop before disappearing through strips of plastic into the darkness. When I was a little kid, whenever we went to visit Gramps, I'd jump on the conveyor belt, squealing in delight as it carried me round. Dad would always grab me before I got whisked into that scary dark hole. The last thing I want to do is go in there now, but that must be where the luggage is stored before it's loaded on and off the plane. Could Gary have crawled back there to find Julian's bag? And does that mean I'm going to have to go in there to look for him?

I scan the walls until I find what must be the controls for the conveyor belt. I flip open the panel to see a green button and a red button. Pretty self-explanatory, I think, slamming my fist on the green one. There's a whirring noise, then the carousel suddenly jolts into life.

I stand there staring at it for a minute, waiting to see if any bags come out. Slowly, items begin to appear. An old luggage label. Odd bits of tape. A child's shoe.

I'm about to climb on, when the plastic flaps covering the hole lift up, like the machine is giving birth. Something large begins to emerge, but it doesn't look like luggage…

'What *is* that?' I say out loud as what looks like a big heap of clothes trundles down the conveyor belt towards me.

I squint at it, taking a step closer. Maybe someone's bag split open?

Wait.

As it trundles towards me, I can see that it's *not* a pile of clothes at all.

It's a body.

It's turned away from me, but when it comes round the bend of the carousel, I see it from the front. My stomach retches as I stumble backwards. Behind me, I hear someone running down the corridor, and I turn to see Emil burst into the room.

'What are you—'

He stops mid-sentence, his eyes widening when he sees what's on the carousel. Quick as a flash, he whacks the red button on the wall. The conveyor belt judders to a halt, leaving Gary lying right in front of us, his eyes bulging out of his head, tongue lolling out of his open mouth.

The luggage straps that were previously tied round his wrists are now pulled tightly around his neck.

I stand there, frozen, unable to move. There's no voice left in me, otherwise they'd hear my screams from here to England.

- EPISODE FOUR -
MEETING THE FAMILY

PETWORTH, SUSSEX

(Marc and his father, Malcolm Van Batten, sit next to each other in two identical yellow chairs)

Producer (off camera):
What does your family think about you taking part in the show, Marc?

Marc Van Batten:
My family are... (looks at his father) well, let's just say they're protective of me. Do I need their approval? No. I'm thirty years old. I don't need their approval for *anything*. You know, I got into extreme sports after university. Skydiving, base jumping, you know, lots of stupid stuff that might kill me. Skiing was my real passion. I was a semi-pro, and there was even talk of the Olympics for a while. My stepmother is constantly terrified I'm going to die, but I like doing things

that scare me. And doing this show is a bit like that. Is it going to piss off certain members of my family? Probably. But it's not like they've never done something dumb, is it? We Van Battens have had our share of scandals over the years, and I think this show will help people see that we're normal, we make mistakes. We're not just evil, soulless robots who love money. I mean, maybe my stepmother is. (laughs) But, well, hopefully you'll see a different side to us. I mean, what's the worst that could happen?

Producer (to Malcolm):
Why don't you introduce yourself?

Malcolm Van Batten:
Do I really need to? (laughs) Been on TV enough, haven't I? I'm Malcolm Van Batten, the distinguished, and rather dashing, CEO of VanCamp Drinks.

Producer:
Are you looking forward to meeting your daughter-in-law tomorrow?

Malcolm Van Batten:
(looks off camera to his left) We're having lunch, is that right?

Producer:
That's right. And how are you feeling about the wedding?

Malcolm Van Batten:
Well, it's about time, isn't it? Christ, I'd been married ten years and had a child by his age. Marc has always had an

eye for the ladies, I suppose. Got in a bit of trouble with the last one. (laughs) Joy keeps telling me it's my fault, my swashbuckler genes. (coughs) I could never sit still, always looking for the next adventure, the next deal. Joy thinks I'm—

Producer:
Sorry, do you mean Stephanie?

Malcolm Van Batten:
What? I didn't... yes, Stephanie. That's what I said, didn't I?

Marc Van Batten (standing up):
Alright, um, maybe we should stop here. Can we stop, please? Are you okay, Dad?

Producer (to camera operator):
Okay, cut there. Mr Van Batten, do you want to take a break? We can re-take that question.

Malcolm Van Batten:
I don't have time for that. Could we wrap this up? I have some calls to make and—

Producer:
Yes, of course, let's call it a day there. Thank you for your time, Mr Van Batten.

As doorsteps went, the Van Battens' was immense. Purple wisteria snaked its way around the porch, dangling over the huge Edwardian door that I was taking my sweet time looking at.

From the air, this place had looked tiny. Up close, it put Downton Abbey to shame. A proper country manor with sprawling grounds. I wouldn't have been shocked if there was a stable out the back. Or a helipad.

Clutching the bouquet of supermarket flowers that I already regretted bringing, I wondered if it was too late to back out. Because if knocking on the door of Marc's house was this difficult, God knows how I was going to cope with actually meeting his family. Especially Marc's father, the bigshot CEO of the VanCamp Corporation.

When I was growing up, Malcolm Van Batten was often on TV, a Richard Branson 'flamboyant entrepreneur' type, happy to make himself the public face of the company. Would he be the charismatic entrepreneur I'd seen on telly, or the ruthless businessman he was rumoured to be behind closed doors?

As I placed my hand on the big, brass door knocker, my wristband flashed.

'Hey, Hazel! How are you today? Your pulse indicates that you are very nervous,' CILLA said.

'Uh yeah, just a bit,' I replied. Still smarting from my first date with Marc, I'd plucked the most inoffensive outfit out of my wardrobe: a pale blue dress paired with a white cardigan. The perfect daughter-in-law outfit.

'Did you know that sixty-four per cent of people say that meeting the in-laws for the first time is more nerve-wracking than a job interview?' CILLA said. 'A positive relationship with your partner's family can strengthen the bond between you and your fiancé. So pay attention to what they say and respond thoughtfully. And don't forget to express gratitude for their hospitality!'

'Okay, thanks,' I said.

'And, Hazel,' CILLA added, 'whatever you do, don't swear.'

Great, she's obviously been listening to me when I'm late for work.

Behind me, a cameraman waited patiently. I knew there'd be another on the other side of the door, poised to capture my stupefied expression when greeted with the inevitable opulence inside. Well, sod that, I wasn't about to give them the pleasure. I fixed my best confident, assured expression and, with a deep breath, lifted the door knocker. Seconds later, the door swung open, revealing a small woman, dressed smartly in a grey smock, who beckoned me inside.

'Oh, hello!' I said, shoving the flowers towards her. 'I'm Hazel. Lovely to meet you, Mrs Van Batten.'

She looked at me, bemused, took the flowers and deposited them on a nearby table.

'May I take your coat please, Miss Harper?' she asked.

'Oh,' I said, my cheeks burning as I handed it to her. 'Right, of course.'

I heard the cameras on either side of me whir, capturing my humiliation from two different angles.

Awesome start, Hazel. If I didn't know better, I'd swear Lion's Jaw chose someone like me on purpose, just so they could make a fool of me. But I *did* know better, so I took a breath and reset.

Smile, say thank you, and whatever you do, don't swear.

The maid led me through the hallway and into a room with a grand piano in one corner, and in the other, sitting in a large green armchair like a throne, was undoubtedly Stephanie Van Batten. Immaculately dressed in a knee-length pristine-white dress, with glossy dark hair that framed her pinched features perfectly, she had the air of a seasoned Hollywood actress. At her feet was a large Great Dane, stretched out and fast asleep, its stomach gently rising and falling.

Beside them, lounging on a chaise longue of the same green velvet, was a man of about Marc's age with a floppy fringe and a bored expression. He was wearing a white polo shirt and shorts, as if he'd just finished a game of tennis. Or indeed polo, for all I knew. Next to him was Marc, who quickly got up as soon as he saw me.

'Hazel,' he said, kissing me on the cheek. 'So glad you could make it. Let me introduce you to my family.' He leant in a little closer and whispered, 'The ones who agreed to be on camera, at least.'

Stephanie coughed loudly. 'I'm quite capable of introducing myself,' she said, standing up and offering her hand. 'I'm Stephanie Van Batten, Marc's stepmother.'

'Lovely to meet you,' I said, resisting the huge urge to curtsy. 'Marc's told me so much about you.'

As soon as I said that, I realised he actually hadn't. The only things I knew about her was what I'd read on Malcolm Van Batten's Wikipedia page, in the – extremely scant – 'Personal Life' section: Stephanie had been head of the family's PR team, but had married Malcolm Van Batten shortly after Marc's mother died.

'And this is my cousin, Dante,' Marc said, pointing to the man in the shorts.

'AKA the best man,' Dante said, not getting up.

'That's right,' Marc said. 'Dante has very kindly volunteered his services in that department. But he's promised to be on his best behaviour.'

'And apparently that includes censoring all the juicy bits out of the speech, right, mate?' Dante stood up and slapped

Marc on the back. I half expected him to give him a wedgie. 'Don't worry, I'll skip the part about him sneaking out of three different girls' rooms in one weekend back at college. We wouldn't want another viral moment, would we, old chap?'

Marc ignored him and bent down to address the dog. 'And this,' he said, rubbing its head, 'is Boris, everyone's favourite Van Batten.'

Boris opened his eyes and looked up at me, suspiciously.

'Say hello, he's friendly,' Marc told me.

I reached down and gingerly patted Boris's head and he let out a low growl.

'I don't think he likes me,' I said.

'That's interesting,' Stephanie remarked. 'He's usually an excellent judge of character.'

'Maybe he's just hungry,' I offered, attempting a weak smile.

'Perhaps,' Stephanie replied, her gaze never moving from mine. 'But he's only just been fed.'

She left that hanging in the air, and I looked desperately at Marc for support.

'Er, you have a pet, don't you, Hazel?' he asked, helpfully changing the subject.

'Yes! A cat,' I said, too enthusiastically. 'Fergie. She was a stray who used to hang around on our estate. One day I started feeding her and after that she never left. It's her flat now, I just live in it.'

Not that I had anything against dogs, but I'd always been more of a cat person. They did their own thing, they didn't rely on anyone for anything, and best of all, you didn't have to clean up their shit after them.

'Fergie? After Sarah Ferguson?' Stephanie asked.

'Um, no, Fergie from the Black Eyed Peas,' I said.

Stephanie stared at me like I was speaking Mandarin.

'Uh, well,' Marc said, before the awkward silence completely engulfed us, 'I actually dread to think who Boris here is named after. I mean, he's Dad's dog, really, so you can probably guess. But he's a good boy, aren't you?'

He took the dog's head between his hands and scratched behind his ears. Boris whimpered appreciatively, then slumped to the floor.

'Will your dad be joining us today?' I asked, and immediately regretted it, as yet another awkward pause followed, this time coupled with some anxious glances.

Thankfully, at that moment, the maid appeared at the door and announced that lunch was being served. She led the way as we trotted back down the hallway, followed by the cameras, into a grand room with a long, beautifully dressed table. Oil paintings hung on the oak-panelled walls and a large window looked out onto the grounds, a perfectly manicured lawn surrounded by neatly trimmed hedges. Marc pulled out a chair for me and I sat down, while another maid brought out bowls of soup, placing one in front of each of us.

Everyone sat in silence, and after a moment, I wondered if they were waiting for me to start. I dipped my spoon in the soup and tasted it.

'Delicious,' I said, then, remembering CILLA's advice, added, 'Thank you.'

No one said anything, so I continued eating. Finally, Stephanie spoke.

'We normally like to say grace before we eat,' she said, as if she were speaking to a child.

'Oh, right, of course,' I said, freezing with my spoon in midair. I slowly lowered it back down and sat up straight.

'Would you like to do the honours?' Stephanie asked, her lips pursed into a faint smile.

'Um, okay.' I placed my elbows on the table and bowed my head. The others followed suit, and I cleared my throat as I tried to remember what I'd seen on American TV shows. 'Well, first of all I'd like to say thank you, to the, um, Lord, for this delicious—' I looked down at my bowl. 'Tomato soup? I think? That we are about to, uh, eat. It's a, uh, massive honour.'

Marc peeked at me through his fingers and gave me a 'what the fuck?' smile. I shrugged back.

'And thank you to Stephanie for this amazing lunch we're about to enjoy,' I added.

'It's not like she cooked it,' I heard Dante say under his breath, but loud enough for everyone to hear.

'Oh right, yes, of course,' I said. 'Thank you to the cook and all the staff here for looking after us today.'

Stephanie sighed loudly and opened her eyes. 'They've been generously remunerated for their services,' she said, picking up her spoon.

Apparently, that was our signal to begin, as Dante and Marc immediately started eating.

'Where are your family from, Hazel?' Stephanie asked.

'South London,' I replied. 'I grew up about twenty miles from here, actually.'

Stephanie placed her spoon down next to her bowl. 'Originally I mean.'

I saw Marc's face stiffen, but I placed my hand on his knee and forced a smile.

'South London,' I repeated.

Stephanie's gaze didn't flinch. 'And when are we going to meet them?' she asked. 'We can't very well just bump into them at the wedding, can we?'

I froze. What was I supposed to say? That my dad pissed off back to the Caribbean as soon as he got out of jail? That I'd barely spoken to my mum since I'd moved out aged sixteen?

'Ah, well, I'm not actually that close to my parents…' I tailed off. 'There's my Aunt Clara, but she's not been well, so…'

Marc put a hand on my knee and gave it a squeeze. I gave him an appreciative glance.

'I see,' Stephanie said, her lips pursed so tightly, I wondered how any soup was ever going to get in there.

'But my friend Tilly will be there,' I added, brightly. 'She's a manicurist.'

'Delightful,' Stephanie said, without any emotion whatsoever.

'You're only bringing one guest?' Marc asked, turning to me.

'Don't worry, Tilly is enough to make up for twenty people, trust me. You'll love her. She's the sort of person who tells her dirty dishes it's bath time.'

Marc looked at me doubtfully, and I knew I'd have to come up with a better excuse than that.

The next course, a large joint of roast lamb with all the trimmings, arrived, seamlessly. But as the maid carved off a slice and placed it on my plate, my heart sank. Now was probably not the best time to tell them I didn't eat meat. I looked down at my plate and shuffled a Yorkshire pudding round my peas with my fork.

'You know what it's like,' I went on. 'Not everyone is totally supportive of the whole TV wedding thing. I mean,

I'm basically marrying a stranger. Most people I know think it's completely crazy to be honest.'

'They're not the only ones,' Stephanie sniffed as she cut a tiny piece of lamb with her knife.

'Hey, now, come on,' Marc said. 'We talked about this, remember? And we all agreed that, yeah, it was a little out there, but we were all going to get on board. I know it's not how people did things in your day, but—'

'Her day?' Dante sniggered. 'In her day she was probably clubbed over the head and dragged to the nearest cave.'

Stephanie let her knife fall to her plate loudly, and Dante immediately stopped laughing.

'Thank you, Dante,' she said. 'Remember what we said about being our best selves today?'

Dante scowled and reached for the wine bottle. I'd noticed, when we sat down, the maid had filled each of our glasses but left his empty. But before he could grab it, Stephanie shot him a look, and he froze.

'I don't think so,' she said. 'There's plenty of soda if you're thirsty.'

'Jesus, I'm not a twelve-year-old,' he snorted.

'Stop behaving like one then,' Stephanie snapped.

Dante folded his arms and pulled a sulky face.

'Dante is on a bit of a, uh, health kick,' Marc explained. 'Minor car accident in the summer, so he's taking it easy for a bit, aren't you, mate?'

'Doctor's orders,' Dante said to me, miming a yawn.

'I'm sorry it's so tedious to you, Dante, but we have guests today,' said Stephanie, motioning to the two camera operators. 'And we don't want to embarrass ourselves, do we?'

'Yes, that's the *last* thing we'd want to do,' he sneered.

'Wouldn't want the family to be humiliated on Marc's special TV show, would we?'

Stephanie glared at him for what seemed like a millennium, and while everyone was looking at Dante, I took the chance to carefully slip the lamb off my plate onto a napkin, then let it drop into my open handbag.

Suddenly, there was a loud noise from the corridor, like someone had fallen down some stairs, and Stephanie looked up, a flash of panic in her eyes.

'Excuse me,' Stephanie said eventually, her voice icy as Antarctica. 'I need to go and check on dessert.'

With that, she got up and walked through the door to the kitchens, leaving the rest of us sitting in more awkward silence. I glanced down at the lump of meat in my handbag, currently dripping gravy onto my make-up.

'I'm, uh, just going to use the bathroom,' I whispered to Marc, pushing back my chair.

'Oh, yeah, sure,' he said. 'Down the corridor on the right.'

Slipping past the camera crew, I went back down the hallway and immediately gulped down air, like I'd been suffocating. Little red lights winked at me from the corners – more cameras. I had to find somewhere private to get rid of this lamb. I wandered down one corridor, then another, searching for a bathroom. The place was enormous; I was starting to worry I'd get lost trying to find my way back.

Suddenly, I heard muffled voices coming from the end of the corridor, like two people having an argument. I stopped and ducked behind a large rubber plant. Peeking out, I saw two figures having an animated conversation. Their voices were low, hissed whispers, but I recognised Stephanie's immediately. The other belonged to an older man with wispy grey hair and a short, wiry beard, wearing a dressing gown. To be fair, it was an extremely nice silk dressing gown, but there was no escaping the fact that it was three in the afternoon.

A tingle ran through me. I was only yards away from Malcolm Van Batten, famous entrepreneur and part-time adventurer, albeit thinner and frailer than the man I remembered from TV. He didn't exactly look like an action man now, more like a man who'd put his glasses down a second ago and now couldn't remember where.

'...we'll deal with her, just like we dealt with Portia... you need to keep it together, otherwise they'll find out...' I heard Stephanie say, but Malcolm was shaking his head, seemingly confused. Or maybe just annoyed.

I leant out from the plant and tried to hear the rest of the conversation.

'Now listen to me,' Malcolm was saying. 'I'm quite capable of—'

But before I could catch the end of his sentence, I felt something wet on the back of my hand and almost jumped out of my skin. I spun round to see the Great Dane, standing behind me with his big slobbering tongue hanging out of his mouth.

'Boris!' I hissed. 'What are you doing here?'

He tilted his head at me and growled.

'Oh, no, no, no, shush!' I whispered. But Boris drew back his gums, baring his teeth, and a large glob of saliva dripped from his mouth.

I glanced back at Stephanie and Malcolm, who were now walking down the hallway towards me.

Shit.

Quickly, I took the slice of lamb out of my handbag, unwrapped the napkin and gingerly held it out for Boris. He took one look at it, gobbled it up in a single gulp, then trotted off in the other direction.

I dashed back to the dining room. Just as I took my seat, Stephanie came striding in, closely followed by Malcolm, still looking flustered from their conversation. Malcolm angrily pointed at the cameramen.

'What's all the noise down here?' he demanded. 'And who are all these people?'

'It's the TV crew, Dad,' Marc explained gently. 'They're filming today, remember?'

Malcolm ignored him and sat down at the end of the table, seemingly oblivious to the baffled production crew, and stared at me.

'I'll do it myself then, shall I?' he said eventually, as though exasperated by my apparent inaction, and went about pouring himself a glass of wine.

Marc's dad looked like him, older, of course, with unkempt eyebrows, hanging jowls and without the brightness in his eyes that his son had. He still had the traces of a Dutch accent, dimmed by the years living between England and America.

When he began spooning Brussels sprouts on to his plate, Stephanie coughed loudly.

'Malcolm, if you're going to be joining us for lunch, perhaps you might want to go and get dressed first?'

'I'm fine,' he said, continuing to pile his plate with food without looking up. 'Don't fuss.'

I noticed the cameras turning to focus on him.

'Can we stop filming, please?' Marc said.

'Don't worry, we can cut this in the edit,' the camera operator told him. 'But we need to keep the cameras rolling for continuity.'

Malcolm's eyes landed on me, and he suddenly stopped, like he'd just noticed I was there.

'Who's that?' he asked.

'This is my fiancée, Dad,' Marc told him gently.

His dad looked at him like he'd just told him he was changing his name to Bozo and joining the circus.

'Don't be stupid. You're marrying Portia, not this woman who can't even afford a decent dress.'

'Portia and I aren't seeing each other anymore, Dad.'

Stephanie's expression remained exactly the same. If I didn't know better, I'd have suspected she was enjoying this.

'Shame,' Dante said, leaning over the new potatoes. 'Absolute fitty. Love of his life, too, until she called off the engagement.'

Marc and Portia were engaged? He conveniently left out that part up in the balloon.

'Give it a rest, Dante,' Marc snapped.

'So what did happen to Portia?' I asked, as innocently as possible.

'Decided being an influencer was unfulfilling,' Dante said. 'So she pissed off to Nepal to hang out with some monks instead. Found a higher calling, apparently.'

That sounded odd. From the look of her old videos, her main calling had been spin classes followed by Aperol Spritzes with the girls.

Malcolm was standing up now, reaching for the carving knife. It was strange to see this man, who by all accounts had been a titan of industry, a self-made millionaire, standing in his dressing gown doing a terrible job of carving a slice of lamb.

'Malcolm, sit down, please,' Stephanie said. 'The maid can handle that.'

'I can do it myself,' Malcolm said. 'I'm not an invalid. God knows I do everything else around here. You know I built this damn business from the ground up. And I mean literally.'

'Oh, not this again,' Dante sighed, throwing his head back theatrically. 'And you were worried about me embarrassing everyone!'

'I lost everything, right at the beginning, you know. Business partner pissed off at the first sign of trouble. Didn't have everything handed to me like these two,' Malcolm went on. 'I built it, all over again, like a—'

'Phoenix from the flames,' Marc finished his father's sentence. 'We've heard this story before, Dad. Come on, let's get you back to bed, shall we?'

Marc stood up, put his arm around his father's shoulders and tried to lead him gently towards the door. Malcolm wasn't having any of it. He stopped in the middle of the room and pointed out of the window.

'There's someone in the garden!' he shouted. 'Some fool in a big red jacket.'

'Oh for goodness' sake, Malcolm!' Stephanie snapped. 'That's enough now.'

Marc tugged on his father's arm. 'Dad, there's no one in the garden,' he said patiently.

'There bloody is,' Dante said, standing up.

We all turned to the window, just in time to see a big bulky object flying towards it. Suddenly there was an almighty crash as it smashed through the glass, sending shards flying over the table. Potatoes and carrots scattered everywhere as plates and cutlery clattered onto the floor. Stephanie was shouting for security while the camera operators spun around, desperately trying to capture everything. Dante and Marc ran to the broken window, trying to see who was out there.

I stood frozen to the spot, my hands shielding my face. When I lowered them, I saw a large brick had landed in the middle of the dining table. There was a piece of paper fastened around it with a single elastic band.

Another note.

Gingerly, I reached out and picked up the brick from among the smashed crockery. Hands shaking, I peeled the paper off and flattened it out on the table. There were only four words, scribbled in thick black marker pen. My heart started thumping as I read them out loud.

Marry him and die

'What the actual fuck?' I yelled, then immediately covered my mouth with my hand.

There was a beep from my wristband. 'Hazel!' CILLA scolded. 'I told you not to swear!'

TWELVE

SKARDBALT AIRPORT

The airport cafeteria is tiny, with an extremely limited choice of refreshments and some truly terrible 1980s décor. Some very nondescript photography adorns the walls – snowy landscapes, a smiling couple holding hands – along with a poster boasting the café's exorbitant coffee, sandwich and muffin deal. Behind the counter, there's an array of stale-looking pastries withering under an electric heater.

Central Perk it is not. In fact, I doubt this place has ever had much of a cosy-cappuccinos-and-muffins vibe going on, let alone at quarter past three in the morning when its only patrons are wondering if they're all going to die.

Sitting around one of the small, circular tables, staring at each other in silence, we could easily be bored passengers waiting for their gate to be called. Instead, we're cold, confused and scared. And there's something else I'm worried we're about to become: victims.

We've moved from the gate to the café, which has the advantage of marginally more comfortable seating and a toilet without a dead body in it. Between them, Emil and Marc have spent the last hour searching the whole airport, and they couldn't find a single soul.

While Marc tries to work out how to use the coffee machine, Dante wobbles the table with his elbow, making the salt and pepper shakers clank against each other. Emil is pacing around the café, occasionally straightening a picture. His nervous energy, combined with the shaking table, is making me want to scream all over again. Eventually, Stephanie clips Dante around the ear, and he stops, folds his arms and sulks quietly.

'Sorry, couldn't figure the coffee out,' Marc says, dumping a collection of fizzy-drink cans and stale pastries on the table. 'And I'm afraid these look like they've been there for a while.'

Stephanie picks up a croissant between her finger and thumb like it's a dead mouse and inspects it grimly. Dante goes straight for the sole cinnamon bun and sticks it in his mouth, chewing loudly. Me? I've lost my appetite. Finding two dead bodies will do that to you.

'I can't believe he's dead,' I mumble, staring at a blueberry muffin. I haven't dared close my eyes since I found Gary, because every time I do, all I can see is his swollen face, a spiderweb of broken capillaries across his cheeks. And worst of all, that thick, red tongue, hanging out between his lips like he's taunting me.

'Chubby sack of shit had it coming,' Dante says through a mouthful of crumbs, and I'm immediately back in the room.

'Wow, way to not sound like a murderer, mate,' Marc says, slapping him on the back.

'Just saying.' Dante shrugs. 'Not exactly a big loss, is it? The guy was a small-time drug dealer and a shit magician. Can't say I'll miss him.'

'Again, maybe don't tell the police that when they get here,' Marc says.

'*If* they ever get here,' Stephanie says, with a trademark eye roll. The blizzard is still raging outside and doesn't look like it's settling down anytime soon.

'They will be here,' Emil says. 'I promise you.'

I wrinkle my nose at him. 'Will they though?' I lift my wristband to my mouth. 'CILLA,' I say, 'what are the chances of us leaving this airport alive?'

The display lights up, and CILLA begins to speak. 'Hey, Hazel! Great question! With the current weather forecast, I estimate the emergency services will reach the airport in approximately seven hours. At the rate of two deaths per hour so far, all of you will be dead before help can arrive. Hope that helps!'

An eerie silence fills the room, and Dante starts wobbling the table again. We sit there for a second, listening to the *clank clank clank* of the metal table leg hitting the tiled floor. If the mood wasn't dreadful before, it's like a morgue in here now.

Sorry, bad choice of words, but you get my drift.

Two people are dead. We're trapped in a nightmare – no, worse than that, a legitimate tragedy. But to these people, it seems like it's just another inconvenience before they get back to their penthouses and property portfolios. I'm beginning to wonder if getting murdered by a psychopath might be preferable to another seven hours of this.

'We need to face facts,' I say. 'Gary and Julian are dead. Do you think whoever killed them is going to stop there? If we want to survive, we can't just sit around here eating pastries.'

Dante stands up. 'You're right. We're going to need something a lot stronger than shitty out-of-date doughnuts.' He goes behind the counter and grabs a bottle of beer from the refrigerator. 'Hiding these, were you, cousin?'

'Dante, please!' Stephanie snaps. 'You know you're not supposed to be drinking.'

'Oh, give it a rest, there are no cameras here.' He sits back down, flips the ring pull and swings his feet up on the table. 'We're all going to die tonight anyway, according to CILLA, so what the hell.'

I get up and go over to the black-and-white photo of the smiling couple on the wall. In another universe, could that have been me and Marc, grinning inanely at each other, the loved-up married couple? Or were we always destined for an unhappy ending?

'Marry him and die,' I say out loud.

'What?' Emil asks.

I tap my finger on the photograph. 'During filming, someone sent us a message, via a brick through a window,' I explain. '"Marry him and die".'

Those words will be etched onto my brain forever, like lovers' initials in the bark of an old tree. At the time, I thought it was a warning, but now I wonder, was it a threat?

Emil drags his palm over his face. 'And you did not think to mention this earlier?'

'It was just some idiot trying to sabotage the wedding,' Marc tells him. 'Stupid anonymous notes, warning us not to go through with it. We figured it was probably a jealous ex.'

'No shortage of those in your dating history,' Dante says, swigging some beer.

'It wasn't just the notes, was it? Remember the person in the red coat, lurking around while we were filming?' I ask Marc. 'And after the incident at the stag do, I swear I saw someone in a red coat running off.'

Marc gets up and starts walking around the cafeteria, his brain clearly going at full pelt now.

'You're saying whoever it is was here on the island?'

'And maybe they still are,' I say. 'They couldn't get to us with all those cameras and Lion's Jaw's security. But what if they followed us to the airport, where we're sitting ducks? And now they're hunting us down one by one.'

'Ludicrous,' Stephanie says. 'Why would anyone want to hurt us?'

'We are kind of hateable, to be honest,' Marc says. 'How many people has the company screwed over in the last thirty years?'

Stephanie's face sours when he says that, but she doesn't argue.

'You say "the company", what you really mean is Malcolm Van Batten,' I say. 'And the people he very literally screwed over.'

'Excuse me, but didn't your daddy dearest murder someone?' Dante asks, coyly.

I freeze, my fingers curling around my Fanta can. Without realising it, I've squeezed it so hard, I've crushed the can. Part of me wishes it was Dante's throat.

'Who told you that?' I say, my gaze spinning to Marc, who holds his hands up in an expression of innocence.

'Don't worry, it wasn't lover boy there. Julian let it slip,' Dante says. 'Didn't go into all the gory details though.

Just told me he was a wrong 'un. Maybe the apple doesn't fall too far from the tree?' Dante puts on a horrible Essex accent when he says 'wrong 'un' that makes my blood boil.

'Talking of fathers,' I snap, 'at least I know exactly where he is – thousands of miles away on some Caribbean beach. Can you say the same for Malcolm?'

'He's at home. You know very well he couldn't make it to the wedding,' says Stephanie.

'This is academic,' Emil says. 'We have searched the whole airport. There is no one here.'

'Okay... so what if they're out *there*,' I say, pointing to the photo of the snowy landscape.

'Out there in the blizzard?' Emil says. 'That is not possible. No one could be out in that weather for more than a few minutes.'

Marc nods. 'He's right. Every skier knows it's whiteout weather.'

'Whiteout?' I ask.

'It's when the blizzard becomes so powerful, you can't tell the sky from the ground. All you can see, from any direction, up or down, left or right, is white. You can't even see your hand in front of your face. Everything around you is blank.'

I close my eyes and try to imagine it. But of course, that just makes everything black.

'Not many survive it,' Marc goes on. 'Wind kicks up the ice, tosses it into the air, destroys visibility, you can't see six inches in front of you, can't tell the ground from the sky. People freeze to death, their bodies found a foot from safety and warmth. Die because they couldn't see the front door.'

The way he describes it, a whiteout sounds equally terrifying and incredible.

'But Emil, you said someone could handle the snow for a

few minutes out there, right?' I ask. 'Is there another way into the baggage area, other than through the airport?'

Last night, I thought the killer had to be one of us, because the gate door was locked. But what about the other door, the one leading out to the plane on the tarmac?

'Yes, of course,' he says. 'It can be accessed from outside. The ground crew load luggage on and off the planes on the apron. That is what we call the area where the planes are parked. Here, I shall show you.' Emil takes the salt and pepper shakers and places them in the middle of the table. 'This is us here, in the cafeteria.' He picks up my crushed Fanta can and places it a few centimetres left of the shakers. 'And this can,' he continues, 'is the baggage reclaim where we found Gary. The gate where you were waiting is down here, past security.' He picks up the metal box of tissues and places it below the other items. Then he traces a route with his finger from the box around the table to the Fanta can. 'So, if you can go out of the gate here, where we normally board the plane, you could walk across the apron, past the control tower to the baggage reclaim, like this. It is only a short distance, see?'

I stare at the random collection of items on the table and something occurs to me. I grab the salt shaker.

'But what about,' I pour out the salt in a generous circle around the items, 'the snow? Could someone make it in this weather?'

'It would not be easy, perhaps, but it could be done. But this is all theoretical, of course. There is no way of knowing.'

'Maybe there is.' I lick my finger and tap it through the salt, making a little trail as I go.

'Footprints?' Emil says, shaking his head. 'They would be

covered almost immediately by fresh snow. There would be no trace of them left.'

'Outside, yes, but what about inside?'

'What are you talking about?' Stephanie sighs. 'I've had just about enough of this, honestly. I can feel a migraine coming on.'

I interrupt her by lifting my index finger. Grains of salt are stuck to the tip. With the same finger, I point at Dante's sneakers.

They're soaking wet.

'If the shoe fits, right, Dante?' I say.

THIRTEEN

SKARDBALT AIRPORT

Dante looks at his feet, and freezes for a second, like someone has pressed pause on his face. Then he snorts, like I'm an idiot for even pointing it out.

'It's lager, obviously,' he says. 'I spilt it. This piece of crap is about as stable as the global economy.' He grabs the edge of the table and wobbles it to accentuate his point.

Marc slams his palm down hard on the table, bringing it to a shuddering halt. 'I didn't see you spill anything, mate.'

Dante shrugs as if that's not his problem.

'Did you leave the gate?' Marc asks. 'Is that why your shoes are soaking?'

'Soaking? Give me a break,' Dante scoffs. 'They're a little damp, at most. You are not pinning two murders on me because of some soggy sneakers.'

Marc picks up Dante's beer can and shakes it, as if he's trying to ascertain how much is left in there. I'm still staring at the array of utensils on the table and wondering if someone would be able to get from the gate round to baggage reclaim and back without anyone noticing.

'Dante was waiting at the gate with me,' Stephanie says, as if reading my mind (and honestly, I wouldn't be surprised if she had been a witch in past life).

'All of the time?' Emil asks. 'He did not leave at any point?'

'No,' she replies, but I see her eyes quickly flick downwards, and one of *my* special powers is knowing when someone is protecting their piece-of-shit nephew.

'You sure about that?' I ask.

Now it's Stephanie's turn to blush. 'Well, I must admit, I did have my eye mask on, very briefly. I mean, it's past three in the morning, a woman is entitled to her beauty sleep. But I'm sure that Dante wouldn't have—'

'Have snuck out without you noticing?' Marc says. 'Because that actually sounds like a *total* Dante move.'

Dante petulantly rocks the table with his foot. 'Typ-i-cal,' he says, drawing out the word syllable by syllable. 'Let's go ahead and blame it on Dante. That's the Van Batten way, isn't it? What about you, Marc? You scarpered off after your little girlfriend Hazel when she ran off. But oh, it's never Marc the golden boy, is it, hmmm? This is because of what happened before, isn't it? You think I'm a killer, just because—'

'Dante!' Stephanie snaps. 'That's enough.'

He sinks back into his seat and petulantly suckles his beer like it's a baby bottle.

I look around the cafeteria. If Emil and Marc ran after me, and Stephanie had her eye mask on, then no one here could verify Dante's movements. Hell, no one could verify *anyone's* movements.

'This isn't getting us anywhere,' I say. 'We need an impartial opinion.'

'Don't even think about it!' Dante cries. 'We are not asking that thing again.'

'CILLA,' I say, ignoring him as my wristband's display lights up.

'Hey, Hazel!' CILLA says. 'How are you today? Brrr! Is it cold in here? I'm registering a temperature of nine degrees Celsius, so I would advise wrapping up warm.'

'Uh, thanks, CILLA, we have a bigger problem, actually. There has been another murder,' I say. 'Gary is dead. We need to figure out who killed him.'

'So sorry to hear that, Hazel. Did you know that ninety-nine per cent of murderers are male? Another interesting fact is that sixty-eight per cent of murderers are known drug users...'

Dante makes a swipe for my wrist. 'For Christ's sake, give me that thing, I'm going to stamp the shit out of it.'

'While eighty per cent have previously demonstrated anger issues,' CILLA continues, as I swifty move my arm out of Dante's reach.

'That is such bullshit.' Dante rolls his eyes and tosses his fringe back. 'Why are we listening to a robot, anyway?'

'Because I trust CILLA more than any of you right now,' I tell him. 'I think Gary went looking for Julian's luggage. And if there was footage of you buying drugs off him on those memory cards, you'd have a good reason to follow him. Because if that gets out, you'll be in big trouble, won't you?'

Dante pushes his chair back and looks around the room for someone else to blame, eventually settling on Emil.

'What about our flight attendant here, with his fucking pre-school diorama of the world's shittiest airport?' he snaps. 'Where was he when good old Uncle Gary got his head bashed in?'

'Strangled,' Emil says. 'He was strangled.'

'See? Wouldn't I know that if I'd killed the fat fucker? But this guy knows all about it. And he knew *exactly where* to go.' Dante points at the arrangement of utensils on the table.

'Yes, because I work here,' Emil says calmly, but there's a glint of fury in his eyes.

'Oh yeah, that's right, isn't it?' Dante says, jabbing a finger towards him. 'You're the one who told us to stay in the airport in the first place. We'd all be sipping on hot chocolate back at the hotel if it wasn't for you.'

'It was your choice to stay overnight,' Emil says calmly. 'The airline makes it very clear in their terms and conditions that they are not responsible for passengers who choose to sleep at the gate. And I think, Mr Van Batten, you would be sipping on something considerably stronger than hot chocolate, would you not?'

Dante jumps up, strides over to Emil and pokes him in the chest.

'I've got your number, pal,' he hisses in Emil's face, standing on tiptoes, as he's a good foot shorter than him. 'You're standing there in your pretty little uniform with your silly little waistcoat. You think you're better than us, just because you have a badge and clipboard?'

Dante flicks Emil's name badge with his finger.

'Well, let me re-educate you on that point, dickweed. You are nothing but a glorified waiter. You're a phoney, and I can see straight through you. All I have to do is click my fingers and you'll be back stacking shelves in whatever shitty Norwegian mini-mart you came from. As soon as this screw-up is over,

I am going to be straight on the phone to the head of the fucking airline, ripping you a brand-new arsehole.'

With that, Dante pours the remaining beer from his can over Emil's shoes.

'Oh, now, look who else has wet shoes?' Dante says.

Emil stands there, lips pursed, not reacting, but I can see his cheeks burning red. They stare at each other for a moment, neither saying a word. Dante is right in his face, their noses almost touching. I watch as Emil struggles to maintain his serene demeanour, his fists curling into balls. I wonder if he's finally going to snap, but after a tense moment, Dante backs off, his sneering expression turning to panic. Perhaps he's sensing that he's about to get lamped.

'I said that's enough!' Stephanie stands up now and pushes in between the two men. 'Dante Van Batten, you are becoming an embarrassment to this family.'

'Oh really? I'm the embarrassment, am I? Not viral sensation Marcy Marc here?' He makes a kiss-kiss face at Marc. 'Or our glorious leader, Mr MVB senior himself, groping every tart he's ever been within three feet of? And what about you, evil stepmother? Maybe it's time we came clean with all the family secrets, hmm? Would you like that?'

Marc and Stephanie exchange a glance. I've dealt with enough drunks at Eight Ball to recognise that moment when they shift from coherent to chaotic, and Dante is way past that point.

'Don't you dare do anything so stupid,' Stephanie says. 'Just sit down and stop talking like that.'

Dante's face twists in indignation. 'No. I'm done doing what you tell me to do. I'd be better off in prison, locked away. That's where I should be. That's where I'm supposed to be, not on a stupid TV show, not at his stupid wedding and not stuck in an arse-end-of-nowhere dump of an airport with you.' He points at Stephanie. 'All *you* care about is how we look to everyone else. The reputation of the Van fucking Battens. Well, I've got news for you, you're not even a real Van Batten, are you? You were a nobody before you married into this family. Worse than a nobody, a fucking PR consultant. And now you're just another one of Malcolm's whores.'

With that, Dante puts a hand under the table and tips it over, sending everything crashing to the floor. Stephanie's face is clenched so tightly, the muscles in her jaw are visibly straining, but she doesn't utter another word. Instead, she just stares at Dante as he steps over the mix of broken china and half-eaten pastries and heads out of the cafeteria.

'Wait,' Emil calls after him, with a flat, sarcastic tone. 'Do not go, please.'

'Sorry, did I spoil your little model village?' Dante calls over his shoulder.

Before anyone can stop him, he stomps off into the main concourse.

'Damn it,' I hiss, running after him.

I hear Marc's voice calling out to me. But I don't listen.

'There's nowhere to go, Dante,' I shout. 'We're all stuck here. If you hurt Gary, you might as well tell us the truth. Once the police get here, they're going to figure it all out anyway.'

He ignores me and goes over to the amnesty box by the security checkpoint. He looks through the glass, like he's surveying the random items inside and deciding which is the most murdery. Then he lifts his leg and kicks it, hard, and repeats the action again and again, until eventually the glass cracks. A final stomp, and it shatters, and he's able to reach in and grab the pair of scissors resting on the top.

'Don't come any closer,' he snarls, waving the sharp ends towards me.

I hear Marc running up behind me. He stops at my side when he sees the scissors and holds up his hands. 'Woah, mate,' he says. 'Come on. Just come back to the café and we'll talk it over, okay?'

'Talk it over with your stupid little chatbot? I'll pass, thanks.' Dante laughs, but it's hollow and mirthless.

When I take a step closer, he jabs the scissors in my direction. I stop dead in my tracks, but my eyes flick to his hands. They're shaking. I've seen Dante bolshy; I've seen him lose his temper. But I've never seen him like this – he's scared.

Sensing my chance, I reach over to the smashed amnesty box and carefully stick my hand in. Avoiding the sharp shards of glass, I push past the corkscrews and the cans of deodorant, until my hand finds the flare gun I saw earlier. I fish it out and point it at him, knowing full well I'd never have the guts to pull the trigger. I've never seen a gun in real life before, let alone fired one.

Dante's eyes widen as beads of sweat form on his brow.

'I didn't hurt anyone,' he says, his tone a lot less aggressive now he's in danger of a flare to the face.

'Then why are you running?' I ask.

'Because if there's a killer here, it's not me. Which means…' He gulps. 'Which means it's one of you. And I am not sticking around to find out if I'm next.'

'You know something, don't you?' I lower the gun. 'Do you know who's doing this?'

He pauses, looks at me, and for a second I think he's going to say something. But before he can open his mouth, the lights suddenly flicker. I look up, and as I do, every light goes out, plunging the room into complete darkness.

FOURTEEN

SKARDBALT AIRPORT

Dante disappears into the gloom of the main concourse. I run after him.

'Hazel!' Marc yells after me. 'Don't!'

But I'm not listening. I have a horrible feeling that Dante knows who's doing this, and either he's running away, or he's running straight into danger. Whichever it is, I'm going after him.

Dante is a hothead, alright, especially when he's been drinking, but I've never seen him freak out like that. Even after we found Julian and Gary, he kept up the cocky-little-shit act. But just now, he looked like he'd seen a ghost.

The arrivals lounge is almost pitch black. He could be anywhere. I consider firing the flare just to scare the shit out of him. Get him to scream. Let me know where he is.

'Dante!' My voice echoes through the lounge. 'Don't be stupid. There's nowhere to run.'

I swing around, wildly waving the flare gun like I'm a rookie cop in a bad action movie. My eyes slowly adjust to the dark. I can't see much, but enough to make my way around the arrivals lounge. The entrance doors to the airport are closed. If Dante has gone out there, I'll never catch up with him. But considering the weather, maybe I wouldn't need to. Marc's right, no one could last longer than five minutes out there. I stand in the middle of the lobby and shout again. He can't have gone far.

Suddenly, there's a loud noise from behind me. A crash, like something falling over. I spin around, but everything is as still and dark as before.

And then… a gurgle? Definitely a human sound. And it came from the direction of the gift shop.

'Dante?' I shout.

I suddenly wonder if Marc followed me. Or did he go back to Stephanie and Emil in the cafeteria? Or is someone else in the lobby with me?

'Marc? Is that you?' I yell.

I walk slowly towards the gift shop, still holding the flare gun out in front of me. The store is tiny, basically just a small room with no shop front, so I can walk straight in. There's a bunch of branded sweatshirts hanging on the walls, but the floor is covered with keyrings, trinkets and mugs. It looks like there was a scuffle here.

There's another noise, like footsteps, and I swing round, pointing the flare gun into the thin air behind me. There's no one there. But there was. *There must have been.*

My heart is pounding now. Clutching the flare gun in one hand, I reach for my phone from my hoodie pocket with my other. I tap the screen but it remains black. Out of battery.

'CILLA?' I say, and my wristband display lights up. 'Just be quiet, but keep the light on, will you?'

She doesn't say anything.

'CILLA? Did you hear me?'

'Yes, Hazel, you told me to be quiet.'

'Right, yes, thank you,' I sigh.

The dim glow of CILLA's display reveals a pile of oversized fluffy polar bears in the corner, I HEART NORWAY proudly stamped on their bellies. I slowly step closer, holding my arm out as I go. The light from my wristband catches something, a streak of red across their white faux-fur.

What is that?

I peer closer, running my hand across the bears. They're wet to the touch. I bring my fingers up to my face, and my body starts to shake. It's blood. Gingerly, I nudge the flare gun into the pile of toys, pushing them aside. There's something under there…

Or someone.

Sticking the gun in my pocket, I frantically start grabbing polar bears and chucking them behind me. Gradually, what's lying under there is revealed. First a nose, then a cheek bone, and finally a mouth gaping open like a fish gasping for air. *Dante.* I kneel down, sweep the rest of the toys off him, and place my hands around his head, gently lifting it up.

'Dante!' I cry. 'Are you…'

His eyes flicker open.

He's alive, thank God.

I rest his head on a polar bear and turn over my shoulder to yell, hoping the others can hear me.

'Help!' I shout. 'It's Dante, he's hurt.'

I was right. I knew it. There is someone in this airport hunting us down, one by one, and they're not going to stop until we are all dead. I turn back to Dante. He's clasping on to his neck with one hand.

'How do I look?' he croaks, a twisted smile spreading across his face.

'Dante, shut up and tell me who did this to you,' I say, pushing his fringe away from his damp forehead.

'Too dark... didn't see... came from behind, took the scissors and...'

Dante lifts his hand away from his neck, just slightly, and blood starts to gush through his fingers. I can see a large gash in the side of his throat.

'Right in the jugular...' He coughs, placing his hand back over the wound.

I scan the floor for the scissors, but it's too dark to see much.

'Just hold on,' I say. 'I'll get the others, we can—'

'No!' he cries, then his voice drops to a murmur. There's a look of sheer terror in his eyes. 'Not the others. Stay with me, please...'

'But Dante, I can't...' I stutter. 'I... I don't know what to do.'

He grabs onto my hoodie with both hands, releasing the pressure on his neck again. Crimson blood spurts out all over me, turning my ivory dress red. Dante ignores it and pulls me closer.

'Just... listen to me.' He coughs, spitting blood as he tries to talk. 'I think... I think... it's impossible but it must be...'

He reaches out with his index finger and, with a juddering motion, scrawls a thick line of blood on the shiny floor of the gift shop. Then, with his last gasp of energy, he lifts his finger again and draws another line crossing through the first. And with that, the life disappears from his eyes, and he's gone.

I stand up, shining the dim light of my wristband at the symbol on the floor. My heart thumps as I realise what it is.

An X.

- EPISODE FIVE -
THE FIRST DANCE

STREATHAM, SOUTH LONDON

Marc put his hand on my waist and we locked eyes, poised like two statues.

As the opening bars of the plodding rock ballad drifted across the basketball court, he pulled me into his chest, then after a beat, leant me backwards.

He then took a step back with his left foot, while I took a step forward with my right. But as I transferred my weight, he tried to twirl me too soon, and I fell into him, toppling him backwards. We landed on the ground in a tangled heap. Again.

'Let's take five there,' the dance instructor said, shaking his head.

Before we could even get up, Julian poked his head from around the camera, like an over-coiffured meerkat. 'You're absolutely welcome to take another break,' he began.

'Great,' I said, getting up and brushing myself off. Marc sat on the floor, exhausted.

'But that would necessitate shooting into the evening, which means our poor crew won't get home to their families tonight. But if that's okay with you, then by all means "take five". Take ten, if you feel comfortable with that.'

I scowled at him.

'Okay,' I sighed, sticking my hand out and pulling Marc up. 'Let's go again. We'll get it this time.'

'Only if you're totally happy to,' Julian said. 'At Lion's Jaw, our contributors' health and well-being is always foremost in our minds.'

'Yeah, sure it is,' I said. That must be why we're still filming despite a death threat through a window. 'Just start the music, will you?'

It's fair to say the practice sessions for our first dance at the wedding were not going well. Julian had envisioned a *Dirty Dancing*-esque training montage, so every rehearsal had to be captured on camera. It was an unseasonably warm afternoon, and after many repeated (and failed) attempts to get it right, I was dripping with sweat and resentment.

Worse, after the brick incident at the Van Batten house, our compatibility rating had plummeted to a mediocre 68 per cent, and our pitiful attempt at dancing was doing nothing to improve it.

The song was an orchestral version of 'Use Somebody' by Kings of Leon, a sort of soft-rock waltz, and not something I'd previously been familiar with. Although now, after hearing it approximately two hundred times in a row, I was pretty sure I never wanted to hear it again.

We were filming in an empty basketball court in south

London, which Julian insisted would look 'really urban and contemporary', but I suspected the real reason was that Lion's Jaw didn't have the budget to hire a proper dance studio. Unfortunately, that meant that every time we got the steps wrong, we'd end up falling on rough concrete.

The song began again, but as we started going through the steps, I saw something in the distance. There was a guy in the car park. At least, I thought it was a guy. They were too far away for me to make out their features. Every time Marc spun me round, the stranger was in my eyeline, just standing there, pointing his phone at us.

Distracted, I missed the beat, and Marc immediately stepped on my foot. I broke away, wiping the sweat from my forehead.

'Who is that?' I cried, pointing to the car park, where the figure, wearing a red puffa jacket, was leaning against a white van. 'He's been watching us the whole time!'

The crew turned round to look, and the guy lowered his phone.

'Everyone, stand down until we sort this out,' Julian barked. 'Security! Can we check this chap out please?'

After the incident at the Van Battens', Lion's Jaw had hired a security firm to oversee the production, which Julian had made very clear they couldn't really afford, but our safety was, *of course*, paramount, and the costs could be deducted from our wedding budget.

A burly security officer marched over to the car park, and we watched as Puffa Jacket Guy protested, and even shoved him, which was a bad idea, because then it was his turn to end up on his arse. The security guard pulled his phone off him and chucked it in the road. Puffa Jacket Guy shouted something I couldn't hear, then scrambled after his phone, before disappearing into a side street.

I realised I was shaking, and Julian was staring at me with a look of mild panic.

'O-*kay*, maybe we should have a little break,' he said, ushering the crew off to their trailer and leaving me and Marc standing in the middle of the court.

'First the brick through the window, now this. Who is doing this?' I asked.

Marc looked sheepish. 'I don't think you should worry,' he said. 'Price of fame. When I was growing up, we'd get all kinds of crazy letters asking for handouts posted to the house.'

'Through the window?' I asked.

Marc gave me a look. 'No, but sometimes they could get pretty nasty. Dad always said people were just jealous, that when you have his sort of money, people come for it. And when they don't get it, they come for you.'

'You mean blackmail?' I asked. 'Don't you have to have done something wrong to get blackmailed?'

'Okay, look,' he said. 'I didn't want to mention it before, because of the wedding and the show and everything. But there's been a bit of, uh, trouble at the company. A woman has come forward with a story about Dad.'

'What sort of story?' A wave of nausea rippled through me. This already sounded bad.

'She's saying she had an affair with him while she worked for the company, then he fired her when it got too serious. She's posted a video online about it. He's not been named, of course, but it's not hard to figure out who she's talking about. We've had calls from journalists, asking questions. They say they have more women ready to talk, a lot more.

They're saying Dad propositioned them too. Our lawyers are looking into it. The women signed NDAs, apparently, not that they're worth the paper they're written on these days. But if it gets traction, it could destroy him. It could destroy the whole business. Malcolm Van Batten is the face of the company, hell, he's the face of the damn drink.'

'And you think that's what the brick was about?'

'Maybe a journalist did it, or one of the accusers?' he suggested.

'Accusers? So you don't believe them?'

Marc runs a hand through his hair. 'Dad's always been a bit, uh, old school. Off-colour jokes at public appearances, flirting with the promo girls, that sort of thing. But I never thought he was capable of anything like this.'

'Old school? Seriously, that's what you're going with?' I said. I was shocked. What the hell was I marrying into?

'He's my dad, Hazel. What do you want me to say? He's the devil? I can't just... You saw him at the lunch. He's not doing so great. He's been getting worse recently. Forgetting things. Must just be the stress of the accusations, I guess.'

I walked to the edge of the court, where there was an ice cooler of, you guessed it, Boom. I grabbed two cans, and we sat on the warm concrete.

'Whatever happens, I've made a decision,' Marc said. 'I don't want to be associated with VanCamp Drinks anymore. I'm going to go out on my own with the foundation.'

'You're going to walk away from a billion-dollar company?' I couldn't hide my smile. 'For what it's worth, I think you're doing the right thing.' I cheersed cans with him.

'Wait a second, are you saying I'm *not* a prosecco fascist?'

'Well, maybe I was a little hasty,' I said.

He took a big swig of Boom, then grimaced. 'And I mean, have you tasted this shit?' He laughed. 'It's basically caffeinated dishwater.'

I laughed too. 'Hey, I thought the ingredients were super-secret!'

I took a gulp from my can. Boom did have an, um, *unique* flavour. But that didn't seem to put people off drinking gallons of the stuff.

'The super-secret ingredients that are listed on the back of the can, you mean?' He tapped his can. 'It's all bullshit. People think it *has* to be special because it costs so much and tastes so weird. But the real secret is that there *is* no secret. My dad somehow managed to convince people that drinking this crap would magically make them run faster or jump higher, that's all.'

'Built by adventurers, for adventurers, right?' I said. That's what Boom claimed on the label. And from what I remembered, Malcolm Van Batten had always painted himself as a swashbuckling daredevil, who created the drink for thrill-seekers like him to help them reach their full potential.

'Adventurer,' Marc said. 'You ever looked that word up in the dictionary? "Someone willing to take risks". Well, that's Dad to a tee. Right at the beginning, he almost lost everything. The Boom factory in London burnt down and he had to start from scratch all over again. Some of the workers died in the fire, and Dad's business partner pulled out. Everyone wrote him off but, actually, if it hadn't been for that fire, Boom might never have taken off the way it did. Dad moved production to South-East Asia after that, started mass producing the drink. He always says the tragedy spurred him on to make it a success, against all the odds. A phoenix from the flames.'

'So, your family owes all this to a fire?' I said.

Marc shrugged. 'Guess so.'

'Nothing to do with Thailand's cheap labour and, um, let's say *flexible*, employment laws then?' I asked.

'Dad's a businessman, through and through,' he said. 'He's always put the company first, above everything. Even me, you know? I got into the extreme sports stuff just to try and impress him, I think, but I sucked at the business side of things, which meant I was always a disappointment to Dad. He never stopped telling me how he built VanCamp single-handedly from nothing. Sometimes I think the foundation isn't for my mum at all. It's me trying to prove I can do something without him, in spite of him.'

I threaded my fingers through his and squeezed his hand. 'Maybe it doesn't matter why you're doing it; it just matters that you're doing it.'

He held my gaze and nodded. 'Shall we get back to it?' he asked.

I groaned. 'Do we have to?'

'We just need to get in sync,' Marc said.

'Right, love synced,' I said. 'CILLA, can you help us?'

'Hey, Hazel!' CILLA said. 'Of course, I am always here to help you! Dancing is about trust. Let go of hesitation and doubt. Trust builds connection, and connection builds trust – it's a beautiful rhythm!'

'That's the problem,' Marc said. 'We don't trust each other yet.'

I shook my head. 'Nah, it's not that, it's the song. Does it have to be *this* song? It's so slow!'

'This is our song!' Marc cried.

'What do you mean? We don't have a song.'

'Well, CILLA chose it,' he said. 'She looked through all our Spotify playlists to find what we had in common.'

'Oh, right,' I said.

'You don't like it?'

'It's just, well, it's not really *our* song, is it?' I said. 'Right now, it's just the anthem of me falling on my arse.'

Marc laughed. 'Does it really matter what song it is? We just need to learn the steps.'

'No!' I said. 'A first dance is supposed to be to a song that's special to us, right? But we don't have any shared memories or experiences yet. Music is all about memories. Here, let me show you.'

I went to the edge of the court and pulled my phone out of my bag. After tapping away on Spotify, I turned up the volume and the tinny tones of 'Dilemma' filled the court.

Marc tilted his head, confused.

'Nelly and Kelly? Come on!' I cried. 'Back in the day, we played the shit out of this! It always reminds me of my two best friends in school. Mia and Naomi. Mia had a crush on this guy who she reckoned looked like Nelly. We even made up a dance routine in my bedroom.'

'Go on then.'

'What?' I asked.

'Show me,' he said, folding his arms, a grin spreading across his face.

'Alright,' I said.

I stood in the middle of the court, rolled my left shoulder back, and stepped forward with my right foot, then my left.

As I did, I twisted my body to the side, then twisted to the centre on the step back.

'Come on, you try,' I said, taking both his hands and dragging him to the centre of the court. 'Watch my feet.'

Clumsily, he copied my steps.

'No!' I cried. 'Jesus, you're like a zombie. You have to loosen up, okay? Don't worry so much about looking stupid. Dance like no one's watching, remember?'

'But millions of people will be watching!' He laughed.

'Forget about that! Just keep looking at me. Now, roll your shoulder in time with the music, like this.'

He rolled his shoulder back, just as Kelly sang about being with her 'boo'.

'Now step forward.' I laughed. 'That's it! You're doing it!'

I let go of his hands, and we did the steps in unison. As the song came to an end, I gave him a high five.

'Shared memory unlocked!' I cried.

'Is it a *good* memory though?' he asked. 'Let's see what CILLA thinks.' He shook his wristband.

'Hi, Marc! Smooth moves!' CILLA said. 'That's the connection I was talking about. You currently have an eighty-six per cent chance of a successful partnership.'

As we went to embrace, Julian came striding over. He whipped off his sunglasses and looked us up and down like we were naughty children skipping school.

'Break's over, kiddos,' he said. 'The light is fading, and we still haven't nailed this.'

The Kings of Leon song filled the air, and we went to our starting positions. I put my hand on Marc's waist.

'Ready?' he asked.

'You know what,' I said, meeting his eyes. 'I think I am.'

And as we danced, finally getting the steps right as the sun set behind us, Marc leant in, and I felt the stubble on his cheek graze my neck. I wondered if the time was right to give Julian his dream shot: Marc and I, sharing a kiss, silhouetted against the dipped sun.

Despite every impulse in my body telling me to do the opposite, I couldn't help myself. I was falling for him. Had somehow, unbelievably, CILLA been right? But as I lifted my lips to meet Marc's, I caught a glimpse of something over his shoulder.

In the distance, near the car park, there was a flash of red. Ducking behind one of the Lion's Jaw vans, I could see the person in the red jacket. When they realised I was looking, they stood up. Whoever it was, they were too far away for me to make out their features. But I was very sure of what I saw next. They held up a finger and, very slowly and deliberately, drew it across their throat.

My blood ran cold, and I let go of Marc.

'What's wrong?' he asked.

'Look,' I gasped, grabbing his shoulder and spinning him around. 'The guy from before, he's...'

But it was too late. All we could see was the red jacket fading out of view as it merged into the crimson sunset.

FIFTEEN

SKARDBALT AIRPORT

Three of us, dead. And all I can think is: *who's next?*

I stumble out of the gift shop in a daze, Dante's blood still warm on my skin. It's probably only a few hundred yards back to the cafeteria, but the way the darkness stretches endlessly ahead of me, it might as well be two thousand.

And somewhere in that darkness is a killer, waiting to pounce.

I should try to find my way back to the cafeteria. But, as I couldn't see the scissors in the gift shop, that likely means whoever did that to Dante still has them, and probably cannot wait to plunge them into my back. My hand goes to my pocket, and my fingers curl around the handle of the flare gun. The killer might have a pair of rusty scissors, but I have this, and if anyone comes near me, I'll fire a flare into their forehead.

The heating must have failed at the same time as the lights, because as the shock of finding Dante wears off, the cold sinks its teeth into me. I look down at my dress, streaked with dark red, and zip up my hoodie. I wrap my arms around myself and kick my feet up and down. Anything to keep my blood circulating.

I shuffle back into a corner, pressing my back against the wall and pull the gun out, pointing it into the darkness.

'Come and get me, dickhead,' I hiss into the emptiness.

After a couple of minutes, my arms start to get tired, and I let myself slip down against the cold, unforgiving wall of the airport lounge until I'm sitting on the floor. My eyelids are growing heavy. I need to stay awake. Stay alert. I wipe the splashes of Dante's blood off my wristband with my hoodie sleeve, and it lights up again, illuminating the condensation from my breath in the darkness.

'Hey, Hazel! How's your day going so far?' CILLA's voice says.

What a question. And one that I have no idea how to answer.

'I honestly don't know, CILLA. You said we were all going to die here, and I think you were right.'

'Would you like some advice, or we can just chat if you'd like?' CILLA asks. 'If you need to talk, I am always here to listen.'

'I just want someone to tell me everything is going to be okay,' I say.

'Based on your current predicament, there is a less than thirty per cent chance of everything being okay. What else would you like to chat about?'

I want to laugh, but all that comes out is a dry, regretful snort.

'Alright, here's how my day is going so far. I'm in a deserted airport. It's dark and I'm scared. I'm trapped here, alone. There's a killer on the loose, three of us are already dead, and I don't think anyone is coming to help us. I thought that doing this stupid TV show would change everything. I thought it would finally bring me some closure. But the only closure I'm going to get is a prison cell when the Norwegian police inevitably blame this all on me.'

'Hazel, I have some good news!' CILLA says.

'Yes?' I sit up a bit straighter. 'What?'

'Statistically, based on your current circumstances, you are more likely to die than go to prison.'

I sink my head into my hands and groan loudly. Either way, it's not like I've got much to go back to anyway. I'm going to get fired when I miss my shift, I won't be able to pay the rent, and Fergie will run away and find some other mug to feed her.

CILLA is quiet for a moment.

'Would you like to hear a joke?' she asks, eventually.

'You just told me I'm going to die and now you want to tell me a joke?'

'Sometimes if you're feeling low, a joke can make things feel better,' she says.

'CILLA, trust me, there is no joke that you could possibly tell me that would make this situation better,' I say.

'Why did the pilot break up with his girlfriend?'

'Really? Are we doing this?' I ask.

'Because every time he got close to her, she would take off! Would you like another one?'

Despite myself, I start laughing. Laughing at the ridiculousness of this deeply stupid situation. I've gone from a reality dating show to a horror movie in the space of twenty-four hours. At this point, I'm seriously considering firing the flare into my own brain.

'You see!' CILLA says, almost proudly. 'Humour can help you see things from a different angle and make a challenge seem more manageable.'

'Awesome. I'd *love* a different angle on how I can manage not to end up like Julian, Gary and Dante.'

'Hmm, that's another tricky pickle!' CILLA says. 'The best course of action when you're in danger is to identify the threat and disable it.'

'How can I do that if I don't have any idea who is doing this?' I ask. 'Come on, CILLA, play Watson to my Holmes for a sec, and help me figure this thing out. Who would want to do something like this to us?'

CILLA thinks for a moment, then she speaks again.

'In most homicides, the perpetrator is known to the victim. Is there anyone connected to you or the family with a history of criminal behaviour?'

I roll that question around in my mind a few times before answering.

'My friend Mia used to shoplift make-up from Boots,' I say.

'Hazel, on the second of April 2026, you told Marc Van Batten that your father was jailed, is that correct?' CILLA asks.

The words sting. I know what she's implying, and it makes me want to rip off the wristband and stamp on it. Whatever is going on here, my father has nothing to do with it.

I only went to visit Dad in prison once, but it was enough to know I never wanted to go back. My aunt took me to see him a few weeks after he was convicted. I don't remember much, just fleeting images. The long car ride, even longer queues, being patted down before we went in. Most of all the snarling police dog that was almost as big as me. I was always a bit frightened of dogs after that. It wasn't like the movies, with the glass partition and the telephone, all that stuff – we went into a little room, with just Dad sitting at a table, and a guard watching. Dad seemed so happy to see me. But I was scared. I was scared of that place, I was scared of the guards, but most of all I was scared of him, and I think that broke his heart.

I wanted to give him something, but I wasn't allowed to take anything in. They let me draw while I was there, though, so I drew me, Mum and Dad, and a time machine. Like the one I'd seen on *Doctor Who*. Because that's all I wanted, to go back in time, to before it happened. Or fast forward until it was all over.

When it was time to leave, Dad tried to hug me, but the guards pulled him back. 'I love you,' was the last thing he said to me as we left.

I didn't say it back. I didn't believe him. If he loved me, he wouldn't be there. He wouldn't have left us.

He wouldn't have done what he did.

Mum didn't want me visiting again after that. She told me he hurt people, and eventually I believed her. What he did dropped a bomb on my little world, sending shrapnel through every inch of our lives. Shrapnel I was still picking out.

'If you're suggesting my father is behind this, you're wrong.

He's currently somewhere on a beach in St Lucia,' I snap. 'Next.'

'Have you considered Marc's father?' CILLA asks. 'While never convicted in a criminal case, Malcolm Van Batten has been the subject of multiple fraud investigations, and in 2026 was accused of inappropriate behaviour in the workplace by eight former employees.'

I shake my head, which is dumb because it's not like CILLA can actually see me. 'He's back in London, supposedly.'

'You're not one hundred per cent sure?'

'Uh, well, Marc said he was too ill to come to the wedding,' I say. 'So I guess he's at home. But he'd have no reason to hurt his own nephew, let alone a local drug dealer. Any other bright ideas?'

'Probability-wise, the person with the strongest motive for murder is you, Hazel,' she says. 'You have threatened Julian three times, spoken of your dislike of Dante thirty-two times, and you helped tie Gary to a chair.'

'Give over. You've been on my wrist the whole time,' I say. 'You'd know if I did anything.'

'Correct, I've been listening and recording your actions constantly over the last eight hours, and I am one hundred per cent certain that you have not murdered anyone.'

'Gee, thanks, CILLA, good to know you're on my side,' I say.

'Who else has a grudge against the Van Batten family?' she asks.

'Portia Clarke was Marc's ex-girlfriend before me, and things didn't end well, apparently. But I've seen her TikTok feed. She's into green juices and stretching and shit like that, not strangling people. But then again, Marc did cheat on her and immediately go on a TV show to marry someone else, so... But it *can't* be her. Portia is in Nepal. At least...'

'At least what?'

'At least that's what Marc told me,' I say, a sickening realisation dawning on me.

'Oh! Okay,' CILLA says.

'What?' I say. 'Why did you say "oh!" like that? What does that mean? You think Marc lied to me?'

'Hazel, I do not think. My responses should not be considered as personal opinions or beliefs or a substitute for human judgement or critical thinking.'

'But you would know if he was, right?' I ask. 'Marc has a wristband, just like me—'

I gasp out loud. Of course... *Marc isn't wearing his wristband anymore.*

'One more question, CILLA,' I say as I stand up, even though I think I already know the answer.

The wristband remains quiet for a moment, then flashes again. 'Yes, Hazel?'

'You don't think...' I begin. 'Sorry, can you calculate, or whatever you do, just tell me Marc isn't capable of this... is he?'

The smiley face disappears from the display.

'Great question, Hazel,' she begins. 'The probability of that is—'

She stops mid-sentence.

'Hello?' I cry. 'Is what? What's the probability?'

I tap on the screen, once at first, then again, frantically. But it remains black, just like my phone. She's finally run out of charge. Looks like I am well and truly on my own.

Just then, a low hum fills the lounge, and the strip lights above me flicker, then turn on, one by one, until the entire room is illuminated.

The backup generator. Emil said it would kick in if the power failed, and here it is.

It's time to get out of this hellhole, one way or another.

SIXTEEN

SKARDBALT AIRPORT

I run back through the main concourse towards the gate. Without CILLA, I'm on my own, but it doesn't matter, because I'm not sure I want to solve this mystery anymore. I just want to get home alive.

I have to look after number one. This isn't about avoiding a jail cell anymore; this is about surviving.

I reach the security checkpoint. A worn-out chair sits idle behind an empty desk, with a faded sign reading 'Sikkerhetskontroll' above. There's a lone security scanner standing in the centre, surrounded by empty trays and a single, deserted conveyor belt. Only the distant wind howling outside and the hum of the fluorescent lights overhead break the eerie silence. You couldn't get further from the stress and bustle of trying to get through Heathrow security at half term.

As I am about to walk through, a figure emerges from the direction of the café.

'Hazel,' a voice says. 'Thank God you're okay.'

'Marc,' I say, instinctively hiding the flare gun behind my back. 'What are you doing here? Where are the others?'

'I was, uh, looking for you,' he says, sheepishly, like a schoolboy caught smoking by his teacher. 'Did you find Dante?'

I squint at him. The emergency lighting is low, giving him a sinister appearance. He steps closer and his gaze falls to my hand, and the bright orange handle of the flare gun.

'Are you… okay?' he asks. 'There's blood on your dress.'

'No.' I wipe the sweat from my brow. 'I'm not okay. Dante is dead.'

Marc's face turns ashen grey. 'What are you talking about? Where is he?'

'Lying on the floor of the gift shop in a pool of blood. Stabbed in the neck with a pair of scissors. But maybe you knew that already?'

I lift the flare gun and try my best to hold it steady with both hands.

'Woah,' he says, lifting his hands up. 'What do you mean? I didn't hurt him. Hazel, you couldn't think that—'

'Why are you here on your own?' I cut him off.

'After the power went out, I went after you. Emil said he'd go and check the backup generator. Looks like he got it to work.'

I don't know what to believe.

Or who to trust.

Is Marc a killer? He could be, for all I know. The rest of his family are psychopaths, as far as I'm concerned. Maybe it's in their genes. Maybe getting dumped at the altar was his breaking point, and now he's totally lost his mind. He wouldn't be the first man to kill a woman who'd told them no.

'Have you got the scissors?' I ask.

'What? No, of course not,' he says. 'Please, show me where you found Dante, maybe we can work out what happened together.'

I shake my head. 'Do not fuck with me,' I say. 'I'm the one with the gun.'

'Flare gun,' Marc says. 'Let's not exaggerate here. Have you ever fired one of those things before?'

'You want to find out how a flare in the face feels, Marc?' I point the gun at his head again. 'Then keep mansplaining.'

Who am I kidding? I'll probably fire it straight into the ceiling, my arms are shaking so much.

Still pointing the gun at him, I walk over to the security scanner. As I step through, a single, loud beep rings through the room.

'I'm spending the rest of the night on this side of security,' I tell him, once the alarm subsides. 'If you want to prove to me you don't have the scissors, take off your belt and empty your pockets, then walk through the scanner. If it beeps, I'll shoot.'

He looks at me, speechless, as I steady my aim at his forehead and rest my finger on the trigger.

'What?' Marc stares at me like I'm crazy.

'You heard me. Do it. If you have the scissors, they'll set the alarm off. So, you're going to walk through that scanner. And if I hear that thing beep, God help me, I'll shoot you in the head with a flare.'

'I'm not a killer, Hazel,' he says, his expression twisting

from bewilderment to fury. 'Whatever you think of me, I'd never hurt you. I'm your fiancé, for God's sake.'

'My *ex*-fiancé. And guess what, that makes you statistically the person most likely to murder me.'

'Hazel.' Marc takes a step towards me, his hands spread out in front of him. 'I have no reason to hurt anyone. All I want is to get home safely, just like you.'

Pulling his belt out from his trousers, he drops it on the floor. Then he takes his wallet out of his pocket and does the same.

'No scissors, see?'

I waver, the flare gun suddenly heavy in my hand. My head is spinning. I need to think. Marc might be a womanising piece of shit, but I've never seen him raise his voice in anger, let alone physically attack anyone. He couldn't have been the one leaving those notes, could he? He was in the hot air balloon with me. He was there in the dining room when the brick came through the window. But deep down, I know I can't trust him. I can never trust a Van Batten.

'Keep going, walk through the scanner,' I say.

He stops.

'No,' Marc says. 'This is stupid, I didn't stab anyone with a pair of scissors.'

'What do you mean "no"?' I snap. 'Walk through the scanner or I'll shoot you in the head. This might only be a flare gun, but at this range, it'll kill you. If you want to prove to me that you're telling the truth, walk through.'

'Hazel, I do not have any scissors. I did not hurt anyone. You need to listen to me. Please.'

'I mean it,' I say, but I can't stop my voice from breaking. I motion with the gun. He doesn't move a muscle.

Fuck. Now what do I do?

'I am only going to say this one more time, Marc. Walk through the fucking scanner. Now.'

My finger rests on the trigger; it's wet with my sweat. I cock the hammer with my thumb. There's only one cartridge. One shot. If I miss, I'm finished.

'Fine,' he says, taking a step towards me with his hands still raised.

I flinch. If he goes for me, I'll never be able to fight him off. Do I really have the guts to fire a flare in his face? And am I really sure he deserves one?

Marc walks through the scanner, and there's a moment of eerie silence. For a moment, I relax and lower the gun. And then a loud beep echoes through the airport.

Marc's mouth drops open, like he's trying to form words, but nothing is coming out.

I stand there, paralysed for a second, unable to pull the trigger. Then I do the only thing I can think of.

Run.

I run as fast as I can towards the gate, the high-pitched beep filling the dim, empty corridor behind me. I ignore it and keep going.

Once I reach the gate, I stop in my tracks. There's only one way to go from here.

I see the door out onto the apron. I push through and sprint out into the snow.

SEVENTEEN

SKARDBALT AIRPORT

Cold flecks of icy snow immediately pepper my face, like someone's spraying me with a shaken bottle of ice-cold cava. Pulling my hood over my head, I stomp on through the thick snow. It comes up to my shins, soaking my dress and seeping through my trainers.

Fuck Marc.

Fuck the Van Battens.

I don't care who's doing this anymore. I just want to curl up in a ball and hide until this is all over. Let them kill each other, for all I care. I'll wait it out in the control tower.

It must be nearly dawn now, but you'd never know. The sky is almost completely white, and I can barely see which way I'm going. This is a terrible idea. But if I can reach the control tower, maybe I can barricade myself in there until morning. No one is going to come after me through this blizzard.

I keep thinking about whiteouts, how people would freeze

to death just metres from safety. But in the distance, I can see the control tower lights blinking at me through the snow. The thin tower rises up to a saucer-shaped top floor with windows all the way round. It's not nearly as tall as the ones at big airports. It can't be more than a hundred yards away. I head towards the lights, one step at a time, telling myself over and over: *it's not that far, I can make it.*

By the time I reach the tower, my dress is soaked and my fingers feel like icicles. I'm not sure I could have lasted much longer out here.

My heart leaps when I see a small door, and I quickly grab the metal handle with my bare hand. As soon as I do, a sharp pain shoots through my fingers like an electric shock. It feels like fire. I yelp, jumping back. But when I try to take my hand off, it doesn't budge.

It's stuck.

I lean backwards and push down on the handle again with all my strength, and suddenly, the door flies open.

I scream in pain as my hand rips away from the handle, sending me falling back into the snow with a thump. I scream again into the sky, and stick my hand deep into the snow, hoping the cold will make the red-hot pain subside.

I pull myself up, get inside and quickly shut the door behind me. The immediate gratification of the warmth fades quickly. The place is dark, damp and seemingly deserted. There's nothing here but a metal spiral staircase that leads up to the top of the tower.

'Hello?' I shout upwards, as loudly as I can.

No response. Emil was right, the fuckers have all gone home.

I take a moment to catch my breath and examine my hand.

Slowly, I uncurl my fingers to see that the cold metal of the handle has literally ripped most of the skin from the palm, leaving it red and raw. The snow has numbed the pain, but I can feel it gently throbbing.

I run up the stairs, sending loud, clanking footsteps echoing through the tower. At the top, the door to the control room is closed, and as I go to open it, I hear a noise from inside.

Is that a voice?

It's muffled, sure, but there's definitely someone – or something – in there. I press my ear against the door and listen again.

There it is again, a strangled, wailing moan. I glance back down the stairs. It's either run back down there and into the snow, or face whatever is making that horrible noise behind that door.

'I'm coming in,' I yell.

I grip the handle with my good hand, and with a deep breath, turn it and swing open the door.

My jaw drops. There's a person sitting right in front of me on a swivel chair, staring back with wild, desperate bloodshot eyes.

And they're wearing a large, red puffa jacket.

– EPISODE SIX (PART ONE) –
THE BACH PARTY

OFF-PISTE BAR, SKARDBALT

(Hazel and Marc sit on the big yellow chair)

Producer:
So next week, we're whisking you off to Norway for your dream wedding. But let's address the elephant in the room – your compatibility rating has been dipping. Do you think you two will manage to reach ninety-nine per cent before you walk down the aisle?

Marc:
You know, I really believe that Hazel is my person, so I'm confident—

Hazel:
(puts her head in her hands and mumbles) Please, *please*, never say that phrase again…

Marc:
(ignores her) I'm confident that we'll hit ninety-nine, no problem. We have the stag party—

Hazel:
Bach party.

Marc:
Right, the bach party, which is a karaoke night. That's our thing, right? We both love making fools of ourselves, so we're going to absolutely smash this one.

Producer:
What about you, Hazel? Looking forward to your last night of freedom?

Hazel:
Sorry, am I the only one freaking out here? Shouldn't we be a little bit more concerned about, you know, the actual physical *death threats* rather than our compatibility rating?

Producer:
Hazel, we spoke about this. Not on camera, please. Now, if anything at all about the production is worrying you—

Hazel:
Thank you, Julian. So the thing is—

Producer:
—we have a Contributor Welfare Officer you can speak to.

Hazel:
Oh, great. Where can I find them?

Producer:
Ah, well, unfortunately they only work on Tuesdays. We didn't have enough in the production budget for full time.

Hazel:
(gives a thumbs up to the camera)

The muffled strains of what sounded like a rugby team belting out a power ballad leaked through the bar door.

I paused before reaching for the handle. I'd made it halfway up a bloody mountain, but I wasn't ready to go inside yet.

'CILLA, can you tell me—' I said.

'Hey,' Tilly interrupted me. 'This is your party, why don't you just try and have fun, and not worry about what your Tamagotchi thinks?'

Fun was the last thing on my mind. The wedding was tomorrow, which meant, if I wanted to be walking down the aisle and saying 'I do', I had about fifteen hours to reach the magic 99 per cent. But since seeing the person in the red coat, I hadn't been able to get the image out of my mind. The threats, together with endless wedding prep and Julian constantly on my case, were keeping me awake at night. CILLA must have noticed, because our compatibility rating had slipped to seventy-three.

'I have to worry about what CILLA thinks,' I told Tilly. 'I'm running out of time.'

'You mean "we",' she said. 'It's not just you, Hazel. It's up to both of you. Now let's get inside before I freeze to death.'

While it was hard to take Tilly seriously in her pink, faux fur-lined ski jacket and matching earmuffs, she had a point. But how was singing karaoke and downing Jägerbombs supposed to prove Marc and I were soulmates?

We'd arrived in Skardbalt yesterday, after a stopover at Oslo, and from the moment we stepped off the plane at the tiny airport, the snow hadn't stopped falling. The Van Battens got here a day before, along with most of the production crew. Julian wanted to keep us apart until tonight's party. Calling it a bach party was generous though. As Tilly was the only friend I had here, it was really Marc's stag, and we were just hangers-on.

We'd taken the ski lift up from the hotel, while Marc and his mates had skied down from the top of the mountain after a day on the slopes. Everyone was staying at a 200-year-old converted castle, nestled in the mountains. The whole thing was like something out of *Frozen*, only with seemingly more snow and worse singing.

This was all so far from what I expected my wedding day to be. I mean, I never thought I'd even get married. But here I was, about to get hitched in an actual goddamn castle. I had to hand it to Julian, this place was unbelievable. My mother would lose her shit if she could see this. A wave of sadness hit me. She would see it, but on a TV screen, months from now.

I pushed open the door of the bar and was immediately met by a gust of thick, warm air and the faint smell of hot chocolate. Inside, it was all rustic wood panelling, stomped-in snow by the door, old ski poles hanging from the walls alongside vintage posters. The chosen activity for the evening was, by default, karaoke, given that the bar had a battered old machine and a small stage area in the corner.

Of course, the moment we stepped inside, a camera was shoved in my face, capturing my bemused expression at the scene in front of me. Marc and a group of almost identical-looking mates, gathered round a couple of mics, bellowing out 'Don't Stop Believin''.

Lion's Jaw had a small crew set up, consisting of a camera operator, a lighting guy and a woman with a sound boom. I groaned inwardly. I didn't even sing in the shower, let alone in front of TV cameras.

Spotting me, Marc jumped off the stage and bounded towards us, arms wide. He was still in his salopettes, and the braces accentuated his muscles through his tight white T-shirt. I could tell he'd already had a couple of drinks by his flushed complexion.

'My beautiful bride!' he beamed, grabbing me by the waist and lifting me in an embrace. No matter how down I felt, whenever he held me, a rush of butterflies fluttered through my body, and part of me didn't want him to let go.

He put me down and curtsied to Tilly. 'And her equally beautiful bridesmaid.'

'Maid of honour,' she corrected him.

'Of course.' He smiled. 'You're probably the only honourable one among this bunch of reprobates.'

He turned to the group of preppy-looking men on stage. They didn't look like reprobates to me, at least not compared to the lads down Southend Wetherspoons on a Friday night.

'What about your best man?' I asked. 'Where's he?'

Marc jerked a thumb towards the bar, where Dante was parked on a stool, staring at his phone, seemingly oblivious to everything around him.

'Poor sod is moping cos he's the designated driver,' Marc explained. 'Someone has to drive us all back to the hotel on the snowmobile later.'

'And your dad? Is he here?' I asked.

His jaw twitched. 'Uh, there was a bit of an... episode at Heathrow. Apparently, Dad was really confused and refused to let go of his luggage. Airport security was called, and, well, when they checked his bags, they were completely empty. All on camera, apparently. Stephanie decided it would be better if he sat this one out.'

He looked momentarily disappointed, but quickly shook it off.

'Guess he'll have to watch it on TV with the rest of the country, huh?' he added, forcing a smile. 'Right then, who's up for a duet?'

He picked up a microphone in each hand.

'Only if you'll be the Nelly to my Kelly.' I laughed.

Marc made a face. 'I do *not* think the world is ready to see me rap.'

'I'm more of a solo star anyway.' I smiled. 'Besides, it looks like the rest of the Backstreet Boys are waiting for you.'

Behind him, his group of his friends were calling his name and beckoning him back over as the opening bars of 'I Want It That Way' seeped out from the tiny speakers on the stage.

'Alright,' Marc said. 'Just promise me you're not going to call off the wedding when you hear me sing.'

'That's up to CILLA, not me,' I said. He kissed me on the cheek and headed back to his mates.

Tilly pulled on my sleeve. 'Hun, you're not going to reach ninety-nine per cent standing here,' she hissed in my ear. 'Get up there and sing with him!'

'Nuh-uh,' I told her. 'That's my worst nightmare, right there. Maybe we can get away with just watching?'

'Sorry, babes, your fiancé is great, but I literally cannot listen to one more second of that.' She pointed to the guys on stage yelling 'tell me why'. 'I'm going to the loo. Get me an espresso martini, will you?' She tilted her head towards the bar, squeezed my arm, then disappeared into the crowd.

'I'm not sure they do those here...' I called after her, but she didn't hear me over the strains of Marc and his friends. While the cameras focused on them, I headed towards the bar.

Dante was still there, and I tried to smile at him, but he was engrossed in his phone. As I got closer, his eyes looked bloodshot, almost like he'd been... crying?

I caught the name on the call screen: *Megan*. When he noticed me, his nostrils literally flared, and he quickly stuffed the phone in his pocket.

'Girlfriend not picking up?' I asked, sliding onto the stool next to him.

Dante looked at me with derision and tipped a shot into his mouth. 'Did you have to get married in the middle of the fucking Arctic?' he said. 'There's fuck-all phone reception here.'

I looked at the row of empty shot glasses in front of him. 'You're hitting it hard. Aren't you the designated driver tonight?' I said.

'None of your business,' he snapped.

'Um, yeah, sorry,' I said. 'You're right.'

'No, I mean, none of this is your business.' He waved his hand around the bar. 'In case you hadn't noticed, you don't belong here.'

That stung, because deep down, he was right. Whether we were soulmates or not, Marc and I came from two very different worlds. But I wasn't going to let Dante intimidate me.

'This time tomorrow, I am going to be a Van Batten,' I told him. 'So we're both going to have to get used to that.'

He picked up another shot glass, and for a split second he looked like he wanted to throw his drink in my face. Instead, he tipped it down his throat, set the glass back on the bar and motioned to the barman to refill it.

Then he leant forward like he was going to whisper something in my ear.

'What do you want with my family, you cheap fucking slut?' he slurred.

'You're drunk,' I said, pushing him back. His pupils were dilated, big pools of black. He wasn't just drunk: he was high. God knew how he'd managed to score drugs on a tiny island in the middle of Narnia.

'Yeah, well, haven't you heard? That's kind of my USP,' he said, moving his hand up towards my breast. 'Now, why don't you tell me what your little scheme is… I know you're up to something. It's the money, isn't it? Well, I've got money too, if that's what you want. How much would it take, hmm?' He moved his lips onto my neck. 'What would you charge me for this?'

My skin prickled.

'Get off me,' I said, shoving him away. 'I'm literally marrying your cousin tomorrow.'

He stepped back and started laughing, his demeanour changing in an instant. 'Oh, you didn't think…?'

He put down his glass to put a fist to his mouth to stifle another snigger.

'That's embarrassing for you. I was just trying to cheer you up a bit. Jesus Christ, you look like you need it. Hasn't Marc given you a good seeing to yet?'

My eyes flicked to the stage where Marc was shouting tunelessly into the microphone, oblivious. The cameras were still on them, so hadn't seen what had just happened. Dante had made sure of that.

'Oh, I see… you haven't done the deed, have you?' He laughed out loud. 'Waiting for the wedding night like a good Catholic, is he?'

'Dante, that is none of *your* business,' I said.

He leant close again. 'Newsflash, honey, your whole life is *everybody's* business,' he hissed. 'You're on a fucking reality TV show.'

With that, he sloped off towards the stage, arms aloft, mocking Marc's singing.

'It's a "social experiment",' I mumbled to no one.

My heart was thumping in my chest. Determined not to cry, I stood there on my own for a minute, feeling gross, like I had a film of grease coating me. Everything was a blur for a moment. The room was full of cameras and strangers. What was I even doing here? This whole thing was a huge mistake. I should never have signed up to this stupid reality show. And it *was* a reality show, whatever Julian said. Dante had one thing right: I didn't belong here.

I pushed my way through the crowd to the back of the bar, looking for Tilly, looking for anywhere that wasn't here. There was a single wooden door with 'Toalett' carved into it.

'Tilly!' I yelled, banging my fist on the door. 'Come on, we're leaving!'

The toilet door opened, and instead of Tilly bouncing out, a bearded man holding a cigarette stood in front of me.

'Excuse me,' he said, popping the cigarette in his mouth while he zipped up his flies.

'Oh,' I said, stepping back. 'Sorry. I was looking for my friend.'

'No, no,' he said, turning to chuck his stub into the toilet bowl. 'I should be apologising to you. Sitting in there having a cheeky smoke. Would you like one?' He pulled a packet of cigarettes from his jacket pocket, withdrew one and offered it to me. 'Look like you need one,' he said. 'Or something a little stronger, perhaps?'

'Um, no thanks,' I said. 'Did you see a blonde girl around here? Purple legwarmers? Dramatic eyeshadow?'

'She sounds delightful. But alas, no.'

'You're with the Van Battens?' I asked, noticing his English accent.

'No one is really *with* the Van Battens.' He placed the cigarette in his mouth, lit it and took a long drag. 'One simply is amalgamated by them.'

I nodded. Only I didn't feel I was being amalgamated – I felt like an organ transplant, forced into a body where it didn't belong, always on the cusp of being rejected.

'You can call me Uncle Gary,' he said, sticking out his hand. 'Everybody does.'

'You can call me the bride,' I said, giving him a little wave. 'Hazel.'

He had what I'd call a somewhat dramatic white beard

and was smartly dressed in a blue double-breasted suit with shiny golden buttons.

'You're giving sailor vibes, Uncle Gary,' I said. 'In a good way, of course. I mean, I really like sailors.'

'You do?'

'That sounds all kinds of wrong. But, um, anyway, you look great. Oh God, sorry, I don't know what I'm talking about. It's been a day. Shit, it's been a week. Two weeks, in fact. I don't know where my head's at.'

'All getting a bit too much for you?' he asked.

'Is it that obvious?' I laughed.

'How are you feeling about the wedding?' Uncle Gary asked.

'All things in consideration,' I said, 'I am shitting myself.'

Uncle Gary blushed.

'Sorry,' I said.

He leant in close. He smelt of sandalwood and sweat. Which coincidently was the scent of the Glade plug-in we used at work.

'Don't apologise on my account.' He winked. 'We sailors don't mind a bit of blue language. And for what it's worth, everyone gets cold feet before the big day.'

'So you're not furious at us for doing this stupid show, like the rest of the family?' I asked.

'It's reality TV, isn't it? I think that's fun,' he said. 'I might look like this now, but I was something of a punk rocker back in the Seventies. And this whole thing strikes me as rather punk. You know, when I married my husband, we'd only known each other for six months.'

'And?'

'We separated three weeks afterwards.' He laughed again, which immediately turned into a phlegmy cough. 'But you're not like me, I'm sure. I mean, I was awful. Wasn't ready for it.'

'It shouldn't be this hard though, should it?' I said. 'Marc and I need this AI thing to rate us as compatible, but every time we get close, something gets in the way.'

Gary thought for a moment. 'Remember what The Beatles said – the love you take is equal to the love you make,' he said.

I looked at him blankly.

'They were a band in the Sixties.' He took a drag and hacked again, a guttural bark that reverberated down his throat.

'I know who The Beatles are, thank you, Uncle Gary,' I laughed. 'But I thought you were a punk?'

'One can appreciate the classics. They're saying that you get what you give,' he went on. 'If you want one hundred per cent out, you have to put one hundred per cent in.'

'Well, actually we only have to reach ninety-n—'

Before I could finish my sentence, I felt a firm hand on my shoulder. I looked round to see a Lion's Jaw crew member, holding out a microphone.

'There you are!' he snapped. 'Come on, you're up!'

'What?' I asked.

'It's your turn!' he said, waving the mic at me.

I took it in a daze, desperately looking around for Tilly as he ushered me towards the stage. I hadn't even chosen a song, but the cameras were pointing right at me now, so I didn't have much of a choice.

The unmistakable riff from 'Should I Stay or Should I Go' by The Clash burst out of the speakers. How apt. Too apt, in fact. Someone was having a laugh at my expense – the producers, or Dante more likely – but you know what? *Fine.* I could take a joke.

'Alright, very funny,' I said into the mic. 'I can do this one.'

But as soon as I started chanting along with the lyrics, the song changed abruptly. It took me a second to recognise it as 'Leave Right Now' by Will Young. Okay, this wasn't amusing anymore. With the light shining on the stage, I couldn't see much of the room, but shielding my eyes, I peered into the darkness. The karaoke machine was somewhere back there, but I couldn't see who was fiddling with it.

'I don't know the words to this one!' I shouted into the darkness. Whoever it was, I wasn't going to give them – or the cameras – the satisfaction of walking off stage. 'But I'll do my best!'

Then the song changed again, and my heart jolted. This time I knew it immediately. The backing vocals rang out before I could open my mouth.

Run run run run, run run run away, oh, oh, oh... Psycho Killer...

My hands started to shake. This definitely wasn't funny now. *This was sick.*

'Psycho Killer!' blared out of the speaker again.

I spun around, furiously scanning the faces in front of me, but everything was a blur. A few of them were laughing; some weren't even paying attention, chatting between themselves. I couldn't see Dante at the bar. No sign of Tilly. And where the hell was Marc?

But I did see a flash of red by the karaoke machine.

'Who's there?' I yelled into the mic. The camera crew swung round to see what I was pointing at, and their lights illuminated the crowd. Someone in a red jacket pushed open the door and slipped outside.

A red jacket, just like the guy from the basketball court. *He was here; he'd followed us to the island.*

'Hey! Stop!' I shouted, dropping the mic onto the stage. It rang out with a screech of feedback, soliciting a few annoyed cries from the snowboarders in the corner. I didn't care. I dashed to the door, shoulder-barged it open and ran outside. But all I could see was snow, and a set of fresh footprints leading into the darkness.

Whoever it was, they were gone.

I stood there, my heart pounding, staring into the night. Snow pelted against my face, but I barely felt the cold. Was I going mad? Seeing things? I hadn't slept for days, maybe I really was losing it. My thoughts were broken by a voice behind me.

'What's going on?'

I turned around to see Marc.

'Where the hell were you?' I snapped. 'There was someone here... someone fucking with the karaoke machine... they, they were just here...'

'I was in the bathroom,' he said. 'What happened?'

The bathroom? My body pulsed with anger. He hadn't even stuck around to watch me?

'The songs,' I stuttered. 'They were...'

'They were what?'

I stopped. Suddenly I felt stupid. It must have been Dante messing around with the karaoke machine. Whoever I saw leaving the bar could have been him, or any one of the hundreds of skiers with red jackets.

'Are you okay, Hazel?' Marc asked.

'I'm not sure,' I said.

He put a hand on my shoulder.

'Hey, there's a lot of pressure on us. It's normal to freak out a bit. This whole TV-wedding idea takes a bit of getting used to.'

'It doesn't help that your best man is playing pranks,' I said. 'He messed with the karaoke machine and then legged it out here.'

'It's a stag party,' Marc said. 'Pranks are part of the deal.'

'Joint party. Remember? Except all the pranks seem to be on me, don't they? Just like everything else, in fact. Your stepmother can't stand me, your dad thinks I'm hired help. Your whole family have made it quite clear I'm not welcome.'

He stared at me for a second, like he was deciding how much offence to take from that statement. Then his face stiffened. 'At least my family are taking part.'

Despite the cold, a surge of heat rose through my chest.

'That's not fair,' I said.

'Isn't it? Hazel, *you're* not even taking part. We should have reached ninety-nine per cent days ago. But every step of this process, you've been pulling away.'

'Process?' I scoffed. 'You sound like Julian. This isn't a process, this is my real life.'

'*Our* real life,' he said. 'And it feels like you don't want to be part of it. In the balloon, on the pier, you couldn't even bring yourself to eat the food Stephanie prepared…'

Shit, he'd seen me hide the lamb in my handbag.

'Prepared?' I say. 'That's generous, you had a kitchen full of staff.'

'... You don't even like our wedding song,' he carried on. 'And you're hiding out by the toilets at your own party.'

I shivered. 'Yeah, because your best man basically called me a prostitute.'

'What?' Marc looked shocked.

'He was smashed, talking rubbish,' I said. 'That guy is a train wreck. You should've heard what he said to me—'

'Wait, he's been drinking?'

'And the rest,' I said. 'He looked high as a kite.'

'And he ran out here?'

'I don't know,' I said. 'I thought it must have been him, but I didn't see their face.'

'Fuck.' Marc ran a hand through his hair.

'It's not a big deal, just get the ski lift back,' I said.

'It's not just because he's the designated driver,' Marc said. 'He cannot be drinking – especially not with all these cameras around. Dante just got out of a court-ordered rehab.'

'What?' I cried.

'The car accident I told you about,' Marc said. 'Dante was high on God knows what when he was behind the wheel. And he wasn't the only one in the car. His girlfriend ended up in a coma, and Dante escaped jail by the skin of his teeth.'

I didn't know what to say. I stood there, shivering in the cold.

'I need to find him,' Marc said, grabbing his skis out of the rack.

'You're just going to leave?'

'I have to go after him. Come with me.' He motioned to the ski rack, and I felt a panic rise in my chest.

'I... I can't,' I said.

'Why?' he asked.

'I can't ski, alright?' I snapped. 'I can't bloody ski.'

Marc's face twitched.

'But that doesn't make sense...' He shook his head. 'Forget it. I have to go.'

With that, he pulled on his mask, clipped on his skis, and pushed off. All I could do was stand there and watch him disappear into the darkness, along with any chance of reaching 99 per cent.

We'd come so far, only to fuck it up at the final hurdle.

With a heavy heart, I lifted my wrist.

'CILLA,' I said.

'Hey, Hazel!' CILLA replied as the display lit up. 'Just a few more hours until your wedding day. Are you excited?'

'Not really,' I replied. 'What's our compatibility score?'

'Great question!' she trilled. 'Partners who can manage conflicts in a healthy, constructive way are more likely to have a successful relationship. So right now, your chances have dropped to sixty-one per cent!'

I slumped against the wall of the bar, defeated. From inside, I could hear Marc's friends singing again. I almost laughed when I recognised the song. It was The Beatles, and I remembered weird old Uncle Gary's advice.

If I wanted to rescue any hope of getting married tomorrow, I knew exactly what I had to do.

EIGHTEEN

SKARDBALT AIRPORT

I stand in the control tower, mouth open in shock, frozen to the spot.

In front of me is a woman, swathed in a bulky red jacket, tied to a swivel chair. There's a gag pulled tightly around her mouth and her legs are bare. Her face is partially covered by her long, blonde hair.

'Tilly?' I shout, and she moans back.

No... it can't be, that's impossible. She's not here, she's at the hotel, she's safe... Isn't she?

Heart thumping, I rush over and brush her hair away from her face. I breathe sigh of relief.

It's not Tilly.

I've never seen this woman before in my life. She moans again, eyes bulging with desperation, the anguished wail snapping me out of my trance. I quickly pull the gag down from her mouth, and she gulps down air. I see she's young, in her twenties probably, with full make-up, although her red lipstick has been smudged around her mouth by the gag.

We stare at each other for a moment, equally mystified. Her, by the strange woman in a blood-stained wedding dress who's seemingly come to her rescue. Me, wondering who the hell she is, and why she's wearing the exact same coat as the man who threatened to slit my throat.

'My hands,' she stutters eventually.

She spins the swivel chair round with her legs, and I see her wrists are bound to the chair with thick grey tape.

'Are you okay?' I ask, yanking the tape with my one good hand. 'Who are you?

Finally, I loosen the tape enough for her to slip her slender wrists out, and spin her back round to face me.

'Emily,' she says, with a trace of a Norwegian accent. 'I'm a NordAir flight attendant.'

'What happened, Emily?' I ask.

'A man grabbed me, took my uniform, dragged me out here in the snow and tied me up.'

Emil. I think back to the scuffed name tag on his waistcoat. He must have just scratched off the letter Y. He isn't a flight attendant at all.

'And this is his jacket?' I ask.

She nods, her blonde hair plastered to her face with sweat, despite the freezing cold.

It's him. Emil was the man in the red jacket. The one who left the note, who threw the brick, who's been threatening us from the beginning.

But it's not just threats anymore. He's the one who's been hunting us down and killing us one by one.

Another horrible thought hits me – that means, whoever Emil really is, he never called the authorities. No one knows we're here, and no help is coming.

'I'm Hazel,' I tell Emily. 'I'm a passenger on Flight 247. I'm guessing that was your flight, right? Did you get a look at him, this man? Tall, with short, brown hair?'

'Yes,' she says, rubbing her wrists. 'That's him.'

'Did he say anything else? Did he tell you who he was?' I ask.

She shakes her head. 'He just said he didn't want to hurt me. He took my keycard, said he'd come back for me when he was done.'

Of course, he has a pass, that explains how he's been able to get around the airport so quickly.

I pat down the puffa jacket, ignoring the throb of agony in my hand, but there's nothing in it.

'Over there,' Emily says, pointing to a pile of clothes on the floor under the desk.

I stick my hand in the pockets of the jeans; there's a bunch of keys and – jackpot – a passport. I hold it up to show Emily.

'The idiot left his passport here,' I say, flicking it open to the ID page.

There's a photo of a young man. His hair is combed back, and he's clean-shaven, but there's no doubt it's Emil, despite what the name on the passport says.

'Robert Deboise, American citizen,' I read aloud. 'Do you know who that is?'

'No.' She shakes her head again.

'Whoever he is, he's been pretending to be a steward. He's...' I pause, wondering how much to tell her. 'He's hurt some of my friends. They're still in the airport. Is there a phone here, anything we can use to contact the police?'

'He destroyed all the equipment,' Emily says, her voice shaky.

I look around. She's right: the desk is a mess of wires, pulled out and cut to shreds. I stare out of the panoramic windows that look across the whole airport. It's like a blanket of white out there.

'The roads are closed. All flights are grounded,' I tell her. 'What do we do?'

She looks at me blankly. 'I'm just a steward,' she says. 'I don't know.'

'What happens if there's an emergency?' I ask her. 'You know, like a terrorist attack or something? There must be a protocol?'

She looks flustered for a moment, then her training kicks in.

'If something like that happens on the flight, the pilot uses the transponder.'

'Okay, great,' I say. 'So, um, what's a transponder?'

'A transmitter,' Emily explains hurriedly, like a school kid who's suddenly remembered the correct answer. 'There's one on every plane. The... the pilot uses it to contact the air traffic control if there's a problem on board. Four dials, in the cockpit. Enter the numbers seven seven zero zero. The squawk code. It will alert the nearest functioning air traffic control that you need immediate assistance.'

'Seven seven zero zero, got it. So if I get to the plane and enter the code, they'll send help?'

She looks unsure. 'If they can in this weather,' she says, looking out the window. 'But they'll be able to tell that the plane hasn't taken off, and they'll send an emergency team to the airport as soon as it clears.'

Right. That's the plan. Get to the plane, find the transponder, enter the code, finally go home.

'Stay here, put these on and keep warm,' I say, handing her the rest of Robert's clothes. 'Find something to barricade the door, and don't let anyone in unless it's me, okay?'

'Wait,' she says, looking at me like I'm crazy. 'Where are you going? There's a blizzard out there.'

She's right, but I don't have a choice. If I don't get help, Emil will kill us all.

'It's not too much further to the plane,' I say. 'I'll enter the code, then I'll come back for you.'

I don't want to leave her alone, but right now, this is the safest place in the whole airport.

With that, I close the door to the control room, run down the stairs and step back out into the snow.

NINETEEN

SKARDBALT AIRPORT

Every step through the thick snow feels like a marathon. It must be almost six a.m. now, and strains of sunlight are struggling over the horizon. Even with my hoodie pulled tightly around me, I can feel the cold seeping into my bones. But I have to reach the plane. I have to get help. Get home. I trudge forward, shielding my face from the snow.

But with each step, I think of Marc. I didn't trust him, and worse, I ran away, leaving him there with the real killer. He's been trying to help me, and I pushed him away.

I stop.

What am I doing?

Marc and Stephanie are still in the airport with Emil, or Robert, or whoever he really is. They don't know he is a psychopath. Whatever they've done to me, they don't deserve to die. If I carry on to the plane, I could save myself, but I'll be leaving Marc and Stephanie with a killer.

I have to go to the airport. I have to warn them.

I turn to look behind me. The control tower has disappeared. Hell, the whole world has disappeared. I spin back round. Suddenly, I don't know where I came from. I can't tell where the sky meets the ground. I don't know which way I'm going. And if it weren't for the biting cold, I might even doubt my own existence. Everything is white, like I'm swathed in a blanket of all-encompassing nothingness. The airport could be two feet away or two hundred yards.

When Marc described a whiteout, he said you can't see your hand in front of your face. Gingerly, I hold up my hand and wiggle my fingers. I can barely make them out.

I'm lost.

I fall to my knees, helpless.

I open my mouth to shout, but realise it's pointless. The world is silent; even the hissing of the wind seems hushed. Marc was right: the snow seems to absorb everything, even sound. The only thing I can hear is my own heart beating.

It's so cold, I can't feel my limbs anymore. In fact, I'm not sure I can feel *anything*. My head spins; any second now, I'm going to pass out.

I crane my neck to the sky. As I stare into the sheer blankness above me, I wonder if this is what heaven looks like. If I ever believed there was a god, right about now would be a good time to start praying.

'CILLA,' I mumble. If I can't ask God for help, I have the next best thing – my fairy godmother. 'How do I survive a whiteout?'

Then I look at the black display on my wrist and remember – she's dead. I unclip it and throw it with all my remaining energy into the snow. It lands silently and disappears immediately, fresh snow covering any trace of it ever being there.

This is it. This is the end. Every endless fight, every hard-won battle, all to freeze to death in the middle of nowhere. I could just let the snow bury me here on the tarmac. I close my eyes and a strange calmness washes over me. I'm not sure I can even feel the cold anymore. Marc, his crazy family, the stupid TV show, none of that matters now.

The last time I looked at the sky like this, it was a wash of purples and greens. The night before the wedding, when Marc and I watched the northern lights swirling through the darkness. Thinking about it almost makes me smile. Funny how a distant light in the sky gave me hope that everything would work out.

I don't want to die here alone.

I pat my jacket, my hands moving up and down slowly, like they're being pulled by invisible strings. But my heart soars when I feel the lump in my pocket.

I still have it.

The flare gun.

I drag it out, my hands trembling, and just about manage to get my finger through the trigger. Pulling back the hammer with my thumb, I aim it towards the sky.

But something stops me. There's no way of telling if Marc or Stéphanie are still alive. If I fire the flare, I'll be telling Emil exactly where to find me. He'll either leave me to die or come out here to finish me off.

It's a risk. But I don't have a choice.

I pull the trigger with the last of my strength, and a bright flash of red bursts from the barrel of the gun. It cuts through the white sky like a streak of blood on pale flesh. I turn my head into the snow as it explodes at its zenith.

Then I watch as the light burns out, leaving a sizzling path in its wake. When it finally fizzles out, the sky is blank again. That was my last chance. If no one saw it, I'll die here in the white.

But then, everything goes black.

- EPISODE SIX (PART TWO) -
THE BACH PARTY

THE NIGHT BEFORE THE WEDDING
BORGENHUS FORTRESS HOTEL, SKARDBALT

I'd been sitting in the big, probably very old, leather chair in the hotel lobby, waiting for Marc for at least an hour. Tilly and I had taken the chairlift back to the castle after he skied off, and I was hoping I'd beaten him back here.

I'd been replaying our row over and over in my head. I couldn't let it end like this. I'd come so far. I was so close. It didn't matter that I was having doubts; CILLA was right. I needed to give 100 per cent to this, otherwise there was no hope of it working.

Just then, Marc marched through the entrance, covered in snow. When he saw me, he shook his head, walked straight up to the lift and stepped inside.

As the lift doors were closing, I ran towards them, and at the last moment, stuck my hand in between them. The doors paused, then began to slowly slide back open. Marc sighed as I slipped inside next to him.

'What are you doing, Hazel?' He ran a hand across his face. 'Please, no more arguments tonight. I need to go to bed,' Marc said, hitting the top-floor button. 'It's been a long day.'

'I'm just trying to get away from those damn cameras,' I said. 'This is the only place they can't follow us, and we need to talk.'

I stuck out my finger and pressed 'hold'. The lift shuddered to a stop.

'Did you find Dante?' I asked. 'Is he okay?'

'He's fine. One of the production crew brought him back. He's all tucked up in bed, sleeping it off.'

'Oh, well, I'm glad he's okay,' I said. 'I shouldn't have yelled at you.'

'It's alright,' Marc said. 'I know what Dante's like when he's off his face. I'm sorry he spoke to you like that.'

We began to move upwards, but I quickly punched the hold button again. I had to convince him, convince CILLA, that this was right, that we could work. I couldn't just let everything go now. We were so close.

'Hazel,' he said, 'it's late. And in case you've forgotten, we kind of have a big thing to do tomorrow. That is, if we are actually going to go through with it. Apparently, we are a very long way off being a perfect match.'

'We're not moving until you've heard what I have to say,' I told him.

He shook his head. 'I've heard what you have to say. You were extremely clear about that up on the mountain. And, you know what, that's fine. I can't force you to feel something you're not feeling.'

He reached for the button again, but I grabbed his hand.

'Give me a chance,' I said.

He tensed. 'Alright, I'm listening.'

I took a breath.

'I thought about what you said up there,' I said. 'You're right, I've been freaking out, but I know what I want now.'

'And what do you want, Hazel?' he asked.

I realised I was still holding on to his hand. I pulled him closer to me, until our faces were almost touching.

'This is what I want,' I said, and in that moment, I think I really believed it.

I leant in and kissed him. After a second, I stepped back and looked at him hopefully, unsure what his reaction would be.

'Okay, well, if *that's* what you want,' he said, after a moment. 'We can stay here all evening.'

He slipped a hand around my waist, pulled me into him and kissed me again. I closed my eyes, and tried to forget everything else. The threats, the stepmother, the drunk cousin. Even the feckless producers. Marc was right: they were just part of the deal. All that mattered was how Marc and I felt, right here, right now.

Before I applied for this show, I don't think I truly believed it could work, that an AI could find me my soulmate. But the pull I felt dragging me towards Marc seemed unstoppable, and the more I resisted, the more strongly I seemed to feel it.

Suddenly, the lift lurched, yanking me back to reality. I opened my eyes. We were moving. The bastard had pressed the top-floor button while I was distracted.

'Hey!' I said, shoving him.

'What?' He smiled. 'Did the earth move for you?'

The lift reached its destination with a bump and opened onto a small corridor with just one door. Marc's room was evidently the only one on this floor. The penthouse suite, of course.

'Come on in,' he said, swiping his keycard. 'There are no cameras in here either, promise.'

I followed him inside to be greeted by the sight of a huge suite. A massive four-poster bed, chaise longue, floor-to-ceiling windows and a balcony looking out across the mountains.

'Totally figures that you got the penthouse suite,' I said, poking my head into the bathroom. 'Fuck me, your en suite is bigger than my entire flat.'

'Helps when your family owns the castle.'

'Right, makes sense,' I said, shaking my head. I wondered how much money the Van Battens were putting into the production, and how much sway that gave them over Julian.

Marc went over to the minibar, picked up two crystal tumblers and poured us both a generous helping of whisky. He handed me one, and I sniffed at it, unsure.

'What, a seventeen-year-old single-cask Scotch not good enough for you?' He laughed.

'Is there anything else in there? Like some Pringles and a can of wine or something?'

'Nah, sorry. I mean, maybe there's a Lidl down the road? You could pop out and get some pickled herring or something?'

I picked up a cushion from the bed and threw it at him.

'Hey, careful!' he said. 'That's probably from the eighteenth century.'

'Cool, stick it in your luggage and I'll sell it on eBay when we get back.'

'Great, that'll help pay the minibar bill,' he said, topping up my drink.

I took a sip. To be fair, it tasted pretty good. Perhaps this was a lifestyle I could get used to after all. Marc sat down on the bed.

'So,' he said. 'Does this mean you're planning on saying yes tomorrow?'

'Doesn't really matter what I say unless CILLA signs off on it,' I said, sitting down next to him. 'We need to get to ninety-nine per cent, otherwise it's academic.'

'So how do we do that?' he asked.

'There is one thing we haven't tried yet.' I smiled, slipping my hands around his waist.

'Woah.' He grinned. 'It's the night before the wedding, remember? Isn't there some sort of rule about this?'

'Oh, I think we broke all the normal wedding rules when we signed up for a reality TV show,' I said.

I thought for a moment.

'Okay, what about this?' I held up my wristband and shouted 'I want to marry Marc Van Batten' into it.

It didn't react.

'Sod CILLA,' Marc said. 'Let's try this the old-fashioned way.'

He took a pen and a piece of paper from the hotel notepad on the desk and drew a line down the middle. On one side he wrote '*YES*' and the other side '*NO*'.

'Pros and cons,' he explained. 'Start with the good stuff.'

He wrote '*good hair*' on the paper.

I screwed up my face. 'Me or you?'

'Me, of course,' he replied.

I thought about it for a second. 'Okay, fair,' I said, running my hand through his hair. 'It is good. And you have nice hands.'

He wrote down '*nice hands*' and then scribbled '*actually quite sweet when she wants to be*' underneath. I smiled, but then took the pencil from his hand and started writing in the No column. He took the paper from me when I'd finished.

'It's not real,' he read aloud. He looked at me, his face serious for a moment. 'What's not real, Hazel?'

I bit my bottom lip. 'All this,' I said. 'The TV show. CILLA. I want to trust her, I really do. But what if she got it wrong, and we're not soulmates after all? I mean, it's not exactly been smooth sailing so far, has it? I didn't sign up for *Love Synced* for a fancy wedding or to get on TV. I did it because I wanted to find my person...'

'You said it!' He laughed.

I gave him a playful shove. 'I'm serious. What if we say yes tomorrow and it turns out we're not such a perfect match after all?'

'Hazel, listen to me. I don't need a computer to tell me how I feel about you. I'm grateful CILLA brought us together, but I don't need a compatibility rating to convince me this is right. If we get a fancy wedding tomorrow, great. If not, I don't want that to be the end. I want to keep seeing you. But only if you want that too. And if you don't, tell me now, because if I have to watch you walk away tomorrow, it will break my heart, Hazel.'

He drew me closer, letting the paper fall to the floor, and kissed me. We'd kissed before, of course, but not like this. This kiss had meaning, and that meaning was either a) I want to rip your clothes off right now or b) I'm falling in love with you. Somehow, I found myself really hoping it was c) both.

We fell onto the bed, his hand running up my thigh as his

mouth made its way down my neck. I undid his buckle and pulled his belt out with one quick motion.

The rest happened quickly, urgently. Everything else fell away – the cameras, the experiment, the doubts. Just us. Afterwards, we lay there, not speaking, but glowing with a thin, glistening layer of sweat.

'Got anything to add to the pros list?' he asked, leaning up on one elbow.

'Not really.' I smiled.

'Oh, come on!' He grabbed the piece of paper from the floor. 'I can suggest a few.'

'Oh no you don't.' I laughed, snatching the list off him. 'You don't get a gold star for the bare minimum.'

He tried to grab the list, but I quickly pulled my hand away before he could get it. I straddled him, holding the list above my head out of his reach.

'One second,' I said, grabbing the pencil from the desk. I drew a firm line through the cons column.

'There, fixed it.' I screwed up the paper in my hand and chucked it over my shoulder with a grin.

'No cons?' he asked.

'Well, there is just one thing,' I said, looking down at him. 'What really happened with Portia?'

'Oh that,' he said. 'Well, Stephanie dealt with her.'

I rolled off of him, shocked.

'What does that mean? She bundled her into a van and tied her up in a basement somewhere?'

'No.' He laughed. 'She really is in Nepal. Stephanie persuaded her to delete the video, paid her enough that she didn't need to be an influencer anymore. That's what she always wanted to do, really, travel the world, so I hope she's happy.'

A wave of relief hit me.

'That's Stephanie's MO. With enough money, she can make any problem go away. She did the same for Dante after his drug driving accident.'

'What do you mean?' I asked.

'Boom was sponsoring some teen soap opera in the States, so Dante spent last summer partying in LA. Took one of the actors for a spin in his Porsche, wrapped it round a lamppost. Ran from the scene, left her there. She still hasn't woken up. Our lawyers pulled off a miracle to keep Dante out of jail. He got off with a slap on the wrist, a stint in rehab and a pinky promise to be a good boy from now on. Stephanie paid off the girl's family to stay away from the media.'

That explained why, when I'd looked up the Van Battens online, there was nothing about Dante being in a crash. Stephanie had made sure of that.

'That tactic isn't going to work with your dad's accusers though,' I said. 'If those stories are already out there, they're not going away.'

'Stephanie reckons she has a plan. There's some big meeting with our lawyers after the wedding. But you're right, there's no way back for him after this.'

'Maybe it's time for a new regime,' I said, kissing him gently.

'Me?' he said. 'No, I promise you, after tomorrow, I'm out. I won't stay on at the company after what Dad did. Once the wedding is done, I quit.'

My heart soared. I pulled him closer to me.

'I know I've been flaky but you don't have to worry. I'm

telling you now, no matter what CILLA says, I am all in. I'm going to say I do.'

We held each other close, and eventually Marc fell asleep in my arms. But I couldn't sleep.

Restless, I fished around the pool of clothes on the floor and pulled on Marc's shirt and my socks. I wandered over to the balcony, opened the glass door and stepped outside. The sharpness of the cold air hit me like a thousand needles, but I kinda liked it.

Looking out into the night sky, I rubbed my eyes. There was something strange out there in the blackness. A burst of green light, almost glowing above me. At first I thought I'd just rubbed my eyes too hard. It looked unreal, like someone had painted the sky.

I couldn't quite believe what I was seeing.

The northern lights.

I watched in awe for a second, feeling insignificant, like a tiny ant in the vast cosmos of the universe. Just me, and the Milky Way. I didn't want to take my eyes off the sky. But I forced myself, for just a moment, to turn away and look back at Marc, who was still fast asleep.

'Marc,' I called over my shoulder. 'Wake up, come look at this.'

He didn't stir. I turned back towards the sky and leant against the balcony railing, my toes curling over the edge. I felt like I was in another universe entirely. But part of me didn't want to be in that universe alone. I peeled off a sock, rolled it up and chucked it at Marc's head. It bounced off harmlessly, but his eyelids fluttered open.

'What is it?' he mumbled. 'We have a big day tomorrow, you know? I need my beauty sleep.'

'Get over here, will you?'

He groggily swung his legs out from under the duvet and came over, wearing just his boxer shorts. He threaded his arm around my waist and rubbed his eyes.

'Jesus, it's freezing out here,' he said. 'So what did I miss?'

'You didn't miss anything,' I said, pointing to the sky. 'Look.'

'Wow.' He stood there, dumbfounded for a second. 'That's gotta be a good omen, right?' he said, pulling me closer to him.

'I'm not superstitious, but yeah.' I smiled. 'I think it is.'

The swirling greens and purples filled the night sky, and it was incredible. For a moment, I forgot where I was; the only thing I was aware of was the warmth of Marc's body beside me.

Deep inside, I felt something shift. I didn't feel quite so alone anymore. I was here with him, and we were both part of something bigger. Maybe something better. As the lights began to slowly fade, I leant into Marc, and suddenly I didn't feel cold at all.

'I don't want this to end,' I whispered. Just then, our wrists beeped in unison, breaking the spell.

'Hey, big news guys! Huge!' CILLA chirped. 'You've reached a ninety-nine per cent compatibility rating!'

'We did it,' I said, not quite believing it. 'We actually did it.'

I looked into his eyes and I wondered if CILLA could really know what was between Marc and me. Could that jumble of code, algorithms and data actually understand how two people felt about each other? If you'd have asked me at that moment, I would have said yes, because despite all my defences, all my barriers, right then, I didn't want to be anywhere else in the world.

'Let's see if we can get this thing to one hundred.' He smiled, pulling me back towards the bed.

Twenty minutes later, Marc was fast asleep again, mouth slightly open, his breathing heavy. But I still couldn't relax. I found myself staring at the ceiling.

One more day.

In one more day, this would all be over. And then what? I looked at Marc, peacefully asleep next to me. How would I feel when the cameras were gone, I wondered, when it was just us?

Every time I closed my eyes, I saw the person in the red jacket running a finger across their throat. It had to be them who'd been leaving the threatening notes. And now they'd followed us here, to the island. But who were they? And what did they know?

My thoughts were interrupted by a soft scratching noise by the door. I pulled on a robe and tiptoed towards it. I peered through the peephole, but the corridor was empty. I was about to go back to bed when I looked down. Someone had pushed a folded piece of paper under the door, and it was lying there at my feet.

A shiver ran through me, and I pulled the cord of my robe tighter. I glanced back at Marc, who was still fast asleep, then picked up the note and opened it. Scrawled in biro across hotel paper, just like our list of pros and cons, were seven words:

Get out now. The show is rigged.

I stared at the note for a few seconds, glanced back to make sure Marc was still asleep, then carefully tore the paper into strips. I placed the remains in my robe pocket.

Yes, of course the show was rigged.

I already knew that.

Because I was the one rigging it.

TWENTY

SKARDBALT AIRPORT

My eyelids flicker open, and everything is suddenly bright again. *Too bright*. My whole body feels numb, except for a stinging sensation in my left cheek, like someone's just slapped me, hard. I ignore it, close my eyes and retreat back to the comfort of darkness.

Suddenly, a sharp smack to my right cheek jolts me awake again.

Shit, someone definitely *did* just slap me.

All I can see is the strains of sunlight breaking through the snow, and it takes me a moment to realise I'm staring up at the sky. The blizzard must be over. Then the familiar face of Marc Van Batten looms into my eyeline. I blink, unsure if this is a mirage or the real thing.

'Hazel!' he cries, and lifts his hand to slap my cheek again. I hold my arm in front of my face to stop him.

'You're awake! Thank God,' Marc says. 'I saw the flare,

found you here passed out. Another few minutes, and I don't think you'd have made it.'

'Marc...' My voice comes out scratchy and mumbled. 'I was wrong... I'm sorry, it was Emil, he must have...' I tail off.

'Hazel, slow down, you're slurring,' Marc says. 'Can you walk?'

I honestly don't know the answer, but I nod anyway. He puts his arm under mine and lifts me up. I cling onto him as we traverse slowly through the snow, step by step.

'The storm has died down,' he says. 'But we're still not safe out here. Not in these clothes. We'll freeze to death.'

'Wrong way,' I murmur. 'Need to go back...'

'It's too far. We won't make it. The plane is closer, look.'

He points ahead of us, and I raise my head. Through the snow, I can see glimpses of the blue NordAir logo on the tail fin, then as we step closer, the torso of the plane comes into view. It can't have been more than twenty feet away from me when I collapsed.

'But Stephanie...' I say.

'She's safe. She's in the cafeteria,' Marc explains.

'Not Emil... Doesn't exist... the man in the red coat,' I say, pulling on Marc's sleeve. I'm rambling now, my vision blurry. 'He wasn't a steward at all...'

'Don't try to talk, just hold on to me,' Marc says. 'We're almost there.'

Together, we manage the last few feet to the plane. It's small, not much bigger than a private jet. Marc rests me against one of the tyres while he reaches up and yanks open the door. With a soft hiss of hydraulics, the bottom half of the door begins to unfold downward, like a drawbridge in a fairy tale. The door has stairs on the inside, and he helps me up the steps and inside. The air smells of cleaning solvents and stale coffee, I think, before my legs immediately give way, and I collapse in the aisle.

'You have to get up, Hazel,' Marc says, the low ceiling forcing him to duck his head slightly. 'You're shivering.'

'No I'm not,' I tell him. 'I'm cosy.'

But when I look down at my hands, I'm shocked to see he's right. I can't feel the cold anymore, but my whole body is shaking. I try to sit up, steadying myself on one of the seats, and my head swims.

'Hypothermia,' Marc says, placing a hand on my forehead. 'You're going to go into shock. We need to get you warm, fast.'

'You're a doctor now?'

'I told you, I spent a season as a ski instructor in Aspen,' he says. 'They teach you this stuff.'

I try to meet his eyes, but I can't focus.

'No,' I slur. 'Go find Stephanie. It's Emil… Emil is the killer.'

Marc runs a hand through his hair and blows his cheeks out. His eyes flash to the plane door, then back to me.

'I can't leave you like this,' he says. 'After you ran into the snow, Emil followed you, which means he's out here, somewhere.'

'Safe here, nice and warm, just let me sleep. Please.'

Marc takes one look at me and shakes his head. 'Nope. Not happening. Let me see if I can start the plane and get you warmed up.'

Through blurry eyes, I watch him disappear into the cockpit, then come back out and start rummaging through the metal compartments.

The plane has a single aisle with rows of seats either side, probably less than thirty, upholstered in a vomit-inducing cheap purple fabric, windows spaced at regular intervals. At one end is the cockpit, at the other end the single toilet. When I flew here a few days ago, I was the last one on, cramming my bag into the already stuffed overhead bins, then squeezing past a group of snowboarders into my tiny seat.

Marc comes back with a life jacket and a handful of packets of peanuts.

'All I could find,' he says, slipping my arms through the life jacket. 'But it's better than nothing. Hopefully this should help warm you up.'

He yanks up the zip, then pulls out the cord so the jacket inflates. I look down at myself. If I am going to die today, it looks like I am going to do it in a sodden wedding dress and a bright orange life jacket.

Marc rips open a packet of nuts, and I try to grab a handful. But as I fumble with the packet, I manage to spill half of them, sending a rogue peanut rolling down the aisle. When I make a grab for it, it feels like someone has stamped on my hand. I cry out in pain.

Marc reaches out for my wrist. 'Let me see that.'

I flinch, instinctively trying to tighten my hand into a fist, but my fingers don't obey. All that happens is a sharp stabbing sensation zings through my arm, and I yelp again.

'Hazel,' Marc says, gently taking my wrist. 'You're hurt.'

'It's nothing,' I say, relenting.

Pain shoots through me as I slowly uncurl my fingers, and I see Marc wince at the red, raw skin on my palm.

'Okay, we need warm water.' Marc scans the plane, his gaze landing on the toilet door, right at the other end of the aisle.

I try to stand up, and immediately sit back down again.

My body has stopped shaking, but my head is swimming, like I'm drunk.

'Come on,' he says, helping me up and leading me to the bathroom, and he squeezes in after me. I sit on the toilet while Marc fiddles with the taps.

'Do people actually have sex in these things?' I ask, looking around.

'Well, once I—' he starts.

'Don't answer that,' I say quickly before he can finish.

The bathroom, if you can call it that, is tiny. There's barely enough room for the toilet, let alone a bath. I catch sight of myself in the mirror above the sink, and recoil. My hair, still wet from the snow, is a wild, tangled mess. My cheeks are flushed red but the rest of my skin is deathly pale. As I squint, my vision goes blurry, and my head starts to loll back. I close my eyes and rest my head against the cold, moulded plastic. I just want to go to sleep.

'Hazel, keep your eyes on me,' Marc says. 'You need to stay awake. Give me your hand.'

I comply and he kneels in front of me, waiting for the water to warm up. When it's ready, he holds my hand under the running water, and I grit my teeth in pain as the water hits the raw skin.

'Are you sure this is helping?' I wince.

'Ideally for an ice burn, we should keep your hand submerged,' he says. 'But there's no plug in this sink. Keep pressing the button. You'll just have to hold it under the running water as long as you can.'

My head is really swimming now, and despite all appearances, I'm convinced this toilet is the perfect place to curl up and go to sleep. I try and pull my hand out of the sink again, but Marc holds it in place.

'Hey, look at me, keep talking,' he says. 'Tell me something. Tell me anything. Tell me how much you hate me.'

'The scanner,' I mumble.

'What?'

'Back at the security gate,' I say. 'You set the alarm off.'

With his other hand, Marc reaches into his back pocket and pulls out a black electronic wristband, identical to mine. He holds it up between his finger and thumb, dangling it in front of me like a bad hypnotist.

'Your CILLA!' I say, my eyes widening. 'But you told me you lost it?'

'Well, I didn't,' he says. 'Truth is, after you left me at the altar, I wanted to take a hammer to this useless thing. I was furious with it, with you, with everything. But I just couldn't bring myself to do it. CILLA knows everything about us.' He taps the screen of his wristband. 'Our whole relationship is in here somewhere.'

'All two weeks of it,' I say.

He smiles. 'I know it wasn't exactly long-term, but it was special. To me, anyway. And this was the only thing I had to remember it by. I wanted to blame CILLA, the algorithm, the whole experiment. But the tech didn't fail us. I did. And, well, part of me hoped CILLA could help us fix things once we were back in London, away from the cameras. Pretty dumb, right?'

A wave of guilt clouds my stupid, blurry brain, but I push it down.

'Mine's back there, in the snow,' I tell him.

Marc slips his wristband onto my wrist. 'Here,' he says. 'You have this one. Something to remember me by.'

I look down at him, kneeling in front of me while I sit on an aeroplane toilet in a sodden wedding dress and a life jacket, and wonder if I'm still lying in the whiteout, hallucinating.

No. I shake it off. I'm here. My head is clearing, and I don't need CILLA to tell me that the chances of me dying on a stationary plane toilet are quite high. If the hypothermia doesn't get me, Emil, or Robert, or whatever his name is, is still out there somewhere. We need to move. Get help. I dig into my hoodie pocket and pull out the passport I found at the control tower.

'Found the real steward in the control tower. Emil swapped places with her.' I hand Marc the passport. 'Look at this.'

Marc flips to the photo page, and I see his eyes widen.

'Do you know who he is?' I ask.

'I know that name. I'm sure I've heard it before somewhere, but I can't place it.'

I have an idea.

'CILLA,' I say. 'Who is Robert Deboise?'

The display flashes with a thinking-face emoji.

'Robert Deboise was the bass player in skiffle band The Cranks from 1963 to 1971. He died in 1993 of a heart attack in a fast-food restaurant after a drugs overdose,' CILLA says.

'That's not him,' Marc says. 'CILLA, try, Robbie Deboise.'

'Robbie Deboise is a twenty-six-year-old American actor who has appeared in The CW's *The Last Wave of Summer* TV series in 2025 and a commercial for Starbucks the same year.'

Marc's lips form an O of realisation.

'*The Last Wave of Summer*,' he says. 'That's the show Boom sponsored last year, where Dante met Megan out in LA.'

Megan, that's a name I do recognise… from Dante's phone at the stag do.

'The girl Dante left in a coma after his drug-driving car crash. And now I know where I've seen the name Robbie Deboise,' Marc goes on. 'Robbie was the one who found her after the accident. They were a couple, I think. Until Dante came along, anyway.'

My brain starts somersaulting. Emil – or Robert – was dating the woman Dante put in a coma, who is currently fighting for her life. He has more reason to hate the Van Battens than anybody, *even me*.

'He's... he's been stalking us the whole time,' I mumble. 'At the balloon, the house, our dance practice. He followed us here to the wedding, and now he's here at the airport.'

'No wonder he wanted to sabotage the wedding,' Marc says. 'The Van Battens are playing happy families for the cameras while Megan is lying in a coma.'

'So this is his revenge?' I ask. 'Killing all of us?'

Marc looks at me. 'Dante stole his girlfriend, left her for dead in the street, then got off scot-free. Stephanie and my dad saw to it that Dante avoided jail and paid off the family, but Robert wouldn't have seen a penny. He was just the ex.'

Adrenaline pumps through me as I'm hit by a moment of clarity. 'The... the X,' I stutter. 'Dante drew an X on the floor. I thought he meant Portia, but he meant Megan's ex. He must have figured it out. Too late.'

The pain in my hand begins to subside, but probably only through numbness. I pull my hand out of Marc's grip and begin bandaging it with the paper towels.

'The transponder,' I tell him. 'It's in the cockpit, I think. The real steward gave me an emergency code that'll signal Oslo to send help.'

Before I can get up, Marc spins round, alerted by something.

'Wait,' he says. 'Did you hear that? Don't move.'

'I don't have a choice,' I whisper. 'These things were not built for two people.'

'Shush,' he hisses, putting his hand over my mouth.

We sit in silence for a moment, holding our breath, listening. There it is again. A scraping sound, coming from beneath us.

'The hold,' Marc whispers. 'Someone's in the hold.'

The scraping stops. But it's quickly followed by another, louder noise, and then again – *thump, thump, thump* – and this time, it's not coming from below us. It's coming up the door stairs.

Marc slowly removes his hand from my mouth and very gently pulls the toilet door shut, then puts his ear to it.

'They're in the plane,' he mouths to me.

It's got to be Emil. He's found us and now he's going to kill us both.

Heart racing, I get up, squeeze past Marc and push the toilet door open, just an inch. I peek out. There's a bulky figure at the other end of the plane, pulling something up the door steps and into the plane.

As I watch, they turn to look in my direction, and I see their face.

I gasp. It's not who I am expecting.

It's Stephanie.

– EPISODE SIX (PART THREE) –
THE BACH PARTY

THE NIGHT BEFORE THE WEDDING
BORGENHUS FORTRESS HOTEL

I snuck out of Marc's hotel room and looked both ways down the corridor. Empty. Whoever delivered that note was gone, but they couldn't have gone far. They must have still been somewhere in the hotel. I tiptoed to the lift and pressed the down button.

I had to find them.

I had to find out what exactly what they knew.

Had someone found out what I was really doing? Who I really was? I'd been so careful. Covered my tracks. Left no breadcrumbs.

Before tonight, I'd assumed the person in the red coat was trying to warn me what a bunch of scumbags the Van Battens were. But what if they were actually trying to warn Marc about me?

Did they know how I'd planned all this? How I'd rigged *Love Synced* to settle my scores with the Van Battens once and for all?

No... that couldn't be it. 'Marry him and die' had to be meant for me. Something else was suss with *Love Synced*. I'd always felt that, right from the start. Why would a family like the Van Battens sign up for a dumb reality show? They certainly didn't need the money or attention, so what did they have to gain?

Whoever left me that note clearly didn't want to sit down and have a chat about it. The hotel was a big place; I mean, it was literally a castle. They could be anywhere. Down on the ground floor, it was dark, the hustle and bustle of arrivals earlier replaced by an eerie atmosphere. But there was a soft glow coming from a back room behind the reception area.

I poked my head in and realised it must be Lion Jaw's makeshift production office. Unlocked. Was the person in the red coat leading me here? And if so, what did they want me to find?

I went in and sat on one of the swivel chairs in front of the bank of monitors. It was all set up for the wedding record tomorrow. On the desk in front of me, there was a plastic box of memory cards, marked with dates, and I flipped through them until I found the one I was looking for. The day of the disastrous lunch at the Van Batten house. I overheard something that day – something I shouldn't have.

I stuck the card in the laptop and an image popped up on the screen. I fast-forwarded through the footage until I found what I was looking for – Malcolm and Stephanie's conversation in the hallway, the one I couldn't hear properly before. It was an odd angle, but I could clearly see neither of them were happy. Malcolm was jabbing his finger at Stephanie as she fiddled with his dressing-gown cord.

I turned up the volume.

– No, it's fine, I can do it.
– Leave it open, like this.
– Stop fussing, will you? Damn silly girl. She signed the NDA, but now decides to talk?
– We'll deal with her, just like we dealt with Portia. But you need to keep it together, otherwise they'll find out the truth.
– Yes, yes, I know the plan.
– Marc takes over as CEO, you retire quietly. Just play along for the cameras, call her the wrong name, everything we talked about, yes?
– For God's sake, woman, I'm quite capable of playing a part. Act a bit doolally, wobble about a bit, it's not exactly—
– Wait, quiet. There's someone here.

I pressed pause and sat back in the chair, staring at the screen in disbelief. The frozen image of Malcolm's face stared back at me – alert, calculating, completely lucid.

He didn't have dementia. He was faking it. Every confused look, every bumbling moment, every time he'd seemed lost and frail – it was all an act. A performance for the cameras.

The truth hit me like ice water. Malcolm stepping down; Marc stepping up. He wasn't walking away: he was taking over. Was everything he told me tonight about leaving the company a lie?

Before I could put the puzzle pieces together in my head,

there was a noise from the corridor. Quickly, I pulled out the memory card from the laptop and stuck it in my dressing-gown pocket. Then I slipped out of the office, half expecting to see someone in a red coat holding a knife. But to my surprise, it was Stephanie.

'Hazel.' She looked me up and down like I was a creased shirt at a dry cleaner. 'What are you doing wandering around like a lost dog?'

'I, uh, couldn't sleep,' I replied, instinctively pulling my dressing-gown cord tighter. 'Nervous about tomorrow, I guess.'

What was Stephanie even doing down here so late? I wanted to ask her, but I had to keep it together. I couldn't let on what I'd just seen.

'Well,' she said, with just the faintest of eye rolls. 'I think I have some Xanax in my bag here somewhere…' She began rummaging through her handbag.

'Stephanie,' I said. 'Wait, a second.'

She looked up, her face expectant.

'You orchestrated all this didn't you?' I said. 'The show, the wedding… everything is part of some grand plan to save the company, isn't it?'

She paused, looking me up and down, almost as if she had a new-found respect for me.

'Clever girl,' she said finally.

'Everything except me. I wasn't part of the plan, was I?' I asked.

'With Malcolm's position as CEO at VanCamp no longer… shall we say, *viable*, we needed Marc to step into his shoes. But his playboy past was a problem. He needed a stable, committed relationship, and for some reason he had rejected every suitable match I tried to make for him. But the AI was supposed to find someone suitable... someone who shared his values, his background. A soulmate, that's what Julian assured me.' She looked at me with pity. 'I just didn't think it would be...' She gestured vaguely at my dressing gown and sex-hair.

'Someone like me?' I said.

'The AI was meant to find someone like *us*,' she said.

I could feel my blood rising, heat creeping up my neck.

'Correct me if I'm wrong,' I said. 'But I seem to remember reading that before you married Malcolm, you were just one of the staff. Is that right?'

Her expression tightened, but I kept going.

'But it seems you've really fitted into your new role, huh? I guess you could say you got a promotion. I don't blame you, Stephanie, we all want something better for ourselves. We all want to climb higher. But what I don't get is, why do you want to pull up the ladder behind you?'

She stared at me, and I immediately knew I'd crossed a line. But what she said next shocked me.

'Leave the show now, and I'll make sure you're remunerated very generously.'

'Excuse me?' I stuttered, leaning in closer. Maybe I hadn't heard her properly.

'Fifty thousand pounds, transferred to your bank account first thing in the morning,' she said.

I heard her alright. Fifty grand. That was more than enough money to pay off my credit cards.

'And what am I supposed to tell Marc?' I asked.

'Tell him anything you want. You got cold feet, you changed your mind. I don't really care. Just don't do it in front of the cameras.'

I stared at her for a moment.

'Think what you like about me,' she said. 'All I'm doing is looking out for Marc. I want him to live up to his potential.'

'And you think marrying me isn't living up to his potential?'

'Marc's an adult, he can make his own decisions. But I'll be damned if I'll let him make his own mistakes,' she finished. 'Fifty thousand pounds. Think about it. But not for too long.'

With that, she turned and walked back into the hall, her Jimmy Choos clipping the marble flooring as she went.

TWENTY-ONE

SKARDBALT AIRPORT

I watch through the crack in the toilet door as Stephanie pulls a suitcase up the remaining steps, then pushes it into the aisle of the plane. There are flecks of snow in her miraculously still-glossy hair, and she's wearing a big I HEART NORWAY sweater over her Dior dress – the same ones they had at the gift shop.

Marc looks over my shoulder, trying to see what's going on.

'It's Stephanie,' I hiss. 'She's got a suitcase. It must be from the hold.'

'What? Let me—'

'No, wait,' I say, holding him back. 'She's got something else...'

I can see she's clutching something in her right hand, but I can't quite make out what it is. I push the toilet door just a centimetre wider and put my face right up to the crack. My hand goes to my mouth instinctually as I take a sharp intake of breath. A single ray of sunshine streams through the plane window, catching the glint of metal in her hands, and I suddenly realise what it is.

The scissors.

Marc nudges me aside, and we watch together as Stephanie rests against a seat for a moment. Then she raises the scissors above her head and plunges them down hard into the case. With a great effort, she yanks them through the plastic until she's made a hole and begins rummaging among the contents. Then, when she finds what she's looking for, her face lights up, and she pulls a small plastic box from the case.

'Enough,' Marc says, pushing past me and stepping into the aisle.

Stephanie looks up, momentarily surprised.

'Marc,' she says, recovering her composure. 'Thank goodness you're safe.'

'What are you doing here?' he asks. 'I told you to stay in the café.'

She holds up the box, giving it a little shake. 'I came for these, of course. The memory cards,' she says. 'All the footage from the wedding is on these.'

Of course, that's Julian's suitcase. Our luggage has been here on the plane the whole time. It was never offloaded after the delay. The cards have been in there all along.

'We need to make sure these never get back to London. If the wedding footage were to get out, we will lose everything,' Stephanie went on. 'The business. The house. And you can forget your precious charitable foundation.'

'Are you mad?' Marc asks. 'It's not safe to be out here.'

'I'm not a complete idiot,' she tuts. 'I waited until the worst of the blizzard had passed.'

'Not the storm,' Marc cries. 'Listen to me, forget the memory cards. Emil wasn't who he said he was. We're all in danger.'

I step out from behind Marc, and Stephanie's expression hardens.

'Oh, you're here too.' Stephanie sighs. 'So pleased you survived, Hazel.'

'Only just,' I say, taking a step towards her. 'Where did you get those scissors, Stephanie?'

She looks down at the pair of scissors in her hand, like she's just realising they are there.

'These? I found them on the floor in the airport. I knew I'd need something to get into Julian's case.' She points to the ripped-open suitcase. 'I remembered it has a combination lock, you see.'

'But Dante had those scissors,' I say, not taking my eyes off her. 'And whoever killed him took them from him and stabbed him to death.'

All the blood suddenly rushes from her face. 'What do you mean, dead?' She looks at Marc. 'What's she talking about?'

Marc shakes his head slowly. 'I'm sorry, Stephanie. He's… he's gone. Why don't you just give us the scissors? We're going to get help, and we'll all be going home very soon.'

The door of the plane is still open, and a cold wind whips through the aisle, pushing Stephanie's hair across her face.

'You think I killed my own nephew?' she says, her voice shocked at first, then breaking into an incredulous laugh. 'You don't seriously think I could be capable of that? I'm a fifty-three-year-old woman with a bad hip and a constant migraine. I haven't killed anyone.'

'Just give me the scissors,' Marc says. 'No one is accusing you of anything.'

'We'll see about that,' I say, stepping in front of Marc and holding up my arm. 'CILLA, is it Stephanie? Is she the one who's been doing this?'

The display flashes, and CILLA's crisp, cheery voice fills the plane.

'Hi, Hazel! Great question!' she says. 'Based on your conversations, Stephanie Van Batten has a very strong motive for murder.'

'If you think I'm going to let a computer convict me, you're stupider than you look,' Stephanie hisses. She takes a step towards us, waving the scissors at me. 'Why would I hurt Dante? After everything I've done for this family.'

'You mean like faking Malcolm's dementia?'

Her lips tighten. 'You should be very careful, young lady,' she says coldly. 'You've already made a number of spurious accusations today.'

'Except they *weren't* spurious, were they?' I say. 'It took me a while to piece it together, but I finally figured out why the Van Battens signed up for *Love Synced*.'

'Because I wanted the world to see the Van Battens at their best,' Stephanie says.

'But not Malcolm, right? You needed the world to see him at his *worst*. You wanted everyone to believe Malcolm had dementia so he could get away with what he did to all those women.'

'Is it true?' Marc asks. 'Did he really do those things?'

Stephanie looks behind her, like she's considering running back out into the snow, then thinks better of it. She takes a breath.

'Everything those women are saying about your father is true,' she tells Marc. 'He's been doing it for years.'

Marc's face goes pale. 'What are you talking about?'

'Every young girl, every photo shoot, every new intern. When I was the head of public relations, it was my job to get all those NDAs tied up, make sure none of them told a soul what he did.'

'And you just went along with it?' I ask.

She looks down at her feet, and for the first time since I met her, Stephanie seems fragile.

'I was one of them,' she says. 'He did it to me too. But I realised, if I played along, I could make the best of it. I could control the situation. And it turned into love, of a sort. But I can't... I won't let those women destroy this family, Marc. I can't. I've worked too hard. Sacrificed too much. You know that.'

'So you faked Dad's dementia?' Marc cries. 'Jesus Christ, Stephanie.'

'Don't you dare judge me.' She straightens up, regaining her composure. 'The TV show was supposed to fix everything, show the world you were different from him...' She clutches the memory cards tighter. 'If Malcolm seemed confused, harmless, no one would believe he was capable of—'

'Of what he actually did,' I finish.

She nods curtly. 'Diminished responsibility. A doddery old fool who didn't know where he was putting his hands. Then you'd take over the reins, Marc, once you'd married someone appropriate. That's where Julian and his AI came in. We needed to set you up with a nice, appropriate woman, someone you believed was your soulmate. This was all for you, darling. And it still can be.' She flicks open the plastic case and takes out the three memory cards inside. 'Once I've got rid of these.'

'Stephanie, I never wanted any of that. I hate the damn business. Don't you get that? I told you I was quitting as soon as the wedding was over,' Marc says.

My heart lifts. He never wanted it – the money, the company, any of it. He'd been telling the truth the whole time, and I'd doubted him.

But before Stephanie can react, there's a movement behind her. She doesn't see it, but someone is coming up the stairs at the entrance to the plane. It doesn't take me more than a second to recognise the tall frame of Emil.

'Stephanie!' I shout. 'Watch out!'

But it's too late. Before she can turn around, Emil runs up behind her, grabbing her arm. He kicks her leg, sending her knees to the floor, then twists her wrist until she releases her grasp, dropping the scissors. With his other hand, he picks them up and holds them to her throat.

'Well, welcome aboard, everybody, and thank you for choosing NordAir,' he says, with no trace of a Scandinavian accent.

TWENTY-TWO

SKARDBALT AIRPORT

Marc rushes towards them, but Emil pushes the point of the scissors against Stephanie's neck.

'Any closer and these go straight in her neck,' Emil says. 'If you think I won't do it, just ask Dante. Now give me the memory cards.'

Stephanie clenches her fist tightly around the cards as Marc takes a step towards Emil.

'Let her go, now,' he demands.

Emil laughs bitterly. 'I don't think so.'

'We have money, if that's what you want. We can—' Marc says.

'That's your answer for everything, isn't it?' Emil cuts him off. 'You can't buy your way out of this one. This footage is going to be all over the internet. And then the world will know the truth about your family.'

He takes the scissors away from Stephanie's neck and points them at Marc. In that split second, she opens her hand, letting the memory cards fall to the floor. With one big effort, she pulls away from Emil, then raises her heel and brings it down hard. I hear the crunch of plastic splitting as the memory cards shatter under her foot.

Emil's face contorts.

'Bitch, you'll regret that,' he spits, then lifts the scissors high before plunging them deep into Stephanie's neck.

'No!' Marc shouts, charging at him, but he's too late.

'Oh God!' I scream as blood spurts from her neck, spraying bright red across the purple seats of the plane.

Emil lets Stephanie go and she drops to the floor like a dead weight.

Marc kneels down next to her, desperately but fruitlessly trying to stem the bleeding with his hands. 'What did you do?' he stutters. 'What did you do?'

Emil steps back, almost like he's in shock. He bends down and picks up a handful of the broken plastic, letting the pieces fall through his fingers. Almost on cue, Stephanie's body shudders one last time, then lies motionless in Marc's arms.

I stare at Stephanie's lifeless body, her I HEART NORWAY sweatshirt covered in dark splashes of blood, and dry-heave.

'She's gone,' Marc says, looking at me, then at Emil. Tears begin to stream down his face. 'She's gone, you bastard. I'll kill you, I'll kill you, I'll—'

At that, Emil pulls back his foot and kicks it hard into Marc's stomach, winding him. Then he kicks him again, and again.

'Stop it!' I yell. 'You won't get away with this. I know who you are, *Robert*. You're Megan's boyfriend.'

Emil suddenly stops kicking. He steadies himself, one hand pointing the bloody scissors at Marc's head, the other holding the back of a seat.

'I was,' he says. 'Before his piece-of-shit cousin left her wrapped around a lamppost. Megan is dead. The doctors turned off her life support two days ago. But none of you would know that, would you? Because no one from your family ever bothered to visit her, did they? Didn't even send any fucking flowers. Just left her to rot.'

My mind spins. The name on Dante's phone at the stag... *Megan*. He knew. Dante knew she had died. That's why he went off the rails at the stag and bought the drugs from Gary.

'You're the man in the red jacket. You were the one sending the notes.'

'You didn't make it easy. No online presence, no email, no social media. I had to go old school. But I had to warn you about this family,' he spits. 'They poison everyone they touch. This was the proof.' Emil kicks the broken memory cards on the floor. 'Now it's gone.'

I grab one of the metal trays from the galley area next to the toilet, and inch closer towards him. When he waves the scissors at me, I hold the tray up in front of my face and take another step. He's now standing by the cockpit door, blocking me from reaching it. If I can't get past him, I can't get to the transponder.

'I've been watching them for months, ever since the crash. When I saw they were filming a dating show, parading themselves around like the fucking Kardashians, I knew they were lining up their next victim,' he says.

I lower the tray, try and make eye contact, but he's rambling now.

'Did you ever ask yourself what happened to Malcolm's ex-wife? And all the secretaries he fucked then disposed of? And what about Marc's ex-fiancée? Poor Portia Clarke? Where is she? In a ditch somewhere? Convenient, isn't it? People are disposable to the Van Battens. And you would've been next, Hazel, if you'd have married *him*.'

He points the scissors towards Marc, who's lying, breathless, on the floor next to Stephanie's body. While Emil's attention is off me, I take another step closer.

'But I didn't,' I say. 'I didn't marry him, remember? You got what you wanted, the show was ruined and the Van Battens were going to be humiliated.'

'After your performance at the wedding, I thought I was done. I was going to go home for Megan's funeral and try to forget all about the Van Battens. My plan was to get off the island before any of you. But when I got to the airport, I saw their names on the steward's passenger list. I knew if Dante recognised me, I'd have nowhere to run. I panicked.'

'So you took her place?'

'Knocked her out, stashed her in the men's toilets and took her uniform.'

Of course, the gate restroom was never really out of order.

'I moved her to the control tower when you were all asleep. Couldn't have her waking up and blowing my cover. Lucky for me, Dante was too wasted to recognise me in this ridiculous outfit. He'd only seen me a couple of times on set. After all, I was just another extra. Wasn't important or famous enough for someone like him to pay attention to. Not like Megan. So I played the role of a lifetime.' He switches back into his Norwegian lilt. 'As your ever-helpful steward, Emil.'

'He did recognise you eventually, though, didn't he? In the cafeteria? That's why he ran.'

Emil nodded. 'And that's why he had to die. I can't tell you I didn't enjoy it. I wanted to see the whites of his eyes.

I wanted him to admit everything he did. Most of all, I just wanted him to say sorry. But he couldn't even give me that.'

'What about Gary? Why kill him? He was harmless.'

I shuffle forward, holding up the tray. I'm almost close enough now; if I can just distract him for another second, I can make a grab for the scissors.

'If Gary found the memory cards, he was going to destroy them. I never wanted to kill anyone. I wanted to go home, just like you, Hazel. But these people... they're like a poison... I had to make it stop...'

Losing Megan has tipped him over the edge. I take another step closer. The aisle of the small plane is narrow. I can't get past him, but I'm close enough to see the blankness in his gaze. Up close, I can see there's nothing left behind his eyes, like he's been extinguished. Is that what hate does to you, I wonder? I've spent such a long, long time hating this family – obsessively hating them, closing everything, and everyone else, off. Is this what I would've become?

'You're right,' I say. 'You and I aren't that different. I hate this family too. So just put the scissors down. We'll call for help, and when we're back in London, I'll tell them everything I know. But we need Marc to corroborate everything, okay? Let him live and we'll do this the right way. It's not too late.'

I lower the tray, leaving us face to face.

'Robert, listen to me,' I say. 'This won't bring Megan back, and it won't make the pain go away. This isn't justice, Robert, this is revenge.'

And revenge is a very lonely place to be.

Our eyes meet, and just for a second, the tension in his face seems to subside. I swear there's something there, a momentary spark, like maybe what I said got through to him, somehow.

Then his expression hardens again, like he can't fight off the storm, and he lifts the scissors high above his head. I bring up my arm in defence, but he grabs my bad hand, squeezing it. I scream in pain, and he lands the scissors, hard, straight into my chest.

TWENTY-THREE

SKARDBALT AIRPORT

I brace myself for the pain, but it doesn't come.

What the hell?

Instead, there's a whooshing noise from my chest, and I wonder if that's the sound of my lung deflating. Or maybe that's the noise you hear when you die? I always thought it would be angels singing or – if you're lucky – a round of applause for an excellent life lived. But this is like a hissing, a lot like a... oh.

I look down to see the life jacket deflating.

The scissors didn't make it through. *It saved me.*

Emil looks at me, his face contorted in anger. I seize the opportunity and bring my knee up sharply between his legs. He doubles over, shouting expletives, and I yell to Marc.

'Now!'

Seeing his chance, Marc pulls himself up and rugby-tackles Emil into a row of seats.

'Get in the cockpit and lock the door,' Marc shouts.

He holds Emil down and I hurry towards the cockpit. Once inside, I pull the door closed behind me and turn the lock.

I spin round to look at the plane's dashboard. The lights are all off. All around me are little switches, dials and buttons, and I have no idea what any of them do. Sliding into the pilot's seat, I start flicking them at random, hoping one will make the dashboard light up.

My heart is thumping in my chest. The dashboard flickers to life. But I can't see the transponder. Four numbers, Emily said, look for four numbers.

'Come on, come on,' I hiss. It has to be somewhere here, somewhere obvious and easy to access.

Outside the cockpit, I can hear a huge crash, followed by shouting. Can't think about that now. I have to focus. Concentrate. Find the transponder.

On the dashboard, I finally see four numbers in a row, each with a twisty dial underneath, just like Emily described it.

'That must be it,' I say.

Quickly, I turn the dials individually. When I twist the final dial to zero, there's a small, high-pitched – and very reassuring – beep.

It worked. At least, I hope it did...

I flop back in the pilot's seat and catch my breath. Through the windscreen, I can see the sun shining across the apron. I don't know what I was expecting to happen – a fleet of helicopters would suddenly descend on the airport to save us?

I look at the cockpit door. Should I go back out there, try and help Marc?

What if Emil hurts him?

What if I'm stuck in here and Marc's dead and...

I get up, ignore the pain in my hand and reach for the lock. But before I can open it, the noises from the other side suddenly stop. There's an eerie silence as I put my ear up to the door.

'Marc?' I say quietly, too scared to shout.

There's no response.

My hand rests on the handle. What if the wrong one was left standing…

Then there's a knock. A single, loud thump on the door, and I freeze.

TWENTY-FOUR

SKARDBALT AIRPORT

'Hello?' I say tentatively.

'Hazel,' Marc's voice says from outside the door. 'It's me. I'm hurt, let me in.'

I look back at the dashboard. How long is that signal meant to take? Surely someone must have received it by now? Daylight is streaming through the windscreen, hitting my face. It's warm, the first hint of warmth I've felt for hours. The skies are clear, so where are the emergency services?

I turn back to the door. 'What about Emil... I mean, Robert?' I ask. 'Is he...?'

There's another pause.

'It's okay, he's... he's out cold. I hit him with the tray. I had to... Hazel, I need your help, please. I'm bleeding. Open up. It's safe, I promise you.'

My hand lingers over the latch, but something stops me from turning it. There's still one thing that doesn't add up here.

Emil admitted to murdering Dante and Gary, and I saw him kill Stephanie. But what about Julian? He had no reason to kill Julian, who was going to broadcast the wedding and show the world the truth about the Van Battens. Emil would have got everything he wanted, without hurting anyone.

I take my hand from the door and lift the wristband to my mouth.

'CILLA,' I say. 'I need your help, just one last time, please. Tell me, can I trust Marc Van Batten? Can I let him in?'

'Hi, Hazel! That's a great question!' she chirps from my wrist. 'Let me calculate…'

There's an agonising pause while CILLA thinks. After a few seconds, she speaks again.

'There's a ninety-nine per cent chance that if you open that door, Marc Van Batten is going to kill you. Hope that helps!'

- EPISODE SEVEN -
THE WEDDING

BORGENHUS FORTRESS HOTEL

From the window, I could see the guests arriving, knocking bright white snowflakes off their hats as they entered the castle. My hair was up, Tilly had done my nails, and the ivory satin dress clung to my frame.

In just a few minutes, it would be time to walk down the aisle, each step magically transforming me from a nobody to a Van Batten. Everything was set for the perfect wedding.

The perfect deception.

Because I was about to marry the son of the man who destroyed my father.

I went over to my luggage in the corner, all packed, ready for the honeymoon, and took out a slip of paper. I unfolded the letter on the vanity table and read it for what must have been the thousandth time.

Hazel,

I can't give you a time machine. But I can give you this – I guess you could call it a time machine, of sorts.

It's the truth.

A long time ago, when you were just a baby, I made a drink for the labourers at the building site where I worked. Sweetened it with cane sugar. Something to keep us going all day. That's why I put the red hammer on it. Malcolm kept that, at least.

Now, I've seen Malcolm on TV, telling everyone how he created that drink. That's not true. Malcolm Van Batten was a small-time property developer. He came on site and tried the drink one time. Next day, he came back, told me it cured his jetlag. We became friends, then partners. He had the money; I had the recipe. He wanted to pay for a factory to mass produce it. And that's how VanCamp started. And it worked, at least, at first. I handled the product; he handled the selling. We sold a fair bit in those early days. But Malcolm had bigger ideas. Rebrand and expand, he called it. Change the image. Move production abroad. Add a load of E-numbers and caffeine. Sell it to the rich kids who throw themselves off cliffs.

I said no. He said it was his money. His investment. But it was my recipe, my drink. We'd invested all the money in the factory, so he couldn't get at it. I wouldn't sign off on it, and we fell out.

Here is what's important. I want you to know: I never started that fire.

The night after the argument, that's when the fire

started. I can't prove that Malcolm did it. But I do know that I sure as hell didn't.

Maybe he wanted the insurance money. Maybe he just wanted to destroy what he couldn't have. Or maybe it was just a terrible accident.

It didn't matter in the end. The insurance policy was in my name. I had been seen on the premises earlier that night. I already had a criminal record.

Maybe Malcolm just saw an opportunity and took it. I guess that's what he was always good at.

When he testified against me in court, I looked straight into his eyes, and even though I knew he was lying, he almost convinced me. That's how good he was. The devil was in his eyes.

And if you make a deal with the devil, you will always lose in the end.

Even the closest hand can hold a dagger. Remember that.

I love you,

Dad

Since this letter arrived six months ago, I'd read it almost every day. But reading it on the morning of my wedding, the words hit me harder than ever before.

It had arrived on my doorstep just a few days after Dad was released from prison. Since then, my whole life had changed. Dad had been locked away for nearly twenty years, and for most of that, I'd believed he was guilty. When you're twelve, and your mum tells you something enough times, you believe it.

But she was wrong.

After the fire, VanCamp Drinks shifted production to Thailand. Found cheaper, lower-quality ingredients and turned it into that disgusting sports drink. Turned my father's idea into a billion-dollar company while he rotted in jail.

Mum couldn't afford the bills on her own, and a loveless marriage with Steve was the only way to keep a roof over our heads. My aunt, Dad's sister, was penniless in a crumbling council flat in Southend, while these pricks lived it up on the French Riviera.

I always thought that my life would've been a lot different if we'd had that sort of money. But looking at the Van Battens now, I wasn't so sure. If the last two weeks had shown me anything, it was that all the money in the world couldn't stop the Van Battens from hating each other.

Since I got the letter, I'd dedicated myself to finding out everything I could about the Van Battens. Following their activities online. Reading up on their business dealings. Watching where they went, what fancy parties they frequented. When I found out Stephanie was a member at Eight Ball, I applied for a job there. I had to massage my CV a fair bit, but I had the right look and could carry a tray, so they didn't ask too many questions.

I was waiting tables when I saw Stephanie Van Batten come in. I recognised her immediately. You better believe I knew the faces of that family better than I did my own by then.

What I didn't know at the time was that the man she was talking to was Julian Draper. I figured he was just some business acquaintance. They were drunk. Talking. Celebrating. I lingered around their table when I was collecting their glasses. My ears pricked up when I heard them mention a TV series. The Van Battens were doing a reality show? I almost laughed out loud. Did they think they were the Kardashians or something? They kept talking about weddings and mentioned Marc's name. After my shift I found the advert for *Love Synced* online. No prizes for guessing what I did next.

From there, it was actually pretty easy. I had an advantage that none of the other women had: I knew who the mystery man at the heart of *Love Synced* was. Marc Van Batten was the 'Prince Charming' that Lion's Jaw had chosen. And all I had to do was convince a computer than I was his soulmate.

I'd been code-switching since before I even knew what it meant – softening my Essex accent for job interviews, straightening my hair for events at the club, pretending to laugh at guys' jokes that weren't funny. Fooling CILLA was just another performance. I became the sporty, dog-loving, meat-eating, posh girl of Marc's dreams. In a way, I'd been preparing for the role my whole life.

Everything had brought me here – to a snow-covered castle on a remote Norwegian island, about to marry into the twenty-third richest family in Great Britain. I'd only have to stick it out for a couple of months. Once I dropped the pretence, he'd be desperate for a divorce. Or, even better, I could just wait for him to cheat on me in some club, like he did with his last fiancée. I'd accept a quickie divorce for half of everything he'd got, and take back some of what was rightfully ours.

I folded the letter as Tilly came back from the bathroom, then slid it back into my bag. It was time.

I was wearing a classic A-line Vera Wang wedding dress with a sweetheart neckline. Ivory satin, side split. Lion's Jaw had paid (the one thing they'd actually splashed the budget on) and let me pick it myself, with Tilly's help, back in London. I knew it was all for a sickly montage, us sipping fizzy wine and gasping at the excitement of it all, but truth be told, I loved the dress.

When I stood up and looked in the full-length mirror, I barely recognised the woman looking back at me. Elegant. Composed. She looked like a Van Batten, and in a few minutes, she would be. At Eight Ball, we all wore all black, designed so we'd blend into the background, unseen, unheard. But here, I was on show, literally paraded in front of the camera, a princess in white.

Stop. Don't get caught up in the fairytale.

Last night, under the northern lights, I'd let myself believe, just for a moment, that maybe this could be real. But then I found the footage. Malcolm, perfectly lucid, conspiring with Stephanie. Either Marc didn't know, or he was lying to me. First and foremost, he was a Van Batten, and there was one thing I knew about Van Battens: they lied.

'Okay, what's wrong?' Tilly asked, interrupting my thoughts. 'And don't say nothing, because you're doing that thing with your face.'

'My face?'

'That thing you do when you're pretending everything is fine, but actually you're freaking out inside. Pretty much your standard expression, to be fair, but today's your wedding day, Hazel!'

I turned away, fussing with my train. 'Just wedding jitters.'

'Hazel.' She put her hand on my shoulder, forcing me to look at her. 'You do love him, don't you?'

The question hung in the air between us.

I'd asked myself that question a hundred times since last night. CILLA was certainly convinced we were soulmates. Was I really that good of an actor? Or could I have actually fallen for this man who represented everything I despised?

It didn't matter. Just a bit longer, and I'd have the ring on my finger. Legal. Binding. That was why I was here, not for fairy tales. For justice.

I opened my mouth to reply, but at that moment, there was a knock at the door, and Julian stuck his head in.

'Are you girls ready?' he said. 'Chop-chop! We're all set up out here.'

Behind him, a camera person was standing by, ready to capture my big entrance.

'I don't know what you and Marc got up to last night,' Julian went on. 'Somehow you clawed your way to ninety-nine per cent, right at the last possible moment. If only you'd done it on bloody camera!' He clapped his hands to hurry us up. 'Let's do this, people! We have an internet to break.'

I stepped towards the door, but Tilly stopped me.

'Remember, whatever happens, stay possy out there,' she said. 'It's a bit like manifesting. If you believe things are going to turn out well, and then they do. That's the power of possy.'

'Very scientific, Tils,' I said. 'Don't worry, I am feeling *super* possy right now.'

'Then let your face know, okay?'

I plastered a big dumb grin on my face and Tilly gave me a big thumbs up.

'Alright, let's do this,' I said, mustering as much courage as I could.

She held out her hand, but before I could take it, Julian stuck his head out from behind the camera.

'Could you say that again?' the director asked. 'But with a little more conviction this time?'

I took a breath, did my best Blue Steel, and flicked my eyes towards that damn red light.

'I said, let's fucking do this. That good enough for you?'

A few minutes later, I walked through the doors of the chapel.

Thirty-seven people I'd never met lined both sides of the aisle – men in expensive suits and women wearing pretty floral dresses, despite the cold. It looked so different to yesterday. Flowers adorned every wall and strains of daylight shone through the stained-glass windows as a harpist picked a gentle melody that echoed off the stone walls of the chapel.

A hush fell over the assembled onlookers as they turned their heads in unison to watch me. I gripped Tilly's hand, and we walked slowly towards the priest. As we did, the harpist stopped picking and started playing a different melody. When I realised what it was, I almost doubled over laughing.

Nelly and Kelly. 'Dilemma'.

I glanced down the aisle at Marc, impossibly handsome in an impeccably tailored dark navy suit. His face blushed through his light tan when he saw me, and I couldn't help but look down, an involuntary smile spread across my lips. *He remembered.*

My gaze fell on Stephanie in the front row – and the empty seat beside her. Malcolm's seat.

I tried to concentrate on taking one step after another, towards Marc, towards my destiny. I knew when I reached the end, that was it, no turning back. When I got to the altar,

I turned to face Marc, my heart thumping so hard I could swear the whole congregation could hear it.

The priest greeted me with a gentle smile. With wispy grey hair and little half-rimmed glasses, he looked like he'd stepped straight out of a Nineties Richard Curtis rom-com. I half wondered if he was a real priest or just some extra that Julian had dug up.

After reading a prayer and blessing the rings, he turned to Marc. 'Do you, Marc Van Batten, take this woman to be your wife?' the priest said.

'I do,' he said, grinning at me with that same big, dimpled smile I remembered from the proposal.

'And do you, Hazel Harper, take this man to be your lawfully wedded husband?'

I paused, my eyes glancing nervously around the room.

Hazel Harper. That was me, right? He was talking to me. This was my bit.

Marc looked at me, his eyes imploring me to say something, *anything*.

The silence around the chapel was deafening, and in my head, it had lasted for approximately one million years. I bit my bottom lip. Suddenly, everything around me blurred, and I felt a rush of blood to my head. I blinked twice, like I was trying to restart the world. But nothing changed: thirty-seven people were still staring at me, waiting for me to say something, to do anything other than stand there gaping like an idiot.

'Would you like me to repeat the question?' the priest asked. There was a polite, awkward titter from the onlookers.

I swallowed the ocean of saliva that had now collected in my mouth, and met Marc's eye. He looked back at me with a mixture of confusion and encouragement. It felt like the entire congregation was holding their breath.

Two words. Two words and it would be done. Justice for Dad. Everything we lost, returned. I looked at Marc, at the hope in his eyes, the slight tremor in his hand as he held out the ring. I'd wanted revenge. I'd wanted what was rightfully mine. But most of all, I'd wanted to take something away from the Van Battens, something they loved. Turned out, it wasn't their money, it was their son. But somewhere along the line, I'd stopped seeing him as a Van Batten, and started seeing him as Marc.

And I couldn't do this to him. This wasn't justice, this was revenge.

'I'm sorry,' I mouthed, and saw his face go instantly pale, the look of bewilderment replaced by panic in an instant.

I turned around and began the thousand-mile walk back to the door, tears streaming down my face, my train dragging behind me. Gasps echoed through the hall as camera lights flashed from all angles. In the sea of faces, Stephanie's was the only one I saw clearly. And it was full of pure, unyielding hate.

I was almost halfway down the aisle when Julian jumped out right in front of me. He had a camera operator beside him, probably getting a nice, big close-up of my wretched, tear-stained face.

'Stop filming,' I told him.

Julian just stared back at me, a sort of twisted smile forming on his face. Was this what he wanted? Was this the finale to his stupid 'social experiment' he planned all along?

'I said, stop filming. Please. Turn the cameras off.'

'No,' he said, bluntly.

I could feel the fury boiling up inside me. I stomped straight up to the camera operator and tried to wrestle the camera off him. He pulled it away from me.

'I knew it,' I heard Dante's voice from behind me. 'Fucking trash.'

Something inside me snapped. Two weeks of smiling when I should've been screaming. Two weeks of being treated like I was less than them, like I should feel lucky to be here, like I didn't deserve any of this.

Well, fuck that.

'Fine,' I said, my voice stronger now. 'If you want to film something, then film this.'

I turned to the others.

'You want to know the truth about the Van Battens?' I cried. 'Well, Dante here is wasted. Look at him. That court-ordered rehab didn't exactly work out, did it? Well and truly off the wagon. Don't drive home, mate.'

'You fucking bitch, I'll—' Dante jumped off the pew and lurched at me, but missed wildly and fell onto the hard stone floor of the chapel.

Next, I walked right up to Stephanie.

'Let's not forget Stephanie Van Batten. Pillar of the community. What could she have possibly done wrong? Why don't you ask her why her sexual-predator husband is faking dementia?'

Stephanie didn't react at first; she just stared at me. I'd never seen so much contempt in a person's eyes before. It was almost enough to make me lose my nerve. But the hellfire was too strong now.

'Hazel.' I hear a voice from behind me, and turn to see Marc, completely crestfallen.

'What are you doing?' he asked.

'I'm sorry, Marc. But the truth is…'

I took a breath. I wasn't even sure I knew what the truth was anymore.

'I think we should see other people,' I told him.

I turned back to face Julian. 'Get out of my way,' I said firmly.

The cameraman pulled back to get us both in shot. Now Julian was in front of the cameras for the first time since we'd started filming.

'Didn't you forget someone?' he said. 'Don't you want to insult *me* on camera? Why not make a complete set, hmm?'

The bastard was goading me. He knew his fairytale ending was ruined, and now he wanted the nuclear option. Alright, fine. Show me the big red button.

'This isn't a social experiment,' I said. 'It's a freak show. And I'm your freak, right? You designed it to make fun of the poor girl, to let everyone watch her flounder in front of all the rich people. Well, I hope you got the results you wanted.'

I expected Julian to yell at me, but he just smirked.

'That's great,' he said. 'Come on, give us some more. Tell us what you *really* think. We're still filming.'

Dad was right. If you make a deal with the devil, you always lose.

I didn't answer him. Instead, I drew back my arm and slammed my fist straight into his face.

The insults, the death threats, the pain of the last two weeks, all rolled up into one punch.

Julian tumbled back, falling into a group of older ladies in large hats.

He got up, clutching his face, and *now* he started shouting at me.

'You fucking cow!' he yelled. 'I'll ruin you.'

I couldn't hear what he said after that; I was already striding down the aisle without looking back. I kept walking, out of the chapel, out of the castle and into the grounds, my wedding dress blurring into the falling snow.

I knew one thing for sure. I was never going to see any of the Van Battens ever again.

TWENTY-FIVE

SKARDBALT AIRPORT

Marc thumps on the cockpit door again.

'Hazel, let me in.'

I don't say anything. My mind is spinning at a million miles per hour. I can't think, I can't focus. I stumble back from the door, steadying myself on the pilot's chair.

'Hazel!' Marc is shouting now. 'What's going on in there? Did you find the transponder?'

'Can I trust you?' I shout back.

'What are you talking about?' Marc yells. 'Of course you can bloody trust me. You just need to let me in. Emil got me in the stomach with the scissors, I'm losing blood. Is help coming? Did it work?'

I don't answer. I try to blot out everything else and think back through everything that has happened tonight, everything that CILLA has told me. First, she pointed the finger at Gary, then Dante, then Stephanie. She's been wrong every time, and now she is saying Marc is a killer.

'CILLA,' I say into my wristband. 'What did you mean, exactly? Why do you think Marc is going to hurt me?'

'Hey, Hazel! You told me that Marc Van Batten was the devil. You said anyone in the Van Batten family would kill rather than give up their money. Therefore, I can say with ninety-nine per cent accuracy that Marc is a murderer.'

'Right,' I say. 'So you're just basing all this on stuff *I* told you?'

'Great questi—'

'CILLA, I know it's a great question, just tell me the answer.'

'Of course, Hazel. I use statistical models and probability scenarios to make predictions based on previous events.'

'Okay, in English, please.'

'That was in English, Hazel,' CILLA says. 'Would you like it in another language?'

'Just explain it to me like I'm stupid, okay?'

'Understood. In short, in reference to the killings, I only have access to the data that you have provided, and therefore I have drawn conclusions based purely on that information. For example, you told me that Gary was creepy. You told me that Dante had wet shoes. You told me Stephanie would do anything to protect her family. And you told me that Marc was the worst man you ever met.'

'All this time, you were just making educated guesses?' I say. 'Jesus, CILLA, you're basically one step up from the self-service check-out at Tesco!'

'If I do not have the correct answer, I estimate the most probable result based on the information you've provided. Can I help you with another question, Hazel?'

Without saying another word, I lift up my arm, unclip the wristband and toss it on the pilot's seat.

Maybe I could just stay in here forever, safe behind this locked door. Never trust anyone again. Never risk being hurt. Or I could drop my defences and accept the consequences.

I reach for the latch on the door.

'I'm going to let you in,' I shout to Marc. 'But first, there's something I have to tell you.'

I rest my forehead against the cold metal of the cockpit door.

'I knew who you were,' I say. 'I always knew. Before the show, before the wristbands, I found out everything about you. Then I tricked CILLA into matching us by copying your lifestyle.'

'You knew?' he says, his voice cracking. 'But how…'

'I needed to make CILLA think we were soulmates so that I would be picked for the show. That profile of you in *Cosmopolitan* magazine came in really handy. Your social media feed told me the rest. Your Instagram is full of the hipster bars and coffee shops you hang out at. TikTok showed me your gym routine and meal plans. Spotify your music tastes. Letterboxd for movies. Then I used the data to become your "person". I spent three weeks falling on my arse at the dry ski slope in Croydon, every Wednesday night. Hours and hours listening to that godawful band you like. Even volunteered with Tilly, trying to fundraise for bloody orangutans in Borneo. And hung out with her silly little Cockapoo puppy so CILLA would think I loved dogs, even though I am definitely, definitely a cat person. I bought meat in my online grocery shop so CILLA wouldn't know I was a vegetarian. I watched every bloody *Mission: Impossible* movie, just because you liked them. I even drank about a pint of coffee before the reveal, just to make sure my heart was thumping, so CILLA would read that as attraction.'

Marc doesn't say anything for what seems like forever. Eventually he speaks, just one word.

'Why?'

I take another deep breath. This is it. There's no point in pretending anymore. I might as well tell him everything, but somehow, it's easier if I don't have to look him in the eye when I do it.

'I'm Jon Campbell's daughter,' I say.

There's a pause.

'I'm sorry, am I supposed to know who that is?'

I grit my teeth, and slam my fist against the cockpit door, momentarily forgetting my snow burn, then stick it in my mouth to stop myself yelping in pain.

'Maybe you should ask your dad,' I say, after the pain subsides.

'What are you talking about, Hazel?' he asks. 'Just open the door and we can talk properly.'

I can feel my blood boiling, almost enough to make me forget the throbbing pain in my hand.

'I'm talking about Jon Campbell. Twenty years ago, he was your father's business partner. Not just his partner. His friend. But I'm not surprised your dad never mentioned him.'

Marc is silent for a moment. 'There was a partner, years ago, before Dad took the company public. But he always said that guy did a runner after the fire, left him in the lurch when things got tough. That's when Dad had to rebuild everything.'

'That's not how it happened,' I tell him. 'Jon Campbell invented Boom, long before your dad turned up. All Malcolm did was provide a bit of capital, but when the drink started selling, he wanted Jon out of the way. Jon didn't want to hike up the price and move production abroad. The fire in the factory your dad told you about? It was your dad who started it.'

'That... that can't be true,' I hear Marc murmur.

I know how this goes. Stage one, denial.

'Only he didn't know there were still workers inside,' I went on. 'Two people died, and when the police got involved, your dad pinned it all on Jon. Even testified against him in court. Malcolm burnt everything down that got in his way, then rebuilt it the way he wanted it. Erased my father from history. Everything you have is built on what my father did. But while he rotted in jail, your dad went on to conquer the world. That was his so-called phoenix from the flames.'

Marc is silent. To be fair, I've just told him his fiancée has been lying to him since the moment they met, and then followed that up with a 'your dad's a murderer' bombshell. So, I can't really blame him for taking a moment.

When he does speak, the uncertainty in his voice is gone, replaced by a crackling fury, fuelled by confusion and indignation.

'So, the wedding, the TV show... that was meant to be what? Your revenge?' he says. 'Trick your way into marrying me, break my heart and take my money? Am I getting that right?'

Stage two, anger.

'When I found out you were the mystery man on the show, it was too good an opportunity to pass up. Marry you, wait for you to either cheat on me, or until you couldn't actually stand living with the real me, and then get a quickie divorce and, with it, a big chunk of your money. Or, actually, my money. The money that should have rightfully been my dad's.'

'So all this, it was all about money?'

'I wanted to take something from you. Something *you* loved. Because your family took the thing I loved most in the world from me, at the time I needed it the most.'

'I'm not my father,' he says. 'I didn't do this to you.'

Stage three, shifting the blame.

'Maybe not. But you sure took the spoils, didn't you? The big houses, the yachts, designer clothes. Did you ever question where all that came from? My family fell apart while yours took over the world. Dad rotting in prison. Mum ended up marrying a man she didn't love because she couldn't afford the bills on her own, turfing me out when I was just a kid. And all the while, the Van Battens were falling out of night clubs and crashing sports cars.'

Now it's his turn to thump his fist on the cockpit door.

'That's not fair, Hazel,' Marc says. 'It wasn't like that. I never knew any of this, what my dad did back then, or Stephanie's stupid scheme to make me take over. Open the door and let me talk to you.'

Stage four, bargaining.

I rest my hand on the door handle, but I don't open it.

'You really thought I was in on this?' he asks. 'That I wanted to follow in my father's footsteps? That's why you left me at the altar?'

I take a deep breath.

'Something happened that I *didn't* plan,' I say. 'And when it did, I couldn't bring myself to go through with it.'

'What?' he says. 'What happened?'

'When I found out Stephanie wanted you to take over as CEO, I thought you'd lied to me… and, well, that broke my heart, Marc.'

'Why?'

I want to scream. This is torture.

'Why do you think?' I cry. 'Because I fell in love with you, you idiot.'

There's another pause, and this one seems to last for a million years.

'Then open the door,' Marc says eventually. 'And let me in.'

With my good hand, I pull the handle and open the door to see Marc leaning against the wall of the plane, clutching his side, blood seeping through his shirt.

I look up at him, his eyes unreadable, his face lit up by the flashing lights on the dashboard.

'I fell in love with you, too,' he says.

I fall into him, exhausted, broken, but finally safe. He puts his hand on my face, wipes away the tears I didn't even realise were there, and kisses me.

There's a moment of silence, which is broken by a familiar tinny voice.

'Congratulations,' CILLA says from the pilot's seat. 'You are a one hundred per cent match!'

'You have to be kidding.' I laugh.

I sit down, and Marc takes the co-pilot's seat next to me. Together we look out of the windscreen. The sun is bursting through the clouds, filling the cockpit with light. It's no northern lights, but it's one hell of a view.

EPILOGUE

THE REUNION

SKARDBALT AIRPORT

'OMG, you have got to be freaking kidding me!' Tilly squeals, running towards me with her arms open.

'Woah,' I say, laughing. 'Watch the hand.'

She ignores me and wraps me in a huge hug.

'Jesus, girl, I thought I told you to keep it possy! What the hell happened? It took me *ages* to even get the police to agree to let me see you. They said there's been a murder?'

It's been three hours since the emergency services arrived from Oslo. An air ambulance has taken Emil, AKA Robert, back to the mainland. Apparently, he's going to make it. Emily, the real flight steward, and I have been sitting at the gate, wrapped in blankets and drinking hot coffee, while Marc's talking to the police. I'm waiting for my turn.

'Uh, yeah,' I say. I pull Tilly over to the vending machine. 'More than one actually. But listen, there's some stuff I need to tell you—'

I don't actually know where to start. After we rescued Emily from the control tower, Marc and I got back to the gate and waited for help to arrive. That gave us a lot of time to talk, yell at each other and ultimately hold each other tightly under a blanket and thank God we were actually alive.

The airport is now full of police officers and forensic tape. My hand is properly bandaged, and they've given me fresh, dry clothes. But there's still one thing I don't understand. Julian was locked in the toilet cubicle. If Robert Deboise did kill him, how did he get in there and, more importantly, why? He literally had no motive to do it. In fact, he had the *opposite* of a motive. Julian was going to broadcast the whole wedding, and Robert would have got exactly what he wanted: the Van Battens humiliated on global television.

Thankfully, before I can even begin to tell Tilly all this, we're interrupted by a uniformed police officer, who's accompanied by a plain-clothes detective.

'If you'd like to come with us,' the detective says in slightly stilted English. 'We have something to show you.'

I kiss Tilly on the cheek. 'Hey, do me a favour. That's Emily over there, I reckon she could really use a bit of possy right now.'

Tilly nods and bounds over to her, and I follow the detective into the main concourse. She shows me into the security office, where there's a bank of monitors. One screen shows the cafeteria, and I immediately recognise the figure nursing a coffee in the corner. *Luggage Twat*. I watch as he notices the delay announcement. He stands up, downs his coffee, then stomps off furiously towards the exit, completely unaware of how close he came to never leaving at all.

'The CCTV footage from last night,' I say. 'Do you have footage from the gate bathroom?'

'Not the cubicle,' the detective explains. 'But we can see the sink area.'

She taps on the keyboard and a black-and-white image appears on the screen. It's fuzzy, but after a couple of seconds, a figure walks into the bathroom.

My jaw drops. *It's Marc.*

'It can't be,' I start. 'Marc isn't... He's not—'

'Wait,' the detective says. 'Keep watching.'

She clicks the mouse, and the footage plays on double speed. We see Marc go into the cubicle, then emerge a second later and wash his hands. As he goes to leave, the door opens and Julian walks in. Marc nods to him in acknowledgement, but Julian brushes past him.

A wave of relief rushes through me as I watch Marc leave the bathroom. Then we see Julian look around, then take a packet from his pocket, lay out a line of white powder next to the sink, and snort it up his nose. Then he takes the Toblerone into the cubicle, and we hear the lock click shut. The next thing we see is me come in, force the lock and start screaming. The detective clicks the mouse again; the image of me, mouth wide open in horror, freezes.

'We will have to wait for the full autopsy for the official cause of death,' the detective says. 'But the medical team say they found huge amounts of ketamine in his system. It seems likely he suffered a massive heart attack while eating chocolate on the toilet.'

'Just like Elvis,' I murmur. 'Or that guy from The Cranks...'

The detective tilts her head at me, confused. 'We suspect Gary Knowles, the local dealer we found in the baggage area, sold him the drugs. We have had our eye on him for a while,' she says.

Shit. Gary said he managed to offload his supply; I guess Julian was the happy customer. So, Julian's death wasn't a murder at all, just a drugs overdose. But of course, CILLA wasn't present when Gary sold him the drugs, so there was no way she could have known that.

The detective then shows me the CCTV footage from baggage reclaim. I can hardly bear to look at it. There's Emil, pouncing on Gary and pulling the luggage straps around his neck. The detective opens another video, and we see the gift shop. It's dark, but we see Emil grab Dante from behind, grab the scissors and then shove them into his neck.

'Stop,' I say eventually. I can't watch anymore. 'Please, I just want to go home. When is the next flight out of here?'

I need to tell Aunt Clara everything. I'm going to need her help to track down Dad. There's something I need to tell him. Something I should have told him twenty years ago.

'Miss Harper,' the detective says, with zero emotion in her voice. 'After what happened here last night, I do not think the airport is going to be open for a while. Now, let's start at the beginning…'

After going through the whole thing, several times and in excruciating detail, she eventually lets me go back to the gate. Tilly and Emily are getting on fantastically, but I can't see Marc anywhere. Then I feel a tap on my shoulder.

'I got you some of these from the vending machine,' he says, holding out a packet of crisps. His wound has been dressed, and though he looks exhausted, there's hope in his eyes.

I pop open the packet and eat one.

'What the hell flavour is this, anyway?' I ask, holding the packet up to the light. 'I mean, it could be a pickle, it could be broccoli…'

'And there's something else,' he says, ignoring my excellent crisp-packet analysis. 'The police found this out on the apron.' He hands me my wristband. 'I thought you might want it back?'

I hold it up and see my face reflected in the shiny black mirror of the display.

'Hi, CILLA,' I say.

The screen doesn't light up, and she remains silent, out of charge. And maybe that's for the best.

'I've been thinking about how you managed to fool her,' Marc says. 'And how you fooled me...'

'Marc, I just got grilled for an hour by a pair of aggressively Norwegian police officers, maybe we could—'

'Wait,' he interrupts. 'Let me finish. You might have fooled CILLA into thinking you were someone else, but you didn't fool me. Over the last two weeks, I *did* see the real you. Almost throwing up in the balloon, saving me from suffocating, trying your best to say grace at lunch. Not to mention your absolutely superb dance moves. *That's* the Hazel I fell in love with. Not the meat-eating, dog-loving girl. I think, even through the lies, I saw the real Hazel. The one who dips her fries in peanut butter. The one who trespasses on the pier. And I think I'd like the chance to see more of her, without all the cameras.'

I pop another crisp into my mouth. 'And all the murders?'

'Yeah.' He smiles. 'We could try to cut down on those too.'

I look at him, blinking. 'Marc, I'm going to have *severe* post-traumatic stress for years. That's going to take a hell of a lot of therapy to get over.'

Marc nods. 'Yeah, but what about *after* that?'

I don't reply. Instead, I reach into my hoodie pocket and

pull out something. I unfold my hand to reveal the memory card, the one I took from the production office in the castle. The one with the evidence that Malcolm has been faking his illness.

His brow furrows. 'But I thought Stephanie destroyed them...'

'Not this one,' I say. 'It's footage from your house, and it proves your dad faked his illness.'

He just stares at it, lying there on my palm. Just like my dad used to say, the closest hand holds a dagger, and this tiny piece of plastic holds the power to unravel everything Marc has ever known – his inheritance, his family name, his father's legacy. I'm handing him the weapon to tear them apart from the inside, asking him to choose between protecting his family and doing what's right.

'Take it,' I say. 'But understand what I'm asking you to do. This will destroy your family. Are you ready for that?'

He hesitates.

'It's not that easy,' he stutters. 'My dad, the business, there's so much—'

'It's not supposed to be easy,' I tell him. 'The footage on here is just the start. After that, there needs to be a reparations fund for Malcolm's victims, an investigation into the factory fire, doing the right thing by Megan's family. You've got a hell of a lot to do.'

He looks at me, eyes wide with trepidation.

'Need some help?' I ask.

'Yeah,' he says, putting his hand over my outstretched palm and squeezing. 'I think I'd like that.'

For a while, we sit there in silence as police swarm around us. My gaze falls to our hands, fingers intertwined, and for the first time in ages, I don't feel cold. It's true, sometimes airports do turn people into arseholes. But sometimes, they get you where you need to go.

ACKNOWLEDGEMENTS

Thank *you* for reading this book. I hoped you liked it.

Thank you to Danielle, my 100% match.

I'd also like to thank my fantastic agent, James Wills.

My brilliant editor, Peyton Stableford.

Megan McCreanor and everyone at Watson, Little.

Polly Grice, Zoe Giles, Lydia Gittins and everyone at Head of Zeus.

My family: Linda, Kenneth, Ewan, Benjamin, Uxue, Laura, Alex and Amaia.

Lucy Rainer, Vicki Laycock, Elliot Stubbs, Laura Bassett, Sian Drinkwater, Rebecca Dawkins, Amber Harwood, Rosie Mullender, Helen Wright, Robert Fenech, the cast of *Love is Blind UK* season 2, Dani times 97, Bucky and Binx.

READ ON
FOR AN EXTRACT OF

DON'T SWIPE RIGHT

ONE

I've done some bad things.

I don't mean your everyday, run-of-the-mill misdemeanours. Listen, I'll freely admit I've got at least two more credit cards than I need, a mild crisp addiction and I really, really need to work on my core. No, I'm talking about the *truly* awful things, the ones you'd like to bury so deep that you can pretend they never actually happened.

Rough estimate, I'd say I'd done, maybe fourteen things, total, that Mary Berry would raise a concerned eyebrow at. But out of all of them, I'd say the *second* worst thing I'd ever done was currently unfolding right in front of me: my best friend's hen do, a.k.a. the hen do from hell (I say hell, but I was pretty sure even the devil had never been forced to drink Bellinis out of penis-shaped straws at 8.30 p.m. in Cameo's on a Thursday evening).

And, plot twist, as maid of honour, it was totally my own fault. My excellent plans for karaoke and Chinese food had been deemed 'untraditional' by Sarah's old school-mates, as if dressing in T-shirts emblazoned with the badly photoshopped face of the groom was what Henry VIII had envisioned when he invented hen dos (I'm assuming he had something to do with it along the line). So, this was what I'd come up with instead, and it was currently dying on its arse.

'Everyone! Time for Mr and Mrs!' shouted Amy (I was pretty sure her name was Amy, but it could equally well have been Helen or Anne. Or Daisy).

The six of us were sitting awkwardly around an overly shiny table in one of the U-shaped booths that surrounded Cameo's (currently very empty) light-up dance floor. It was too early to be busy, and we pretty much had the place to ourselves, save for a couple of businessmen at the bar, who looked about two vodka and Red Bulls away from wrapping their ties around their heads and attempting the haka.

'So... question one, what is Richard's shoe size?' Amy/Helen/Anne/Daisy asked.

I closed my eyes and sank into the faux-leather, hoping it would envelop me.

'Fuck knows,' Sarah slurred as she fiddled with the Bride-to-be sash that hung around her shoulders, her face turning a ripe shade of beetroot. 'Ask me something dirtier!'

'Okay, umm...' Amy (probably) said, frantically looking down the list of questions for something suitably risqué before giving up. 'Err, what's his favourite position in bed?'

I couldn't take any more of this. As the group groaned in unison into their Bellinis, I pulled myself out of my seat and took slow steps backwards into the clouds of dry ice that billowed up from the dance floor. Guided by the neon lights that spelled out 'Create your own adventure' across the wall, I made my way to the sanctuary of the bathrooms, praying someone had dug an escape tunnel behind the condom machine.

Once there, I found an empty stall, nudged the toilet seat

closed with my foot and sat down. As the thumping bass of the generic house music faded to a dull thud, I pulled my phone out and opened Connector, the dating app *du jour* that was either: a) thwarting any chance I had of a sensible post-break-up recovery, or b) providing a useful distraction from my increasingly dubious life choices, depending on who you listened to.

After a good ten minutes of swiping through the endless stream of almost identical men looking far too fresh after climbing Machu Picchu, I was interrupted by the sound of the bathroom door swinging open. Seconds later, I heard Sarah's voice echoing off the tiles.

'Gwen! Are you hiding in here? You're going to miss Pin the Cock on the Groom!'

'Shit,' I mouthed, quickly stuffing the phone back in my bag and poking my head out from the stall to see Sarah standing in the middle of the bathroom holding two plastic champagne flutes.

'Ah, there you are,' she said, handing one to me. 'Please tell me you've not been sat in there playing on dating apps again?'

'No, just reading the graffiti,' I lied.

Sarah looked at me the same way people look at a really cute puppy that's peed on the floor.

'I know what this is about,' she said, shaking her head and smiling sadly. 'I was worried all this might be a bit much for you. It's only been a couple of months since, well, you know. You don't have to stay if you don't want to…'

'What, and miss sticking a cardboard penis on a picture of your naked fiancé? No way! I mean, I'd only be doing the exact same thing at home anyway.'

'Gwen,' Sarah sighed. 'You can drop the act with me. It's okay to be upset about Noah, you don't have to—'

'I keep telling you, it's fine, I'm fine, really, everything is *fine*,' I said.

Usually, I found that if I repeated the word fine often enough, I could at least convince myself that everything would be, well, you know, fine.

'Okay, well, good, I guess,' she said. 'Come on then, I need you out there, I'm getting totally mullered at Mr and Mrs.'

'I'm not surprised,' I said, hopping up onto the bank of sinks so I was at her eye level. Sarah was a good three inches taller than me, even without the block heels. 'Sar, are you really sure about all this?'

'The hen night?' Sarah said. 'No, not really, it's awful, but you said Flares wouldn't let us in again after you—'

'No, no, not the hen. I mean, are you sure about *this*.' I pointed to her neon-pink bride-to-be sash. 'The wedding, Richard…'

'Oh for God's sake, not this again.' She rolled her eyes. 'I know you and Richard aren't exactly BFFs, but you don't know him that well yet—'

'Do you?' I interrupted.

After some bad experiences with dodgy boyfriends at uni, Sarah had mastered the art of spotting red flags, immediately jettisoning any man who showed even the slightest indication of being a tosspot. That's why I'd been surprised when she fell for Richard so quickly. While there was nothing intrinsically wrong with him, beyond his obvious good looks and trust fund, there was nothing very right with him either. I guessed that's what she liked about him – he was completely average. Their romance had snowballed since meeting (in real life, just like our grandparents used to!) at a work conference last summer. Shortly afterwards, Richard had surprised her during a hike up some random hill with a ring secreted in one of the many, many pockets boasted by his favourite cagoule.

And now, six months later, Sarah was about to move out of our shared flat, leaving me to face the horrors of singledom without her. And that was absolutely fine. I was totally, totally okay with it and anyone who suggested otherwise didn't know me very well *at all*.

'We may not have been together long, but I do know he's one of the good ones,' Sarah said. 'And God knows there's not many of those around. So I would love it if you two at least tried to get along.'

I looked down at my scruffy Converse. As I opened my mouth to say something, a telltale beep rang out from the depths of my bag, cutting me off. Sarah's eyes swivelled towards it like a trained sniper.

'I knew it!' she cried as I reached for my phone. 'You *have* been swiping! Can you leave that thing alone for just one evening? This is supposed to be the best night of my life!'

'Um, isn't that the wedding night?'

'No, that's the second best. The best night,' she said slowly, taking my wrist and pulling it gently from my bag, 'is dancing 'til two a.m. with your closest friend in Eastbourne's second worst club and getting pissed on champagne.'

'Hun, this is not champagne,' I said, waving my plastic flute at her.

'Whatever.' Sarah released my wrist. 'It's the end of an era, right? Sar and Gwen, one last night on the town before I move out. That's just as important to me as the big day.'

'Well then, you really should straighten your tiara, mate, it's all wonky.'

As Sarah turned back towards the bathroom mirror to fix her tiara, I stole the chance to reach into my bag again. That familiar beep only meant one thing: I had a new Connector message, and I was insanely curious to see who it was. But just as my fingers curled around my phone, I heard Sarah exhale loudly, like the air being let out of a tyre.

'For Christ's sake, Gwen, have you forgotten how mirrors work? I can see you!' she snapped. 'Give me that thing!'

'Fine!' I sighed, holding the phone out for her between my thumb and forefinger. 'It's your wedding photos that will look asymmetrical if I don't find a plus-one before next week.'

The wedding was, predictably, on Valentine's Day.

'If it's going to be a dickhead off this thing,' she said, putting down her glass and plucking the phone from my hand, 'I'd rather you didn't bring anyone.'

'Hey, come on, they're not all bad,' I cried.

'Really? What about that guy last week who used hand sanitiser instead of deodorant?'

'Well, at least he was resourceful,' I offered. 'And at least I'm trying to get back out there. It's not easy, you know. We can't all magically bump into the love of our lives in a conference centre in Milton Keynes.'

'The problem isn't *you*,' Sarah said. 'The problem is, this app is chock-full of absolute bellends.'

As if to prove it, she began poking at the screen with her index finger, like a grandmother trying to choose a chocolate biscuit from a selection box.

'See what I mean? They all look like serial killers,' she said.

'Woah, woah, slow down!' I cried as she abstractly swiped

left and right through about twenty profiles. 'You're missing some real potential there!'

Suddenly the phone beeped again.

'Oh look, it says you got a match.' Sarah sighed.

'Gimme that!' I squealed, snatching the phone from her.

I scanned the app frantically, terrified to see who she'd accidentally matched me with. But the image on the screen was surprisingly pleasant. Dirty blond with dark eyebrows, 'Parker, 34, Data Analyst from Eastbourne' had an almost feminine face that made him quite striking.

'Likes going out and staying in, travelling, movies and roasts on a Sunday,' I read out loud.

'And, oh, works in fucking IT, obviously,' Sarah said, looking over my shoulder.

'Well, nobody's perfect.' I shrugged. 'Look, it says here he has a good sense of humour, doesn't take himself too seriously and, as you can see from the excellent selection of photos, he really enjoys laughing in various pubs with two to three different mates.'

'Is there an "unmatch" option?' Sarah said, miming sticking a finger down her throat.

'Well, I could block him, but...'

'Good, and when that's done, turn that thing off and come back to the table.'

When she saw me wavering, her face softened for a second, and she placed her hand on my shoulder.

'You promised to lay off the dating, remember, at least 'til after the wedding. All these silly boys won't replace Noah, you know?'

I bristled. My ex was the last person I wanted to think about right now. I sighed and put my phone face down on the sink.

'Oh, and listen, don't hate me, but Richard's on his way,' Sarah added matter-of-factly.

I flung my head back and groaned dramatically. If there was one thing that could make this night even lamer than it already was, it was Richard.

'Are you fricking kidding me, Sar?' I whined. 'Is that even allowed? What happened to this being a traditional hen night?'

'Oh come on, Gwen, I think it stopped being traditional the second Daisy inhaled the willy-shaped helium balloon.'

'Dammit, I knew her name was Daisy!' I hissed to myself.

'Don't stress, he won't cramp our style,' Sarah continued. 'He can just sit quietly in the corner until we finish the games.'

'Great, can it be the other corner?'

'Gwen! Be nice. It's the twenty-first century, everyone is having a "Sten Do" now. And it's a good chance for him to meet the girls before the wedding. Please try, just for me, okay?'

I folded my arms sulkily. 'Fine. Just gimme a minute to freshen up, will you?'

'You're not going to message that Parker guy, are you?' Sarah said, looking at me suspiciously.

'Definitely 100 per cent not,' I said.

'Smart,' she said, checking her tiara one more time before turning to leave.

'Hey, Sar, wait a sec,' I called out.

'Yeah?' she said, looking back over her shoulder.

'Twelve,' I said.

'What?'

'Richard's shoe size,' I said. 'It's twelve.'

'Shit, of course,' Sarah said. 'Thanks! How do you even know that?'

'Cos I wrote the quiz, you idiot,' I told her. 'Now get out of here.'

And with that, she blew me a kiss and walked out, leaving me sitting on the bank of sinks staring at my distorted reflection in the stainless-steel tap. I might have been stranded in singledom, but I desperately wanted Sarah to have the wedding of her dreams and never, ever have to navigate her way through the minefield of flotsam on a dumb dating app to find a halfway decent human being to share her life with. Deep down though, something about this particular 'happily ever after' didn't feel so, well, *happy*.

I hopped down from the sinks in an attempt to shake the feeling off. As I went to stuff my phone back in my bag, I caught a glimpse of Parker's profile, still open on the screen. I paused, my finger hovering over his face. With my other hand, I grabbed my glass and downed the last of the warm prosecco.

'Fuck it,' I thought, as I typed out a message.

Gwen: wyd? currently stuck at the hen do from hell, fancy giving me an excuse to get out of here?

ABOUT THE AUTHOR

L.M. CHILTON is a journalist with fifteen years' experience working on TV shows for the BBC, ITV and Channel 4 in the UK, as well as writing columns for magazines such as *Cosmopolitan* and *Glamour*, and reporting for national newspapers across the world, everywhere from Doncaster to Delhi. He lives in London, procrastinating. His debut novel, *Don't Swipe Right,* was published by Head of Zeus in 2023, followed by *Everyone in the Group Chat Dies* in 2025.

'Funny, twisty, bloodthirsty' **Julie Mae Cohen**

'An absolute joy of a thriller' **Sarah Bonner**

Kirby Cornell needs a break from everything:

Her crumbling flat in the sleepy town of Crowhurst.
Her dead-end job.
Her slobbish housemates.
And, most of all, the terrible thing they did.

Luckily, that hasn't caught up with her just yet. Until a new message on their old group chat pops up:

Everyone in the group chat will die.

It's the first text her ex-flatmate and social-media sleuth Esme has sent for ages, but that's not the really weird thing.

The *really* weird thing is, Esme died twelve months ago…